I0643265

ALSO by JUDITH A. BARRETT

DONUT LADY COZY MYSTERY SERIES

MAGGIE SLOAN THRILLER SERIES

RILEY MALLOY THRILLER SERIES

GRID DOWN SURVIVAL SERIES

SWEET DEAL CONCEALED

Donut Lady Cozy Mystery

Book 2

Judith A. Barrett

SWEET DEAL CONCEALED

DONUT LADY COZY MYSTERY, BOOK 2

Published in the United States of America by Wobbly Creek, LLC

2019 Florida

wobblycreek.com

SWEET DEAL CONCEALED is a work of fiction. Names, characters, businesses, places, events, locales, and incidents either are the products of the author's imagination or used in a fictitious manner. Any resemblance to actual persons, living or dead, or actual events is purely coincidental.

Edited by Judith Euen Davis

Cover by Wobbly Creek, LLC

ISBN 978-1-7322989-9-6

DEDICATION

SWEET DEAL CONCEALED is dedicated to being fierce, sprinkles, and the color pink.

CHAPTER ONE

The Georgia pre-dawn air was warm and thick with humidity. The snick-snick of my footsteps and the trotting clicks of Colonel, my German shepherd, broke the eerie silence. Shadows swirled in the low-lying fog and scattered when we approached, and a sudden drop in temperature sent a chill through me. I pulled my sweatshirt sleeves over my hands for warmth and quickened my pace to leave the shadows behind.

After I unlocked the front door of my shop, the *Donut Hole*, and flipped on the lights, Mia, my feline shop guard, stalked Colonel. Colonel circled and snuffled the shop perimeter and then flopped down near the counter. Mia leaped over him and dashed to the storeroom. I tied on my signature pink apron and mixed my first batch of dough.

Two hours later, I organized the last tray of maple donuts in the display case and checked the clock. *Plenty of time to put the final touch of pink sprinkles on the donut holes before the book club meeting.*

I glanced toward the front window. Shadows swarmed and billowed at the window and caught me off guard. I shuddered. *What are my nightmare shadows doing here?*

Colonel woofed in his sleep and whined. I knelt next to him and stroked his back. "It's okay, boy." He opened his eyes, stretched, and sauntered to the door.

"You're right, Colonel. Time to open. Donuts before jitters."

Despite my dread, I flipped the sign to OPEN, unlocked the front door, and returned to my sprinkles and my next batch of donuts.

The sharp jingle of the bell over the door startled me. *Something's spooking me.*

Giselle burst in. She wore jeans and a soft green T-shirt with her shop logo, scattered rose petals and twisting ivy, on the pocket.

"You got coffee? And I need three dozen donuts. Whatever kind you've got. Make it four. I got a call last night. The church auxiliary voted to host their annual white elephant sale at my thrift shop, and their sale is today. They're bringing their kitsch and what-nots this morning at seven for a consignment sale."

She fanned herself with a napkin and leaned against the counter. "I need a spot for them. I think a sidewalk sale will work. I've bribed Isaiah and his friend, Thomas, with your donuts if they'll help me set up the tent and drag out some tables. They'll be at the shop in thirty minutes. Have you checked today's weather? I think it'll be mostly cloudy with no rain so it won't be too hot. Hopefully, anyway. Our southwest Georgia weather is unpredictable. I sure got a ramble going, don't I? Lord love a duck, I'm flustered."

Giselle flopped down on a stool at the counter, and I grabbed a coffee cup. Mia slinked out of the storeroom and stalked Giselle. She held her gray tail straight up. She was the feline version of a shark.

"You don't drink coffee, Gee. Want cream and sugar?"

"I don't know. Probably."

I filled her mug halfway with coffee and added milk and four heaping teaspoons of sugar. I put a maple donut on a plate in front of her. She took a sip and a big bite.

She relaxed with a sigh. "Maple donut cures everything. And coffee. Why did I never like coffee? It's sweet and a soft brown, just like me."

"You have my version of Cuban coffee. Extra milk and sweet." I peered at her. "What else is bothering you?"

"My sister drove in last night from Houston. She'll pick up her daughter today and bring her here tomorrow. From prison."

I sat on the stool next to Giselle. She sipped her coffee and continued. "Melissa wants Tiffany to stay with me. The two of them have always been at odds with each other. I don't mind giving Tiffany a job or a place to live, but I can't do both. I know I couldn't be around her all day at work and at night too. One or the other, but not both. I suspect she feels the same."

Mia leaped at Giselle's feet. Gee scooped her up with one hand and plopped Mia onto her lap. Giselle rubbed Mia's ears; Mia purred.

"Awesome, Gee," I said.

"Me and Mia go 'way back. She's stalked me for years." She laughed.

"So what would you prefer? Or should we ask Tiffany?" I said. "Her choices are work in a donut shop and stay with you, or work in a thrift shop and board with a white lady. Will it scare her that I was in prison?"

Giselle broke into her signature grin that began with her eyes and took over her face. "We can only hope she'll be scared. I didn't want to put you on the spot but knew you'd understand. Nobody else for me to ask in town, and Tiffany needs to be occupied. It'd work best for me if she worked at the donut shop and stayed at my house so I can keep my thumb on her. Don't think I could focus on her and work at the same time."

"Then I'll be happy to interview her for a job at the donut shop."

"I have always loved the way you think, Donut Lady." Gee toasted me with her cup. "One more thing. Would you help me with the consignment sale after you close?" She drained her cup and polished off her donut. She licked her fingers and patted her mouth with her napkin.

"Of course. We'll barter a deal later."

"Didn't expect anything less." She set Mia on the floor, and Mia flicked her tail and pranced to the storeroom.

I grinned at how energized I was by the thought of a heated negotiation with Gee, the guru of bartering. After Giselle and I loaded up her donuts, she said, "Look at the time. We better hustle. You need your donut holes ready for the Thursday Book Club, and I've got hungry young men that will disappear if I'm not there when they show up."

Amber showed up thirty minutes before the book club meeting. She wore her black yoga pants and faded Bulldogs T-shirt. *No court appearance today.*

"Ms. Karen, I have some papers for you to sign. I'm sorry this process is slow, but I expect a judge ruling by the first of next month to clear your felony conviction. I have been pleased that it's all been legalese and paperwork, so it hasn't been a burden on you. You available this afternoon?"

"What time were you thinking?" I asked.

"Any time. Drop by the office. Leah has the papers all ready. You and I don't have to get together unless you have any questions. I wrote a summary, and Leah has it."

Amber headed to the pink meeting room. "Oh. One more thing. The club is voting today on whether to meet once a week. Probably the same time. Would that work for you?"

"Just let me know, and I'll put it on the event calendar." I grinned. "The Pink Room is busy most days, thanks to you."

Amber picked up the box of pink-sprinkled donut holes and carried them to the meeting room while I made their first pot of coffee. "Ms. Karen," she called, "may I have a maple donut before anybody shows up?"

I took her two. *Saved myself a trip.*

Shirley bustled into the shop. A few book club members had gathered at the display case. She weaved around them like a motorized scooter in downtown rush hour traffic.

"Hmm. Book club day," Shirley said. "I need a donut with sprinkles."

I handed her a to-go coffee and a sack with her donut with sprinkles and a scone.

"Got any scones?" Shirley peered into the display case.

"Blueberry okay? There's one in your sack." *I know my regulars.*

"Perfect. Are you available next Tuesday afternoon? Woody is receiving a certificate for making the A honor roll at school, and I'd like to be there. He's doing great in school thanks to your tutoring. His teacher said I'm the best foster mother she's ever seen. I'm sure that's not true, but wasn't it nice of her to say that? I got an email from a client this morning who is interested in looking at a house, but the only time she and her husband can be here is smack-dab in the middle of the school event. Could you meet them at the house so they can look at it? All you need to do is unlock the door, and then lock up the house after they've looked at it. You don't have to answer any questions. I can meet them after the school program for a few minutes before they leave town. I haven't met them, but she said her folks used to live here. Being a foster mother is tricky. Did you know boys don't like to wear polo shirts and khaki pants to school? I didn't know that. My parents' group set me straight before I gave them to Woody. And then Woody and I went shopping together, and he got jeans and T-shirts exactly like the ones he already has. I never heard—"

"Shirley. You have an appointment today at nine? You usually do."

"Oh, yes. I gotta run. I'll drop the key off with you before Tuesday."

On her way out, she crashed into a late-arriving book club member. They exchanged fast "excuse-mes" and rushed to their respective destinations.

After I refilled the carafes in the meeting room, the bell jingled, and Sheriff Grady Hayes strolled inside.

He sat at the counter as I poured his coffee. He peered at the menu board. "What's the special today? Coconut-pineapple-raspberry-mai-tai?"

I laughed. "One of these days I'm going to make a crazy concoction donut just for you. When's your birthday again?" I wiggled my eyebrows.

"Gave 'em up. I'll take one of those pink-sprinkled donuts seeing as how it's Thursday." I pointed at the counter where I'd set his Thursday donut in front of him while he looked at the board.

He squinted at me. "Am I that predictable? Never mind."

While I caught up on the dishes, he said, "The air conditioning in here feels great, Ms. Karen. Last week I rode around in my car with the windows down. Not this morning. Too sticky. We might have some bad weather coming our way later today."

"I didn't know that. Giselle's planning on a consignment sale outside her shop."

"I'll check on her."

"Thanks. I've got a feeling." I refilled his cup and poured one for myself. "Nice to sit a minute after my morning rush of making donuts and scones."

The sheriff chuckled. "I need the coffee and donuts as fortification before I hit the streets and get harangued over the latest perceived infraction by somebody's neighbor."

We sipped coffee in companionable silence.

On his way out, the sheriff said, "I'll swing by and talk to Gee."

By eleven, the book club had left, every bit of pastry was gone, and I had cleaned the shop. I locked up, and the south Georgia heat and humidity slapped me in the face when I stepped outside.

"Whew, Colonel. We should have driven to work this morning. I'm going to melt before we get home."

Colonel trotted in front of me, but before I was halfway home, my neck was damp, and my feet were dragging.

When we got home, I filled Colonel's water bowl and poured myself a glass of iced tea. After my peach yogurt and iced tea lunch, I filled a jug with iced tea and left Colonel to nap in the cool house.

The parking lot behind the thrift store was full when I arrived. I parked a half-block away and hauled my jug to Giselle's. Giselle's daughter had hand-painted the sign over the store twenty years ago when she was eleven. FRUGAL AND A LITTLE FANCY. The faded red rose petals and twisting ivy on the neatly lettered sign added to the charm and authenticity of the thrift shop.

"Iced tea or rum?" Giselle called out when she spotted my red container. Her customers laughed along with her.

Gee's face glistened with sweat. "You were smart to wear your pink hat. That wide brim will give you a little shade. It's brutal out here. All the prices are marked, and they are firm. It's cash only, and here's the cash box. No receipts and all sales final. Can you take over here? I'll go inside and rescue Isaiah. He needs to leave for his afternoon class."

"Got it."

After an hour, ominous clouds with a greenish tint darkened the sky, and the humidity was even more oppressive.

Mary Rose, a waitress from Ida's Diner, picked through the table of paperbacks. Her black hair was twisted on top of her head and held in place with a hair clip. She picked up two books and added them to her stack on the table. "We're under a tornado watch."

Our retired dentist, Silas, stood next to Mary Rose and held a small ceramic lamp in one hand and a child's brown felt cowboy hat in the other. "It's summertime in southwest Georgia. When are we not under a storm watch of some kind?" He shielded his eyes with his arm as he scanned the sky. "Although, might be some hail in those clouds."

Gee stepped outside and handed me a tall glass of sweet tea with fresh ice. She surveyed the items left. "Okay, folks. Everything out here is half price for thirty minutes. Go!"

She caused a stampede. I set down my glass to take people's money, and in ten minutes, everything was sold. All the ice cubes in my glass had melted, but I was on the verge of overheating. I gulped down my tea.

"Let's get these tables inside and the tent down before the rain hits." Her customers jumped to help. Two men took down the tent while four women carried tables inside. Her helpers cleared out in anticipation of a thunderstorm.

"Stay here until the storm passes." Gee peered at the sky. "Looks like it's going to be a doozy."

"I think I can beat it home. I want to swing by and pick up Mia. I don't want her to be at the shop alone."

I hurried to my car. By the time I left the donut shop with Mia, the sprinkles of rain had turned to heavy rain. When I reached home, the rain was torrential. I covered Mia with the hometown newspaper I'd left in the car and dashed into the house. Colonel led the way to the kitchen. I opened the kitchen pantry door, and Mia scooted into her home version of the storeroom.

Colonel sat for his treat, and I turned on the burner under the kettle. The wind picked up to a howl, and the rain pounded the windows. I turned on the radio for some music to counter the outside assault.

I sipped on my hot tea, patted the sofa cushion next to me, and Colonel hopped up and stretched out. Something crashed against the side of the house, and Mia bounded onto my lap.

"Did you leap in all the way from the pantry?" I stroked her back, and Colonel leaned harder against me.

The radio blasted the emergency signal. "Tornado warning. Take shelter." The air conditioner stopped running. We lost power, and the wind and rain were deafening. I grabbed my small flashlight.

"Let's go sit in the pantry." I carried Mia, and Colonel followed. I dragged a kitchen chair into the pantry and closed the door.

"Why didn't I buy a house with a basement?" Mia purred.

The air was stuffy in the pantry, but it was quieter than the living room. I flicked the light switch so I'd know when the electricity came back on and turned on my flashlight, but there were too many shadows. I clicked it off and slumped in my chair. *Is it the storm and the low pressure or my busy day that's drained me?*

The thunder rolls escalated to a rumble of never-ending vibrations. My chair shook and scooted toward the wall. I trembled and closed my eyes. *I am beyond fight or flight.* The house shuddered and moaned, and we were engulfed in the deafening roar of a runaway train.

Lord, make it stop.

I felt Mia being lifted from my lap. I clutched her and wrapped my legs around the chair legs. Colonel leaned against me, and I wrapped my arm around his neck.

Lord, take care of Colonel and Mia.

I was tossed to the floor by a blast of tornadic wind that was accompanied by an ear-splitting explosion.

CHAPTER TWO

I was flat on my back, wet, and still clutching Mia. Colonel whined and nudged my shoulder. I looked up through tree branches at the gray sky and realized it was sprinkling. Either the roof was gone, or I was outside. I peered around for the shadows, but there were none.

Sure seemed like a nightmare to me.

Colonel nudged me again. I tried to get up, but boards crisscrossed across my lower torso. I relaxed my hold on Mia. She jumped to the boards that were propped up by my perfectly intact chair wedged next to me and howled. Colonel joined in with barks and howls. I stared at the splintered wood, ripped wallboard, broken glass jars and dented cans around me. *This cannot be real.*

I tried to move, but I had no room to maneuver, and my left arm throbbed with pain. My protectors kept up their din. Men shouted, and Colonel barked even more.

"It's okay, Colonel. We're here. We'll get everybody out," Sheriff Hayes said. "You there, Karen?"

I exhaled in relief. *I didn't know I'd been holding my breath.* "I think I'm pinned under something. And my left arm might be broken." My tears of relief mixed in with the rain.

"Your roof is gone, and a large tree branch is on your house. Don't know where that came from. It'll take a little time to get you out."

There was a lot of noise while the debris around and on me was cleared. *I love the sound of chainsaws and men shouting.*

After two men removed the wall that had collapsed on me, I was rolled onto a backboard and handed out to a waiting stretcher. Mia jumped up on me, and Colonel scrambled out and growled while he stood by my side.

"It's okay, boy," the paramedic said in a soft voice. "Sheriff said you and the cat are support animals. You can ride with us to the hospital."

Colonel trotted alongside the stretcher and accompanied the paramedic to the side door. After Mia and I were inside, Colonel and the paramedic climbed in.

"I'm Carol." She did her assessment and splinted my arm. "All I found was the broken arm. I'm sure they'll x-ray everything at the hospital, and you'll be there for a while. They're really busy."

She was right.

Colonel, Mia, and I had been in the hospital hallway for over three hours. *I could walk out, but where would I go?* I rubbed my head. *Headache from the bright lights.* I inhaled and then coughed from the suffocating odor of disinfectant and stale urine. Unintelligible moans, shouts, whispers, and cries filled the hallway. Gurneys rushed up and down the hallway and occasionally bumped my bed. I jerked awake at the sound of a familiar voice.

"Miss Lady. Where are you?"

Woody.

Colonel gave a yip, and Woody dashed down the hallway followed by Shirley.

"Are you okay, Miss Lady?"

"I'm fine. Especially now that you're here."

Woody grinned. "I'm glad we found you."

"I tried to call you," Shirley said. "Your house is a wreck. We went there to look for you, and I almost had a heart attack, but the sheriff said you were here. Are you okay?"

"I'm fine. Truly. Did you go by the shop?"

"Oh, yes. Woody said we needed to drive by because you would want to know. The shop is fine. The tornado tore a large swath through the residential area on your side of town. I'm glad you're okay. Do you need anything? Coffee?"

"I need out of here. Can you find me a place to stay?"

"Are you sure you can leave? Don't they have to put on a cast or something?"

"For now, the splint's all I need. Doc said the x-rays showed no bone displacement, and he wants the swelling to go down before they put on a cast. I'm waiting for a social worker to find me a place to stay."

"You can stay with us, Miss Lady. Right, Ms. Shirley?" Woody glanced at Shirley and raised his eyebrows. I raised my hand to my chest. *I'm pretty sure my heart just melted from the pleading in his eyes.* From the look on Shirley's face, she felt the same as I did.

"Of course. Karen, stay with us tonight, and I've got a partially furnished small one-bedroom duplex on Flint Street you can rent. It's only four blocks from my house. It has appliances and a kitchen table and chairs. The cleaning crew cleaned it two days ago. They're always thorough. I was going to advertise it next Monday, but it's yours if you like it."

"Let's find somebody and tell them I have a place to stay. Is there anything salvageable at my house, do you think?"

"I don't know," Shirley said. "Let's get you situated then I'll go see. Maybe I can at least get clothes for you."

"I'll come with you."

After being slammed around by a storm and sitting on a gurney for three hours, I was stiff. I sat up and discovered my feet couldn't reach the floor.

"Dagnabbit. This dratted stretcher is too high." I sounded as whiny as I felt.

"Language, Miss Lady." Woody said. Shirley laughed, and I smiled.

Woody grabbed a stepstool from a nearby room, and I planted my feet on the stool.

Woody offered me his arm. "Lean on me, Miss Lady."

Colonel led the way to the parking lot but kept an eye on us in case we changed direction. Shirley carried Mia. The parking lot was a mess of large branches. We were greeted by the sound of chainsaws. I stopped to stare at the size of the limbs on the ground from the oak trees. When we reached Shirley's car, Woody helped me into the passenger's side.

"Are you sure you're up for all this running around, Karen?"

"You might be right. That short walk took a lot out of me. Let's go by my house first."

"Well, we can't just drive by. The roads are blocked with trees, limbs, siding from houses—lots of debris. We had to walk a block and a half to get to your house."

"Maybe tomorrow might be better. Can we go by your rental?"

Shirley's gray duplex with blue shutters and trimmed bushes across the front was small but well-kept.

"I have a rollaway bed you can use until you get a bed. It's comfortable but short, but it'll be fine for you. We can check Gee's for a sofa. A young couple lives on the other side. Ginny's a teacher. Eli's still in school. They have a cat, but I can't remember the cat's name. They've been there for three years. They're great tenants."

Poor Shirley doesn't even know she made a short joke. I glanced at Woody, and he smiled. I snickered.

"You doing okay, Karen?" Shirley asked.

I nodded so I wouldn't laugh out loud. Woody coughed.

We passed Gee's closed shop on our way to the grocery store for dog food. I scrutinized her building for any damage. The solid structure was intact, and even the sign was undisturbed. Our next stop after the grocery store was the donut shop where I ensured Mia was fed and comfortable, and then Shirley drove us to a fast food drive-through for tacos.

After our meal, Shirley changed the linens on her bed, and Woody measured out Colonel's food. "After Colonel eats, I can take him for a walk, right?"

"Don't go too far and don't be gone too long. I worry about you being out in the dark alone. Of course, you won't be alone. Colonel will be with you. That's fine then."

Woody and Colonel dashed outside.

"Do you have a blanket I can use?" I asked. "If you don't mind, I need to lie down. The sofa's fine for me."

"You're sleeping in my bed tonight. You wouldn't be comfortable on the sofa. There's not enough room for your splint. Go on. You look terrible. You need to get some rest. Can I get you anything?"

"Really need to lie down."

"I put a pair of my pajamas on the bed. Go."

I stumbled to her bedroom, put on the pajamas, and collapsed.

* * *

I woke to the smell of coffee. My mind intended to jump out of bed, but I slowly eased my feet over the side of the bed and placed them on the floor. *I need to get to the donut shop.*

I shuffled to Shirley's kitchen. "I need to get dressed and get to work."

She handed me a cup of coffee. "We knew you'd want to open the shop. Here, ya go, and there's clothes you can wear in my bathroom. Woody and I will work with you this morning. School's canceled. We think you can tell us how to make donuts. We might be slow, but people will understand."

After I dressed, the four of us, including Colonel, went to the shop.

Shirley unlocked the door with my spare key. I sat at the counter with the recipe book and barked orders.

The jingling bell announced Amber. "Hey there! I came to help. What do I do? Sign these papers, Karen."

I signed the papers. "Glad you're here. More people to boss around." I grinned. "Although Shirley and Woody have it pretty much under control."

"We could go faster with a third set of hands," Shirley said. "Want to be in charge of the fryer? I can cut out donuts and holes, you can fry, and Woody's a star at making and drizzling icing."

"Sure am glad this isn't Thursday," Woody said over his shoulder. "I don't think I could drizzle and sprinkle. How do you do all this by yourself, Miss Lady?"

"She's a donut beast," Amber said.

The bell jingled, and Mayor Richardson walked in. "Need any help?"

"Make coffee, Dad," Amber said.

The sheriff was our first customer. "I was afraid I'd miss my donut this morning. Y'all are awesome."

I set a cup on the counter, and the mayor filled it. He was wearing one of my pink aprons. He winked at me.

I chuckled. "Sheriff, will I be able to get some things out of my house?"

"I don't think it's safe for you. Okay if I contact a salvage crew? I'll get them working this morning. They're experienced and know what to save."

More customers streamed in. I sat at the cash register on a stool while my efficient crew cranked out donuts.

At ten thirty, we were out of donuts except for the nine we set aside.

"Here's your donut, Miss Lady. More coffee?"

I smiled at the hovering Woody. "Just a splash to go with my donut. You know this breaks my rule, right?"

"Yes, ma'am. You only eat a donut with me on Saturdays, but you aren't breaking your rule." Woody grinned with a maple mustache. "I'm here. This is my second one."

Amber polished off her second maple donut. "I love maple. I'm going to contact your home insurance company about your house. Let me know if your car's okay. Same time tomorrow. See ya."

She and her father walked out together. "Now tomorrow, Dad, I need to get a photo of you with the coffee pot and your apron."

Woody grabbed the broom from the storeroom and swept the floor. Shirley sprayed and wiped the countertop.

"Karen, you have an appointment with the doctor at eleven. After that, we can go to lunch then Gee's. If you're too tired, we can pick up lunch on our way home after you see the doc."

"I'd rather skip the doctor," I grumbled.

Shirley laughed, and I frowned. *I wasn't joking.*

When we walked into the waiting room, a boy and his mother sat together. The boy's right leg was in a cast.

The medical assistant opened the door to the examination rooms. "Paul?"

Paul's mother handed him the crutches that leaned on her chair and helped him up.

I stared at the door after they left. *Guess I'm done with feeling sorry for myself.*

"Ms. Karen?"

"Shall we come with you?" Shirley asked.

"I'll be fine. Thank you."

"The doctor reviewed your x-rays, Ms. Karen, and has ordered more. We can do those here. Down this way."

After my x-rays, I was escorted to my exam room.

"Ms. Karen, good news," the doctor said. "The swelling's down, and we can go with a soft cast. Your next stop is our cast room."

As the medical assistant led me out of the room, the doctor said, "You can pick the color of your cast."

"Pink," I said when I walked into the cast room.

The technician wheeled around, grinned, and pointed. Pink.

"You're awesome," I said.

"I know," he said.

Woody jumped up when I walked into the waiting room. "You got pink? You match the meeting room."

"Ready for lunch? Ida's Diner okay?" Shirley asked. "Might be cherry pie."

I glanced back at Woody, and he nodded.

"Sounds good to us."

After turkey sandwiches and pie, we went to the thrift shop. Shirley pulled in front of the shop. "I'm going to drop you off. I have an appointment. I shouldn't be more than thirty minutes. If you get tired before I'm back, Gee can text me. I was going to ask, but it looks like Woody is going to help you shop. I don't blame him." Woody had already hopped out and opened my car door while Shirley was still talking. Shirley waved as she drove away.

When we walked inside, Woody's face lit up. Isaiah carried an overstuffed chair from the back to an open area near the front.

"Mama, Woody and I will be at the park for a while. We're going to work on his pitching."

Gee came out of the back room and waved her hand. "You've got everything done I needed. Thanks for your help, son. Take it easy on him now, Woody. Isaiah's an old man, you know."

The two sauntered out of the shop, pushing each other and laughing.

"Gee, it's great that Isaiah has taken an interest in Woody and spends time coaching him." I sat on the nearest chair.

"I was worried about Isaiah for a while. I didn't much care for the company he was keeping. Woody's pulled him away from that. Now Isaiah's talking about vet school. Can you believe that? They tell me it's easier to get into medical college." Gee shook her head. "But he's always kept his grades up even during the rough times, so he might make it. He says it'll take him a little longer to save up the money, but he's focusing on science and math at the junior college."

Gee sat next to me and patted my hand. "But here I'm going on, and you're probably exhausted. Like some iced tea? I have some in the back."

She jumped up before I could say anything and returned with two glasses wrapped with paper napkins.

"So what do you need?"

"You know the duplex Shirley has? I'm going to rent one side from her. It's got a refrigerator, washer, and dryer, and that's it. She plans to loan me a rollaway bed. I need something comfortable for Colonel and me to relax on."

Gee gave me a hand up. "Let's take a little walk around the shop. See if anything strikes your fancy."

"What about Tiffany? Did she make it here?" I sat on a forest-green sofa with large orange flowers. "This is ugly, isn't it? But a sweet kind of ugly that makes you want to settle in."

"Are you sure you didn't hit your head? This sofa's so ugly, its mother averts her eyes." Gee sat next to me and spoke in a soft voice. "Tiffany's here. She's hiding out in the back. Tiffany told me she heard you'd killed your husband and went to prison. She said you must be pretty tough. She's afraid of you. When she heard your house collapsed around you and you came out with barely a scratch, she was convinced you're a witch. I think Isaiah embellished a few stories about you. You've got it made, girlfriend." Gee laughed, and I joined her. We were so out of control we had to set down our glasses of tea to keep from spilling them.

I wiped my eyes. "I needed that. Poor thing's going to be disappointed when she sees me."

"Isaiah took care of that too. Witches can change their appearance, you know. At least that's what Isaiah said. I should speak to that young man about teasing his cousin one of these days."

I snorted. "When you get around to it, right? So what about this ugly sofa?"

"I can top this ugly sofa. Want to see its supposedly matching chair? It's orange with small green flowers."

"No."

"Yep. Come look over here."

She was right. The ugly sofa paired up with an even more hideous chair.

"I'll never sell these. They are brand new. The furniture dealer didn't charge me for them. In fact, she gave me a discount on the rest of the items I bought."

"How about twenty dollars for the two of them?" I said.

"Why don't we go to lunch tomorrow, and I'll buy. Oh, and Isaiah will deliver when you want them."

"Did you hit your head? What's wrong with you, Gee?"

"Okay, you win. Lunch tomorrow, and you come to my house for dinner. Bring Shirley and Woody."

"What?" I had trouble controlling my giggles.

"You're beating me down. I got a brand-new mattress and box spring and an old wooden bed frame. I'll throw that in." By this time, Gee was laughing at herself so hard, she couldn't continue. The two of us collapsed on the ugly sofa. *I need silliness in my life more often.*

Gee tried to whisper, but I couldn't understand her. She took a breath and said quietly. "Tiffany is going to be convinced you bewitched me." She grinned. "All Isaiah's idea."

"You two are terrible. Okay, it's a deal on one condition. I need bed linens and towels. I pick out what I want and pay full price."

"Ten percent off, I pick, and you have a deal."

"I give up. You win."

"Really?"

"Yep. Except I pick where we go to lunch, because you didn't include that."

"You aren't a witch, you're just always thinking. No, you're a thinking witch. You relax. I'll grab those bed linens and towels. That'll be fifteen dollars."

"Wait. I have a question. How did you know I'd want the ugly set?"

"Because your mother gave you the wrong name." Gee stared at the ceiling and rubbed her chin.

"What? You're getting to be as off-the-wall as I am."

"You are the twenty-first-century patron saint of lost causes and desperate cases. You should have been named Jude."

I rolled my eyes. "Got me on that one. Now I have another question."

Gee's turn for the eyeroll.

"How did you know about St. Jude?"

"You aren't the only smarty-pants around here. I write crossword puzzles in my spare time."

"You do crossword puzzles?"

"Nope. I write them for other people."

"Wow. I'm impressed." I tilted my head and tried to look pitiful. "About the fifteen—can I owe you? My purse is in the rubble that used to be my house."

"Lawdy, you take the cake. Hey, Tiffany. Come meet the Donut Lady."

Tiffany peeked around the backroom door and stepped tentatively toward the front of the thrift shop. She was tall like Gee, except she was thinner and darker. She wore skinny ankle-length jeans and a man's sage green polo shirt. Her tightly-curled black hair was cut short. Her fingers were long and slender, and I was glad her hands were relaxed. *Wonder if she ever played piano.*

"This is Ms. Karen O'Brien, Tiffany. Why don't you sit and talk? I've got a few things to do." Gee disappeared.

We stood near one of Gee's showcase areas with a sofa, two chairs, two side tables next to the chairs, and lamps. Tiffany sat on the chair farthest from where I stood. She kept her head down. I couldn't see her eyes. I backed up and sat on the sofa. I understood the need for space.

"It'll be better in a week." I spoke in a soft voice.

"What?" She kept her head down. I knew she heard me but didn't believe me.

"Someone told me that my second day out. And it was true. It was better in a week."

She raised her head and narrowed her eyes at me. She didn't believe me, but she wanted to. *Good sign.*

"What did you do? Laundry? Kitchen? TV? Cards?" I held my breath. Her answer would tell me if she was willing to work.

"Kitchen in the morning. Read in the afternoons, ma'am."

I nodded. Her face softened. *She's brave to admit she's a reader.*

"What did you read?"

"History textbooks and historical fiction, ma'am."

I'm not surprised by a lot, but that surprised me, and it must have shown when I raised my eyebrows.

She glared. "Nobody else read them, so I had my pick, and nobody cared."

I laughed. "History can be pretty steamy sometimes."

Her face became very animated. "I know, right? But the cover had just the title. No clothes being torn off, so everybody thought I was some kind of nerdy bookworm."

I like this girl. "Which of course, you are."

Her eyes widened, and she clenched her hands. "What? Why do you say that?"

"Because nobody would even know those words except a nerdy bookworm."

She stared at me. I waited.

She rose and dropped back into her chair. She examined her feet. She put her hand up to her mouth.

Ah ha. I got her. She's covering up a smile.

I snickered. She giggled.

"Want to learn how to make donuts? I need the help. A lot more than I did a week ago." I nodded at my pink arm. "Right now I have an eleven-year-old boy, a realtor, a lawyer, and the mayor helping me. Do you think you could do the work of four people? I go to work early, make the donuts fresh for the day, serve customers, clean up, and leave by noon. How does that sound?"

Tiffany leaned forward. "I can do it if you'll teach me, and sounds like if you can teach a mayor, realtor, and a lawyer, you can teach me. I know Woody. He's smart. Don't know how smart the rest of them are."

I laughed. "They're pretty smart, but they aren't baker material. Can you start in the morning? Be at the shop at four thirty. We'll need a little extra time the first day."

She stood. "I'd like to shake your hand. Aunt Gee says that's important."

We shook hands.

* * *

Later that afternoon, the salvage crew brought fifteen medium-sized boxes of items from my house to Shirley's and stacked them in her living room.

The crew leader, a buxom young woman with bulging arm muscles, handed me a key. NANCY was embroidered on her shirt. I noticed she had fresh bruises on her forearms. I frowned. *Look like defensive bruises.*

"Ms. Karen, we stored your salvageable furniture at the local storage unit. Here's the key and a receipt. You might want to inspect your things and clean them up fairly soon. Your sofa, recliner, and mattresses were soaked and would be mildewed in a day. They're gone."

The sheriff arrived with my purse. "You'll want to unpack your stuff fairly quickly and wash or air them out. We found your car down the block. Not even a scratch. Pretty wild. It's at the tow yard. I'll take you if you like. You feel safe to drive one-handed? Are you taking any pain meds?"

"Yes to safe. No to meds."

"Go ahead and pick up your car, Karen," Shirley said. "If you don't mind, I'll open boxes and get laundry started."

"Can I ride along with Miss Lady?" Woody asked.

Shirley nodded. She was elbow-deep in the boxes and had already tossed towels and clothing into a laundry pile.

When Woody and I returned, he dived in to help Shirley, and I called Gee.

"I'm moving to Shirley's duplex tomorrow. Will Isaiah be able to deliver the furniture sometime in the afternoon?"

"I think he's planning on it. What about lunch? Do you mind if Tiffany joins us?"

"Sounds great. If the weather stays nice, I'd like to picnic at the downtown park near the square. We can pick up sandwiches and drinks."

"And I'll bring homemade brownies. I love it."

* * *

"What sounds good for dinner, Karen?" Shirley stood at the door with her purse and keys. "I'm going to run to the store. We're low on milk, and I need to pick up some salad stuff. Woody always makes us a salad every evening. He says I need vegetables. I never knew that. I thought I'd pick up a pizza. How does that sound to you? What about to drink? Woody drinks milk. I like hot tea. Or I can get some cold tea. Sweet or unsweet? I don't remember which you prefer. Might be unsweet from all your years in Ohio. Is there something else you'd like to eat? I'm still not much of a cook, but Woody and I try different frozen foods I can heat in the oven like lasagna, pot pie—"

"Can you pick up a can of chicken noodle soup and plain crackers at the store? Hot tea sounds good, and maybe I'll have a little of Woody's salad."

"Are you sure? I'll pick up some cheese to go with the crackers. You going with me, Woody? I might need help picking out ice cream."

Woody and Shirley left. I leaned back on the sofa and soaked in the silence. Colonel nudged my hand, and I patted the cushion. I closed my eyes, and Colonel put his head on my knee.

I was on the side of a canal, and I leaned forward with all my weight to pull an ocean liner with a rope. The rope bit into my shoulder, and I was drenched with sweat. Mia fought off the wharf rats. A shadow rolled in ahead of me like a fog. Colonel growled and bared his teeth, and the shadow diverted to my left toward the canal. I strained with the weight of the ship. I heard screams behind me. I glanced back. I froze as the shadow swallowed the boat. The rope went slack, and I fell face forward.

Colonel whined, and I woke. I was damp with sweat and hyperventilating. I breathed in through my nose and blew slow breaths out my pursed lips. Colonel gave a low growl, and I turned my head in the direction he alerted. A shadow receded and disappeared. I glared to be sure it didn't return. I was filled with anger, not fear.

Shirley and Woody burst into the house. Woody carried grocery sacks to the kitchen and returned to sit next to me.

"You okay?" His frown telegraphed concern.

"I'm fine. I need to remember to take it easy." I smiled and patted his hand.

Wise beyond his years sometimes.

Woody jumped up and ran to the kitchen. "Wait, Ms. Shirley. I'll peel the carrots."

Shirley talked to me from the kitchen. I couldn't understand what she said, but I had a bad habit of zoning out when Shirley talked anyway.

I'm injured. I chuckled. *Lame excuse.*

"Dinner is on the table." Woody stood at the doorway. I suspected from the pride on his face and in his voice that he had prepared the can of soup for me.

I watched Shirley brush away imaginary creases in the dark blue tablecloth and place the paler blue cloth napkins square with the blue and white striped placemats.

"Your table setting is beautiful, Shirley."

Shirley blushed. After we were seated, Woody and Shirley bowed their heads, and I followed their example.

"Thank you for our food and family," Woody said. "Amen."

Shirley and I chimed in. "Amen."

Family.

.Woody picked up his pizza but sneaked peeks my way. I put my napkin on my lap and picked up my spoon. I leaned over my bowl and breathed in the soup. "Ahhhh."

I scooped up broth, chicken, and a noodle onto my spoon, blew lightly, and tasted my soup. "Mmmm. This is exactly what I needed."

I glanced at Woody, and he beamed.

"You made my soup, right? It's perfect. A magic elixir. Thank you."

I crumbled a few crackers into my soup, waited for them to become soggy then dug in. I loved the soggy crackers, the salty broth, and the bits of chicken. I slurped the noodles, and Woody laughed.

"I'd say you're a bad example, Karen, but isn't that how noodles are supposed to be eaten?" Shirley asked with a mouthful of pizza.

Woody and I laughed when she threw her hand to her mouth.

"What am I going to do with you two?" Woody tried for a stern tone.

"Well said, Woody." I laughed. "The two of you don't have to come to the shop tomorrow. I've hired an assistant." I was careful to swallow before I spoke.

"Who? Is it somebody we know? I know everybody. Shouldn't we come anyway to make sure your new assistant does everything right? She might need some help on her first day. We did, and we're outstanding. Right, Woody?"

"Okay. You can come to the shop tomorrow." I rolled my eyes. Shirley slipped when she said *she*. "My new assistant is Gee's niece, Tiffany."

"Tiffany is nice," Woody said. "She had some friends that weren't so nice, though."

"You're right about that," Shirley said. "They were thugs. She didn't belong in that crowd."

Woody cleared the table while Shirley dished up ice cream. I felt like royalty. I wasn't a saint, I was a princess.

"We got toffee crunch. That okay with you?" Shirley set our bowls on the table. My eyes widened. Our servings were triple portions.

"Let me know if you need more," Shirley said.

"This is much more than I can eat, but—"

"It's ice cream." Woody finished for me.

After we ate, I set my alarm on my cell phone and collapsed in bed. Before I fell asleep, I glanced at the hall. A shadow lurked in the doorway.

* * *

My alarm went off at four-thirty. Time to go to the shop. I heard Shirley's version of whispering. I wasn't sure I was ready for another full day of Shirley. I really felt I'd had my quota for a week in one day. I rubbed my forehead. *I need to work on being grateful.*

I sure hope Tiffany shows up. I wonder if that's why Shirley and Woody insisted on going to the shop with me. *Only one way to find out.*

CHAPTER THREE

Woody and Colonel rode with me to the donut shop. When we arrived, Tiffany was sitting on the porch. My hands loosened their grip on the steering wheel, and my shoulders relaxed. *I didn't realize I was that worried.*

"Saturdays are usually busy." I unlocked the door. "Woody, would you feed Colonel and Mia and check their water? Maybe take Colonel for a walk after he eats?" Woody hurried to the back.

"Tiffany, let's wash up and grab our aprons. We need to make the dough so it can rise. We don't really have set hours, but sometimes people show up as early as six with a donut emergency."

After I handed Tiffany Mr. Rothenberger's secret recipe book, she read, weighed, measured, and mixed.

"Wait a second, Tiffany. Test question. How long are you going to stir it?"

"Not long. Until it's smooth." She glanced at the book. "Yep, that's it."

I smiled. "You're doing great."

She kept her focus on the dough. "Thanks, Miss Lady."

I made the first pot of coffee with Woody's help. I forgot I had the use of only one hand. *This is going to be annoying.*

"How many batches do I make?" Tiffany pointed to the recipe book. "It says here three to five. I've made three."

"Let's make six. We'll have enough left over to take to some of the crews cleaning up the tornado aftermath."

Woody made a second pot of coffee and handed me a list. "Miss Lady, I checked the inventory. This is what we'll need this next week. Maybe Ms. Shirley could shop this morning if she has time?"

"Thanks, Woody. I'd forgotten it's Saturday. I'll ask her."

The bell jingled, and Shirley stopped in the doorway. "Wow. Looks like everything is under control here. What can I do to help?"

I took a sip of coffee. "Grab a cup of coffee, and I'll check."

"What about it, Tiffany? Need any help?"

Tiffany narrowed her eyes at me. "Not with the donuts. So far, I've just followed the instructions, including the hints for efficiency in the back."

I was impressed. She either flipped through the book or checked the table of contents.

She cocked her head. "What else do you sell besides yeast donuts? There are recipes here for scones and cake donuts."

"Scones," Shirley sat at the counter next to me. She furrowed her brow. "Did I speak out of turn?"

"She's right, Tiff. Sometimes I make scones, but I'd suggest we focus on donuts today."

Tiffany nodded and turned back to her donut production.

"Shirley, on Saturdays Woody takes inventory for what we'll need for the next week. Could you do my shopping today?"

"Absolutely. I could do that. What stores do I go to? I can check and see what time they open." Shirley sipped her coffee and made a face. "Is this how I drink coffee, Karen? It doesn't taste right."

"I put a lot of cream and sugar in your coffee for you. Can you fix it, Woody?" I bit my lip so I wouldn't laugh.

"I can try." Woody took her cup, poured the contents into a larger one, and added cream and sugar.

"Thank you, Woody. I'd forgotten my routine has always been to come to the Donut Hole every morning for coffee, and I guess I forgot how I like my coffee too." Shirley laughed. I was relieved to laugh along with her because I would have exploded if I'd held it in much longer.

Tiffany turned on the fryer to preheat and cut out her first batch of donuts. Even though the fryer showed a temperature of three hundred fifty degrees, she dropped one of the holes into the fryer and watched. The dough floated to the surface.

"Well done, Tiffany. That's one hint I didn't find for a while."

Tiffany grinned and turned back to her donut production. After she had fried the first batch, she walked to the counter. "Miss Lady, the book doesn't say, or at least I can't find it, do I fry all the donuts before I make the toppings?"

I noticed Woody was wiggling and realized he was about to burst. "Woody would like to answer, I think."

"Fry them all and let them drain, and then do toppings. The donuts will still be warm, but not too hot. If it's too hot, the icing melts, but if it's too cold, the icing won't stick." He said the words so fast, I wasn't sure Tiffany understood what he said.

Tiffany smiled. "Thanks, Woody. Want to help me with the icing?"

"That'd be great."

Tiffany and Woody worked on donuts, and Shirley sipped her coffee and checked her phone. I wandered back to the storeroom, checked the calendar for our meeting room, and groaned. *I should have done this sooner.*

I hurried back to the front of the shop and waved the calendar. "Change in plans. We have two meetings this morning. The Quilt In Timers will be here at nine, and the Coming Up Roses meets at ten thirty. The quilters like blueberry scones, and the gardeners like cranberry-orange scones. Let's divide and conquer. Tiffany and Woody, you stay on the donuts. Shirley and I can start on the nine o'clock scones. Then Tiffany, when you and Woody finish the donuts, you can take over the scones."

Tiffany scowled and bowed her head. *She thinks she failed.*

"I'm lucky you all are here. I couldn't have done this by myself, even if I hadn't been injured. If I had the use of both arms, I could have made three batches of donuts and two small batches of scones. But I couldn't have doubled that to six batches of donuts and still made two different kinds of scones. Too many moving parts. Because everyone's here, we'll have donuts for those who are working hard to help others."

Tiffany raised her head. She brushed her cheek with her apron. I met her gaze, and she mouthed, "Better in a week." I nodded and smiled.

"Hurray for the donut team!" Woody said. We all applauded.

"Y'all can party. Woody and I have work to do." Tiffany placed her hands on her hips and grinned.

Shirley stepped close and whispered. "Good save there, girlfriend."

The bell jingled at six thirty. The mayor sauntered in. "What do I do?"

"Coffee duty," I said. "Shirley will keep a pot full for you. We have the quilting group meeting at nine. We'll need you to keep their carafes full and serve their scones. The rose gardeners will be here at ten thirty. Another group for you to look after."

"You know, Ms. Karen, you are a politician's dream. You've given me the schmooze assignment. I can wear my pink apron, right?"

"Yes. I think Amber expects it."

The bell jingled at seven. Amber came in, out of breath. "Sorry, I'm late."

"You're fine," I said. "You'll be working with your dad. We've got two meetings this morning. He's going to keep their carafes full and work the crowd. Right, Mayor?"

"Yep. Crowd-control. That's me."

Amber laughed. "What do I do?"

"Keep the coffee pots full and his honor supplied in coffee. Set up the meeting room with plates and napkins and put scones on a platter for the mayor to serve. You're replacing Shirley. She and Woody are going shopping for supplies."

The bell jingled. Our first customer was the sheriff. "Well, I'm impressed. You've put the entire town to work, Ms. Karen. What's the special?"

I nodded at Tiffany. She cleared her throat. "Two specials today. Classic glazed and chocolate-dipped. Woody decided the specials for the day."

The sheriff peered at the display case while the mayor poured his coffee. "Well, in honor of his honor, why don't I just have one of each?"

Woody served the sheriff his donuts, and Tiffany took his money. I held my breath. *Would she be able to give him change?* Her fingers moved deftly as she counted out the bills and coins. *She calculated the change in her head.*

I flashed a thumbs-up, and Tiffany's mouth twitched a quick smile.

Shirley and Woody returned from shopping. "I have an appointment to show a house," Shirley said. "Do you think—"

"Can I stay?" Woody asked.

I chuckled. "Of course."

"I won't be long," Shirley said as she rushed out.

Amber wheeled the utility cart out of the meeting room. "What now?"

"Everything's done here. Would you and your dad like to take donuts to the city crews? Do you have time?"

"I have time," the mayor said. "Do you know how much our crews will appreciate your donuts? They're used to being grumbled at; nobody ever says thanks. This is great."

"I need to get a few things done today at my office. I know you can handle this, Dad."

"I'll stop by the store and pick up a few cases of bottled water. We'll have a street party for our workers," the mayor said. "Hey, Woody. Would you like to go with me? We'll pick up burgers for our lunch."

Woody looked at me for permission.

"I'll text Shirley and let her know where you are. She'll be proud of you."

Woody grabbed the four dozen donuts we'd packaged for delivery. The mayor stopped at the door. "Ms. Karen. May I take my apron? Please?"

"Of course. Be my guest."

The mayor grinned, returned to the storeroom for his apron, and the two of them headed out on their errand.

Amber, Tiffany, and I looked at each other and burst into laughter.

"You've got a fan, Ms. Karen," Amber said.

"Maybe I need to order his honor and Woody ball caps."

"And me," said Amber.

Tiffany gazed at the floor.

"Yep, and Tiffany too," I said.

Tiffany raised her head; I saw doubt on her face. *Give it a week.*

* * *

I hung my weekend sign on the door, CLOSED SUNDAY. SEE YOU MONDAY! After I locked up, Tiffany and Colonel rode with me to the park. Gee waited for us at a picnic table with a large sack from Gus's Sandwiches and a fabric bag that read *Frugal and a Little Fancy.* I liked the bag idea for the Donut Hole.

"I ordered a variety of sandwiches, a salad, and a treat for Colonel from Gus," Gee said when we got close. "What we don't eat, I'll take to the shop. The boys will finish it off before they deliver your furniture."

Tiffany selected half a roast beef sandwich on rye with horseradish mayo and a Caesar salad. I reached for the half sandwich of roasted chicken and avocado slices on whole grain bread. Gee pulled out her sourdough bread sandwich with mustard, thick slices of liverwurst and red onion. Our dessert was brownies. When Shirley joined us at the park bench, Gee handed her a brownie.

"Mmm, good. Thank you," Shirley said. "Karen, here's your key to your new home. I stayed up last night and finished your laundry. Woody got up early with me, and we packed everything. I took the boxes to Flint Street, but I didn't unpack them because I wasn't sure where you might want things to go. Is that all right? I can come over this evening after dinner at Gee's and help you unpack. You can just tell—"

"Shirley, you are awesome." I couldn't stop the tears. Even Gee had tears slipping down her face. "I don't know how to thank you. You have the kindest heart of anyone I know." I sniffed back my tears.

"Woody said you'd be happy. You're happy, right?"

"Yes, I'm happy."

"Good. I was worried. I hope I folded your clothes the way you like. I packed all the shirts together and tried to match the colors so if you want a blue shirt, it will be with the blue shirts. Oh, look, there's Woody with the mayor."

Woody joined us and waved goodbye to the mayor. He sat on the bench and scratched Colonel's ears.

"You were right, Woody. Karen is happy. We have time to drop off a contract before our family counseling if we leave now."

"Thank you, Woody," I said. "I told Shirley she is awesome, and so are you."

Woody blushed and gulped. "Welcome."

"We gotta run," Shirley said, and the two of them rushed to her car.

"That Shirley is a whirlwind," Gee said. "You're right Karen, she does have a big heart. But lawdy, that woman can talk. And talk and talk."

Tiffany snorted. Gee sacked up the untouched food before she and Tiffany left.

Colonel and I ambled to my car. "Do you think Mia's ready to be a duplex and a shop cat?"

I found Mia's cat carrier in the storeroom inside a large box. When I picked it up, Mia stalked me. I walked to the front door, set it down, and sat on a stool at the counter. "Get in your carrier, Mia."

I frowned. *How do I do this?* Mia flicked her tail, meowed at me, and waltzed into her carrier. I zipped the door closed, and she curled up.

"Did she understand me, Colonel?"

The duplex was in the middle of a residential block. The street was lined with old elm trees, and most homes had flowers near the front door. The old white house on the north side of the unit had a large magnolia tree in the middle of the yard and roses in the side yard. The soft magnolia fragrance took me back to my childhood. *My mama loved magnolia blossoms.* The house on the south side unit was blue with gray shutters and had azalea bushes across the front.

The boxes were in the kitchen and bedroom with the contents of each box listed on the outside. Fresh flowers were on the counter in the kitchen, and clean towels hung on the rack in the bathroom. *Shirley and Woody are unbelievable.* I opened Mia's carrier, and she scooted to the small pantry.

"Sorry it's smaller than ours at home was, Mia. I'm glad it works for you."

I heard a knock at the door. "Miss Lady?" Isaiah stood on the porch. "This is the ugliest furniture I've ever seen, Miss Lady. Mama said she had to pay you to take it away from the shop. Is that so? She said only a saint would take this furniture. Do you really want it?"

"She's pulling your leg. I love it."

"She said you'd say that." Isaiah chuckled. He and his three buddies brought in the sofa and chair.

He and I shifted the furniture around for a placement that suited me while Thomas and the two other friends brought in my bed and set it up. After the four of them left, I sat on the ugly sofa and Colonel stood in front of me.

"Well, come on up." I patted the sofa. He turned to Mia's carrier and stuck his nose inside.

"You won't fit. I'm sure your dog bed is around here somewhere. If it didn't make it out of the house, we'll go shopping tomorrow. You'll get used to the ugly sofa. I'll feed you and Mia, and then we can go for a walk."

Colonel and I walked to the end of the block and back. The neighborhood birds sang a welcome, and butterflies danced in the yards. *I love being outside.*

After we went inside the house, I unpacked boxes. Shirley and Woody had washed all the dishes and pans. It didn't take long to put my things away. Isaiah delivered the bedding with the furniture. The fresh smell of clean sheets tempted me to go to bed early, but I realized I was hungry.

"We're invited to Gee's for dinner. You can go or stay. It's your choice, Colonel."

Colonel padded to the pantry and flopped down near the door.

"Guarding Mia works. I won't be too late."

When I arrived at Gee's, Shirley and Woody were already there. Woody, Tiffany, and Isaiah were playing a board game.

"Ms. Shirley's in the kitchen with Aunt Gee," Tiffany said.

"But it's okay," Woody added. "Aunt Gee is cooking, and Ms. Shirley is keeping her company."

When I walked into the kitchen, Gee was pulling a roasted chicken out of the oven. The aroma of chicken and herbs swirled around me. She wore an apron with her logo *Frugal and a Little Fancy* stitched on the apron's bib. "Hello, Donut Lady. We're about to dish up our food. Would you tell the kids to wash up?"

After we ate, Tiffany, Isaiah, and Woody shooed us out of the kitchen and took over clean up. Shirley, Gee, and I sat on the screened-in porch with our iced tea.

"You worn out yet?" Gee asked.

"Pretty much. I hate to eat and run or make that eat and shuffle, but I really am tired."

"Do you want me to drive you home, Karen? It's not safe to drive when you're so tired. I'll pick you up early in the morning, and we can pick up your car. I know you must—"

"Thanks, Shirley. It's only a few blocks. Thanks for everything you did today. And thanks for dinner, Gee."

* * *

I woke to Colonel's breath on my face. "Good morning, Colonel." The sun streamed in the window, and I glanced at the clock. "Nine o'clock? You let me sleep the entire morning away."

And no nightmares.

After I fed Colonel and Mia, I opened the cereal box I found in the cupboard. The box cover pictured a cascade of multi-colored O-shaped cereal that looked like an explosion of tiny donuts. *I'll bet this is Woody's favorite cereal.*

I opened a box packed by the professionals and found the contents from my file cabinet. When I realized how much paperwork I wouldn't need to recreate, relief washed over me.

"Want to go to our storage unit, Colonel? We'll see if the file cabinet made it."

On the way, we stopped at the hardware store. When Colonel and I checked out, the clerk gave him a doggie treat. "Somebody's got a cleaning project in mind," she giggled as she scanned the multi-purpose cleaner, furniture polish, and paper towels." I returned her smile. *Only in a small town would you get a comment about your purchases at check-out.*

I unlocked the storage unit and stared in disbelief. *I expected to see more than this.* My dining table had a diagonal gash like a sword slice across its length, but the legs were solid. Three of my six dining chairs sat next to it. The file cabinet had a chip on one corner, but the drawers were operational. I smiled at the sight of my two old bookcases. *I need to look for a box with my books.* My family's old steamer trunk didn't have any new damage. I opened it and found a medium-sized box packed by the professionals in it. *My blankets must be in one of the boxes they delivered.* My living room coffee table had four deep gouges on the top. I didn't see my living room end tables. My bedside nightstand and the metal storage shelves from my bedroom closet survived.

I sat on a dining chair and stroked Colonel's back. "Mama's dining room hutch is gone, and so is my old Amish pie safe. No desk; no computer… Shake it off, right Colonel? Let's clean the dirt off what we've got."

I rolled up my sleeves to clean furniture. Colonel flopped down at the door. "Guarding me while I work?" I asked.

* * *

When Colonel and I pulled into my driveway, Gee drove in behind us.

"Where'd you go? I brought you some leftovers for your lunch." She carried a bag of food inside. "I made chicken salad for you and a few other things. You have to eat to heal, you know, so I added brownies."

After I put the food away, I joined her in the living room. She relaxed on the ugly sofa, and I sat on the ugly chair.

"Colonel and I went to the storage locker to check what was saved. It's not much, but we cleaned everything. Do you suppose I could pay Isaiah and Thomas to pick up a few pieces of furniture for me? I don't want them to do it unless I can pay them."

Gee chuckled. "I'll tell Isaiah it's for his college fund. He might be available this afternoon. I'll send him over today if he is. Otherwise, might be later in the week. Is there anything you'd like to get right away that you and I could pick up?"

"Not really. Could I write a check you could put into his college fund? I don't want him to look at it and refuse."

Gee looked at the check after I wrote it. "Karen, this covers his books for a semester. Are you sure you want to pay him this much?"

"Yes, because I want to help his college fund."

"I'll pay you twenty dollars cash for this check."

I stared at Gee. "What kind of crazy negotiation are we in now?"

"I love getting the best of you. You give Isaiah the cash, and I'll deposit the check. Everybody's happy."

"Give me twenty-five, and it's a deal."

"Dang it. You got me. Here's thirty." Gee pulled cash out of her purse. "Take it or rip me off for more."

"You win. You are so good. Bartering with you is sometimes a reverse game in an alternate universe." I laughed, and Gee joined me.

"Nobody plays this game as good as we do, though."

"Nobody else could possibly understand the rules."

* * *

Isaiah delivered my bookcases, dining table and chairs, file cabinet, and bedside nightstand that afternoon. I gave him and his two friends thirty each.

Isaiah refused. "We can't take your money, Miss Lady."

"Trust me. I'll get in trouble with your mama if you don't."

Isaiah narrowed his eyes. He glanced at his friends, and they shrugged. "I don't understand you or mama sometimes, but if you say so. Thank you."

I'll have to tell Gee we got Isaiah and his friends on that deal too.

Toward the end of the day, Shirley and Woody appeared at my door.

"Karen, we went shopping in case you didn't feel well enough to go out. You've got furniture. How did you do that? Isaiah and his friends, right? It looks nice. Except for the ugly sofa and chair. They look. Unique. I'm trying to be more careful with what I say. That was better, right?"

Shirley and Woody stacked grocery sacks on my dining table, and Woody put everything away.

"Want to go for a walk, Colonel?" Woody and Colonel raced to the front door.

"We got you soup, crackers, cheese, some frozen dinners, bread, yogurt, butter, eggs. And some other stuff. If you want soup for your supper, Woody will open the can and put it in your refrigerator. Is there anything else we can do? Do we need to get you an electric can opener? Would that work for you? I have a couple more things in my car for you. I'll be right back."

I smiled. "Take your time."

Woody and Colonel came into the house with Shirley.

"We went to the drug store and picked up a few things too." Shirley carried in a sack. "I didn't know if you could take a shower with your cast, so we got some bubble bath for you and a few other things. I took a picture at the Donut Hole of Woody and Colonel with Mia in the background. It was Woody's idea. We planned to surprise you for your birthday, but Woody thought you'd like to have it now. I had it enlarged, and Woody made a frame."

She handed me the picture, and I dropped to the sofa.

"Wow." Tears slipped down my cheeks. "You two are amazing. Woody, I'd love for you to pick a soup and open the can. I hadn't thought about that."

"Woody's idea. We won't stay because Woody said you would need to rest. And he has school tomorrow."

Woody sat next to me. "Miss Lady, we were scared when we heard about your house. I sure am glad you're okay and you have Tiffany to help you. I trust Tiffany."

I stared at Woody while he opened a can of lentil and vegetable soup. *Interesting word choice for a little boy. Trust.*

Shirley and Woody left, and Colonel flopped to the floor. Mia came out of hiding.

"I'm going to see if I can find a box of books."

Colonel followed me around, and I looked for a box marked *Books*. Mia jumped onto each box I reached for. "Is this our exercise, Mia? I reach; you jump; I scoot you off."

I found two boxes. "Which one should I open, Mia?"

Mia dashed to the kitchen.

"You abandoned me. I'll open this one."

I searched through the box and selected a book. After I poured my can of soup into a pan, I turned to set the table. A shadow was poised in the hallway. I waved my spoon, and it slinked away.

CHAPTER FOUR

A sound woke me. I glanced at the glowing clock. *Two o'clock*. The soft noise was next to my bed. *Under my bed?* I tried to roll to my side, but I couldn't move. Something pinned my feet to the bed. I half-turned, leaned over the bed, and saw Colonel. The sound was his intermittent snore. I pushed myself up on my elbow and peered at the foot of my bed. Mia was sprawled across my feet. The shadow was outside the window. *I've got my protectors. No shadows allowed.*

When my alarm went off at four, I was alone in my room. If what I remembered about Colonel and Mia was a dream, it was a nice break from the nightmares.

I moaned as I dressed. The doctor said I'd ache for a while, and he wasn't kidding. I fed Colonel and Mia and placed Mia's carrier next to the door. Mia walked around the carrier and returned to the pantry.

"No Mia today, Colonel. Let's get to the shop."

Tiffany sat on the curb when we arrived.

"How long have you been waiting?" I worried about her being by herself in the dark.

"Not long, Miss Lady. I never knew how much I enjoyed silence."

"You walk here by yourself?"

"Aunt Gee dropped me off. She claimed she needs the extra time to do paperwork at the shop."

I unlocked the door. "I'll make you a key so you can go inside if the weather turns or you just feel like it."

Tiffany chuckled. "I think Aunt Gee might like that. She hid around the corner until you showed up this morning."

"I'm checking the calendar early, so I don't have a panic attack like I did on Saturday."

Tiffany had the dough for the first batch rising when I returned from the storeroom. "Good thing I checked. We've got a writers' group meeting this morning. It's their first meeting here, so we don't have any experience with them to fall back on. Let's do lemon-blueberry scones and donut holes. What do you want to do for donuts today?"

"Woody said to always do a classic. Either a classic glazed or a strawberry classic, but he said pink is kind of reserved for Thursdays. How about classic glazed and maple. I know I can handle the donuts and scones unless we get another emergency."

"Sounds great. I'll stay on top of the coffee. I don't know what kind of help we'll get today. Woody has school, and I suspect Shirley will have appointments. Which reminds me, she asked me to meet with a client tomorrow afternoon while she goes to school for an award Woody is receiving. We can do the basic cleaning tomorrow and catch up on Wednesday."

"I can scour the equipment and the shop by myself unless you want me to go along with you to meet the client and her husband."

"If you're okay with working solo, that's great. Shirley didn't seem to be concerned about the client, so I'm sure I'll be fine. I'll get the coffee going while you're busy with the donuts and scones."

The bell jingled. Our first customer of the day was the sheriff. I poured his coffee.

"I see you've taken to retirement, Ms. Karen. Maybe Tiffany will make me my pomegranate and coconut donut."

Tiffany's eyes were wide when she looked at me. I winked at her, and she turned to hide a smile.

"We'll have a surprise for you one of these days, Sheriff." I poured myself a cup of coffee.

"We have classic glazed and maple this morning, Sheriff. Here's one of each for you." Tiffany put his plate on the counter.

The sheriff bit into his maple first. "Nothing beats starting off the day like fresh warm donuts and Donut Hole coffee."

I sat next to him and sipped my coffee. Tiffany drizzled the scones with lemon icing. I refilled the sheriff's coffee.

He gazed at the scones. "Those look good, Tiffany. I think I need a scone to go."

Tiffany brought him a sack. "You want a to-go coffee too?"

"No, I'll just pay up and eat this with my lunch. Or maybe a midmorning snack." The bell jingled as he left.

"I hadn't thought of lemon icing for the lemon-blueberry scones, but it really makes sense."

"I thought it might brighten up the flavors of the blueberry and lemon. I added lemon zest into the icing too. I hope it isn't overwhelming."

"We'll see what Shirley has to say about it. You aren't afraid of feedback, are you?" I wiggled my eyebrows.

"I can take it." Tiffany grinned.

The Write Now members poured into the shop a few minutes before nine. We had their carafes filled and donut holes and scones on platters on the buffet table.

A little before ten, Shirley rushed in. Tiffany handed Shirley a to-go coffee and a sack.

"I have a meeting with your insurance agent, Karen. We're going to talk to the adjuster. You need somebody to manage the repairs to your house. I'll find you a good contractor. You'll have papers to sign, but I can take care of everything. I may not be much of a cook, but I know houses. You're okay with this, right? Woody and I talked it over last night and decided this was the best thing we could do for you. Woody's my assistant. We're excited about doing a project together. We'll do a good job. We had a contractor cover the hole in your roof with a blue tarp on Friday morning. That was Woody's idea. He thinks of everything. I have to hurry, or I'll be late."

Shirley handed Tiffany money and ran out.

"That's fine, Shirley. Thank you." I shook my head. *I need to remember she really is good-hearted.*

"She didn't wait for her change." Tiffany looked at the cash in her hand.

"Look at this." I pulled a pint canning jar out from under the counter. In it were a few coins, a handful of one-dollar bills, and a five. "Sometimes she overpays; sometimes she underpays or forgets to pay. This is my Shirley jar. She's ahead more than usual. You can keep that for a tip. If she forgets to pay, take what she owes out of the jar."

"You are totally awesome, Miss Lady." Tiffany grinned. "Aunt Gee told me you know your regulars, and she was right."

The Write Now group filed out. The group leader sat at the counter next to me and settled up. "Ms. Karen, can we reserve the pink room for our meetings? We meet on the third Monday of every month."

"Sure can. I've got a form for you to fill out, and we'll put you on the calendar."

After the leader left, Tiffany called out from the meeting room. "Miss Lady come look at this."

I rushed to the room not knowing what I was going to see.

"They stacked their dishes, wiped down the table, and pushed all the chairs in. The sugar and artificial sweetener packets are all facing the same way in their holders. Do you make all your groups clean up after themselves?"

I dropped into a chair and laughed. "No, but even if I did, I don't think another group could come close to this one."

Tiffany grinned. "At least they didn't make their own donuts. I'd be out of a job." She picked up the tray of dishes and headed toward the dishwasher. "Good thing they don't meet every week. We might start thinking this is how everyone's supposed to leave the pink room."

* * *

My bubbly soak in the tub before bedtime was interrupted by a shadow that drifted past the bathroom door. I struggled out of the tub and dripped down the hall, but I couldn't find the shadow.

"Show yourself. Coward." I growled. I returned to the bathroom and grabbed a towel to dry off. I scooted my towel down the hall with my foot to wipe up the puddles.

After I dressed in my pajamas and threw on a robe, I plopped onto the sofa and propped up my feet to read.

I was surrounded by shadows. They picked up the sofa with me on it and carried it to the door. I was going to jump off the couch, but the blackness below was unending. I grabbed the threshold to stay in the house, but the shadows shoved the sofa outside. Colonel howled, and I dove back into the house. I swam in the blackness toward Colonel's howl using one arm. Something nibbled at my feet, and the shadows tried to pull me under. I looked below and saw Tiffany. I swam down and grabbed her shirt with my teeth and swam toward the surface. The shadows reached for me and pulled Tiffany and me down, down, down.

I woke with my teeth clenched and my sleeve in my mouth. I gulped for air. Colonel whined and put his head on my knee. I stroked his head.

"I hate. Nightmares. I hate them."

Colonel followed me to bed. He circled my room and lay down next to my bed.

I was filled with dread. *What if the shadows come back?* I grabbed my pillow and lay on the floor next to Colonel.

* * *

My alarm went off. I opened my eyes and realized I spent the night on the floor. Every bone in my body ached, but especially my hip from laying on my side. I used the bed to pull myself up. *If the shadows don't get me, lack of sleep will.*

I dressed and stumbled to the kitchen to feed Colonel and Mia. While they ate, I grabbed a creamy peach yogurt and snickered when Mia stalked the cat carrier and curled up inside. I zipped the carrier, and we headed to the shop. *I forgot to make a key for Tiffany.*

Tiffany and Gee waited for me at the shop.

"Gee, if I give you my key, could you have a copy made for Tiffany? I meant to do it yesterday." I unlocked the door and handed her my key.

"I can do that. You look awful. You having trouble sleeping? Didn't your doctor give you something for pain?"

Tiffany grinned.

Gee glared. "I'll get the key made, and maybe I understand Shirley better than I realized." She huffed and drove away.

"Why don't you make the call for donuts today, Miss Lady? What are your favorites?" Tiffany mixed the dough.

"I love maple. There may be three or four cans of coconut in the storeroom. Feel like toasted coconut?"

"Sounds good. You don't happen to have any pomegranate juice, do you?" Tiffany headed to the storeroom. "And Aunt Gee is right. You do look like you didn't sleep at all. Are you okay?"

When she returned, I frowned. "I have nightmares."

She stopped, and I met her gaze. "From being in prison?"

"Yes."

"Those are bad."

"Yes, they are." I shuddered and turned away to make coffee.

The bell jingled. The sheriff was our first customer of the day. Tiffany poured his coffee and placed a plate with two donuts in front of him on the counter.

"What is this?" The sheriff squinted at his plate.

"Maple and toasted termite donuts." Tiffany pointed at the chalkboard where she had written *Today Only! Toasted Termite Donut!*

The sheriff guffawed, and we laughed too. He wiped his eyes. "You got me good, Tiffany. Would you leave it on the board for another half hour? I want to invite my on-duty deputy, Roger, to join me for coffee and donuts."

"Okay. Thirty minutes starting now." Tiffany pointed at the clock.

After the sheriff went outside and used his radio, a patrol car rolled to a stop in front of the shop. A tall deputy with soft brown skin and brown eyes opened the door. Roger glanced up at the specials board when he came inside and froze with his eyes wide.

"How do you like your coffee, Deputy?" Tiffany asked.

"With cream and sugar."

"And a donut for the deputy. Make it two, I'm buying," the sheriff said.

"I'll have what the sheriff has." Roger gulped

"Here ya go. Maple and a special." Tiffany set down his coffee and plate next to the sheriff.

"Are they good toasted?" he eyed his plate.

"The best." I answered while Tiffany erased the board.

Roger took a bite. "This is really good. I never knew termites tasted like coconut."

The sheriff chuckled.

"How did you know?" Tiffany asked.

"I've got two sisters and a brother. We grew up trying to gross each other out, but none of us tried the toasted termites trick. I guess I'll make a pie for our next get-together."

"Make these for Halloween, okay?" the sheriff asked. "I'll need three dozen for the office and the emergency center staff."

"I'll put it on the calendar," I said.

Shirley rushed in. "Is everything okay? I drove by after I dropped Woody off at school, and saw the shop surrounded by cop cars. Is it okay to say cop cars? Should I have said police officer cars? Did I bust in on a special investigation? Here's the key to the house and the address. The client wants to meet at eleven this morning. Can you still do it, Karen? How's it working out with Tiffany? Hi Tiffany. How's it working out with Karen? Sometimes my mouth gets away from me."

Tiffany handed Shirley her coffee and a sack, and she rushed out.

We watched in silence as she drove off.

"Wow," Roger said. "She's on full tilt this morning."

"Welcome to my world," I said. "What's in her sack, Tiffany?"

"A maple donut and a blueberry scone. I'm a coward," she said.

* * *

"I'm heading out to meet Shirley's client. I should be back by eleven thirty or so." I announced at ten thirty.

Tiffany opened the dishwasher. "See you when you get back."

I drove up the long driveway to the house I was showing to Shirley's client. A manicured lawn and trimmed bushes surrounded the two-story white colonial-style house with white columns in front and a wraparound porch. *Nice curb appeal, as they say on TV.* A black SUV sat in the driveway.

A corpulent man in his mid-forties stepped out of the car. He wore a dark gray suit with a light gray shirt and a yellow tie. He had brown hair, a brown mustache, and a scowl on his ruddy face. "What took you so long to get here? My time is valuable."

I raised an eyebrow and walked up the sidewalk. I unlocked and opened the door and stepped back.

He stepped into the house while his passenger climbed out of the car. She was close to six feet tall but was over six feet with her heels. Her short black hair was pushed behind her ears, and she wore a black tailored suit and a turquoise blouse.

"Hi. I'm Carla Simpson. Please forgive my husband. Randall is sometimes short-tempered." She held out her hand, and we shook hands.

"I'm Shirley Warren's friend, Karen O'Brien. I'm not a realtor. Ms. Warren had a conflict and asked me to unlock the house so you could see it. If you have any questions, she said you had her number."

"Carla, get in here. We don't have all day for you to socialize." The man called from inside the house.

Carla rushed in.

His voice was loud enough for me to hear outside. "Carla, why did you drag me all the way out here to see this dump? It's overpriced. Look at this cheap carpet. It's supposed to be brand new. They must have bought it off a truck. Who even puts in carpet anyway? This house is substandard. I shouldn't even be in here. Where's the hardwood floors? Oh great. Look at this kitchen. Granite. Junk. Nobody does granite."

I walked away and stood by my car. I didn't much care what ole Randall thought. I wasn't sure if he was trash-talking to get the price down or if he was as much of a jerk as he sounded.

He walked to the door. "Hey, you. Get in here."

You have lost your ever-loving mind, bud.

Carla limped to the door and waved to me. "I'm okay. I just slipped."

Randall pushed her into the door jamb. "You tripped over the bad flooring. You weren't supposed to get up until our witness saw you. I didn't know your realtor was too ignorant to show a house." He grabbed her arm and shoved her toward the car.

I stepped into my car, locked the doors and called the sheriff.

"Sheriff, it's Karen. I'm showing the colonial house for Shirley out on County Line Road. I'm not sure if I'm a witness to domestic violence or a scam, but I've locked myself in my car."

Randall walked to my car and attempted to open my car door.

"Unlock this door. You need to see this hazard of a house." He slammed his fist on the roof of my car.

"We're on our way," the sheriff growled. "Stay on the line."

Randall kicked my car door and howled. *Hope your toe's broken, Randy Boy.*

"Come on, Randall. You don't like the house. Let's leave." Carla limped to their car.

"You heard me. Unlock this door." He pounded on my hood.

I could hear the sheriff's siren over the phone. I turned on my engine.

"Come on, Randall. It's not good for you to get upset. She's not the realtor. Let's go," Carla said.

"What do you mean, not the realtor? You're an imposter? You trying to rip me off? Get out of that car. I'll show you what I do to people who try to mess with me."

Randall stormed to his SUV and pulled out a tire iron.

"You on County Line Road, Sheriff?"

"Sure am. Ten minutes away."

"He's coming at my car with a tire iron."

"Drive away. Back up and drive over the lawn. Get away."

The sheriff's siren screamed from the main road.

Randall's head jerked. "You sorry snitch. You called the cops?"

He ran to the SUV, tossed the tire iron into the back seat, and sped down the driveway. His tires squealed when he turned onto the highway.

"He left."

"You okay if I go after him?"

"Yes. I need to lock the house. Should I leave or wait here for you?"

"Wait for me."

When I stepped out of my car, I shook with anger. I held onto the car until my muscles settled down. I peeked inside the house and saw what looked like blood on the tile floor near the foyer. A corner of the carpet in the living room near the red liquid had been ripped.

I locked the house door and hurried back to my car. *Most excitement I've had in a while. Glad it was me and not Shirley.*

My phone rang. It was the sheriff.

"I lost him. Do you have his license tag number?"

"Sure do, but I think the car was stolen."

"I'll call it in. Why do you think the car was stolen?"

"It had a bumper sticker that said *Kindness.*"

"Oh lord. I'll be back for you. I want to escort you back to town. One of my deputies is with Shirley. That guy sounded like a nut case."

*   *   *

When the sheriff pulled next to me, his grim face startled me. He rolled down his window. "I'll follow you into town. Go to my office. I'll call Gee to pick up Tiffany."

"I want to pick up Colonel and Mia on the way. Let Gee know. She has my key."

The sheriff pursed his lips and frowned. "Okay. I'll tell Gee we'll make a stop for Colonel and Mia."

We drove the speed limit to the Donut Hole. Gee and Tiffany waited in Gee's car across the street from the shop. The sheriff stepped to Gee's car and retrieved the key.

He unlocked the shop. When I opened the door, Mia circled her carrier and stepped inside. I zipped her up, and Colonel followed me to my car. The sheriff checked the shop and locked the door. I drove to the sheriff's office with the sheriff's car within inches of my bumper.

Once inside the office, I gave the house key to the sheriff. He turned on a recorder, and I described everything I saw and heard. A deputy and a police detective sat on either side of me and listened. When I came to the end and was silent, the sheriff reached over and turned off the recorder.

"Wow," the deputy said.

The sheriff walked us out to my car. "This guy's been pulling scams across three states. There may be more victims that we haven't heard from. Realtors and owners are paying him off to keep him from tainting their reputations and sales. He's not only intimidating, he's violent. We know he beat up at least two realtors."

When I got home, Gee and Tiffany were in Gee's car across the street. They walked with me to my door. Gee's *Frugal and a Little Fancy* sack was full, and Tiffany carried a grocery sack.

"We invited ourselves to an early dinner. I'll bet you didn't have a chance to grab any lunch, did you? We brought dinner and wine," Gee said.

"I am thrilled to see you. I need people normal like me."

Tiffany snorted.

"Talk or not?" Gee asked while she and Tiffany brought in appetizers and wine.

"I'm not sure. My head says not, but we'll see. That okay?"

"Can I tell you what I heard?" Tiffany asked. I nodded. Gee rolled her eyes.

Ah ha. This is going to be good.

"I heard you showed up at the County Line house and this seven-foot guy rushed you. You sidestepped him, and he fell on the ground.

That's where the blood came from. Because there has to be blood, right? While he tried to get up, you strolled to your car and locked yourself in. He beat on your car's hood, door, and roof with his fists to break in. Repeatedly."

I laughed. "This is good and might be pretty close. Keep going."

"Thought so. You got bored and called the sheriff to keep you company. The sheriff drove a hundred and fifty miles an hour or thereabouts to get there. The guy called you a bad name, and you gave him the evil eye. He fell back in fear, crawled to his SUV, and ran over his own foot in his attempt to get away from you. He drove away and now cowers in terror in a cave in Montana. Do I have the details right?"

"That's a great story, Tiff. I love it. And it's almost the way I remember it too."

"Were you scared, Miss Lady?" Tiffany asked in a soft voice.

"No. I was angry. And I was glad I was there, not Shirley. I'm more aware of how to keep myself safe."

"You're amazing, Donut Lady. Not everybody thinks like that. I'm going to pull our dinner together." Gee hurried to the kitchen.

When we were alone, I turned to Tiffany. "Why did you say SUV?"

Tiffany shook her head. "Maybe later."

"I can wait."

After dinner, Tiffany cleaned the kitchen.

"Will you be able to sleep tonight?" Gee asked. "One or both of us can stay with you if you like."

"I'll be fine. Colonel's a good guard dog."

Tiffany walked in. "I need to stay. I'll sleep on the ugly sofa. You can't say no. I need to stay, Miss Lady."

"So?" Gee asked.

Tiffany knows about prison nightmares. Maybe mine will chase away hers and vice versa.

"It's okay. Tiffany can stay."

"Good. Because I brought my overnight clothes." Tiffany grinned and showed me her sack she had stashed near the ugly chair. The shadow near the door slid away.

Gee checked all the window locks and left. I took Colonel out to the backyard. When I returned, Tiffany had made up her bed on the sofa.

I yawned. "I'm going to bed. I'll take a book and read. Thanks for staying. You know you weren't that far off with your story about what happened today except for a few of your embellishments, although it would be nice if he's in Montana. How did word get around so quick?"

"This is a small town, Miss Lady. I wished I'd gone with you, even though you took care of yourself just fine."

"I don't think this is the end. I think there's more coming up. Good night, Tiffany."

* * *

I woke to the smell of hot coffee. I'd forgotten to set my alarm, but it was four. I dressed and rushed to the kitchen.

"How'd you sleep, Miss Lady? I slept all night, and I can't remember the last time that happened."

"I don't think I read one page. I woke up with my book on my pillow. It was wonderful to sleep through the night."

"I fed Colonel and Mia, and Colonel's had his walk. I'm ready when you are."

* * *

Tiffany mixed the dough and brushed her floured hands on her apron. "You need to order your pink ballcaps."

"You're right. We have the Asbury Historical Society this morning at eight thirty. What are you thinking for today's donuts and scones?"

"Did you know our town had one of the first jails in the state? Why don't we do orange for the Historical Society? Cranberry orange scones and an orange drizzle classic. I know, stereotype. Maybe it's a bad idea."

"I love it. Don't be surprised if they figure it out and decide it's their theme color. They are masters at research. And now I want to know how you knew that."

"Nerdy bookworm." Tiffany grinned.

My ballcap order took longer than I expected. I got lost in the rabbit holes of an internet search until I decided to send an email to my apron embroiderer. *Should have thought of her an hour ago.* "Pink adult ballcaps, similar in color to the aprons, with the same logo *Got Sprinkles?* How much for 25 caps?"

The bell jingled. The car dealership sales manager strode in. He wore khaki slacks and a red polo shirt with the dealership logo embroidered on the pocket. "We're number one in sales for the region. I need three dozen celebration donuts. Whatever you've got. We love your donuts."

"Congratulations. What a wonderful accomplishment." I handed him a to-go cup of coffee while Tiffany boxed up his donuts.

"We've got a great team." He stirred sugar into his coffee and beamed.

After he left, I sat at the counter. "I've got a feeling we've got a big day ahead of us. You want to mix up another batch of donuts?"

My phone rang. "Ms. Karen, it's the mayor. I had a big meeting this morning, but it's been canceled. You need any help?" I smiled at his wistful tone.

"The Historical Society will be here at eight thirty. Tiffany's busy making more donuts for the day, and I could use the help with the meeting."

"I'll be there at eight and set up the room for them."

Tiffany covered her rising dough. "He's a smart man with a good heart."

Sometimes I got the feeling Tiffany talked in layers. I heard more words behind what she said.

The bell jingled, and the sheriff stopped inside the doorway and read the specials board. "Just needed to check. Orange isn't code for something else, is it?"

"What a good idea," I said. "Tiffany, what could we do that would be a secret code?"

"Here's your coffee and donuts, Sheriff. Aren't you sorry you said anything?" Tiffany grinned.

"I know it won't be tomorrow. You can't mess with pink sprinkles day."

"You're right about that." I glanced at the front window and saw a shadow lurking outside. *Interesting. No shadows inside the Donut Hole.*

The mayor showed up promptly at eight. He grabbed his apron and carried plates, cups, and napkins to the meeting buffet table.

"Come check, Ms. Karen. Is the buffet table set up right?" The mayor's brow was furrowed.

I peeked in the pink room. "Perfect. Tiffany has your spoons for you, and your coffee's perking. Tiffany will keep your platters full, and I'll make coffee."

"And I'm the pretty face, right?" The mayor grinned and picked up the spoons.

The bell jingled. The mayor's eyes narrowed, and his face hardened.

"Alfred." He growled.

The bank president froze in the doorway. He wore a gray suit, white shirt, and a blue and gray striped tie. He had played football in college twenty-five years ago, but unlike most, he retained his muscular build. "David." He matched the mayor's tone.

A shiver raced down my spine. *No love lost there.*

The bank president strode to the counter, and the mayor crossed his arms at the meeting room door.

"Ms. Karen, I've got a big announcement for the bank staff today and need some celebration donuts. We had a record profit year, and they deserve the recognition." He beamed. "I need four dozen of your best donuts."

The mayor stood like a sentry and clenched his jaw. I glanced at Tiffany and realized she mirrored the mayor's stance. *What's wrong with these people?*

Tiffany boxed up four dozen donuts and handed them to me. I raised my eyebrows, and she turned back to the sink.

"Here you are, Mr. Gibson. Congratulations to your team." I gave him the boxes, and he handed me a check.

After he left, I cocked my head. "So what was that all about?"

"Not a fan." Tiffany scrubbed the already-sparkling sink.

"Me neither. Donuts. Shoulda been dollars. Cheap son of a…" The mayor snorted, stomped into the meeting room, and slammed the spoons in his hand down next to the napkins.

The jingling bell announced the first two meeting attendees. The mayor rushed to the door and greeted them with a smile.

We serve up donuts and drama. Mayor mighta been right about the dollars, though.

After the meeting adjourned, the mayor hung up his apron. "The Historical Society made me an honorary member. If I'm ever voted out of office, can I work as a volunteer for you?"

"You are the official meeting room event coordinator. Any time."

Tiffany cleaned the mixer at the end of the day. "I was relieved we had the extra donuts for the bank staff. But how did you know?"

"I don't know. Just a feeling."

She narrowed her eyes. "Not telling me? I can wait."

She emptied the dishwasher and wiped out the sinks. "If you'll be okay, I'd like to go help Aunt Gee this afternoon. She has some furniture being delivered, and I think she wants to nag me about applying for college."

I laughed. "I'm fine. Thanks for staying last night. I'll be okay tonight."

"If you change your mind, call Aunt Gee. She'll send me right over." She chuckled.

After I closed and locked the shop door, the sheriff parked at the curb.

"Can we go inside and sit? I need to talk to you, and it's cooler in the shop."

We sat at the counter. The sheriff's face was flushed and damp with sweat. I poured a glass of water and handed it to him.

"Thanks. I've been outside most of the morning and drank the water I had." He pulled a napkin from the holder and wiped his neck and face. "We found Simpson's SUV in a ditch. You were right. It was stolen. But we also found Randall Simpson. More accurately, we found his body, and Carla is missing."

CHAPTER FIVE

"Whoa. Glad we came inside to sit. Did Russell lose control of his car? What do you mean missing?"

"Early this morning a farmer reported a car crashed in a foot of water in a ditch with no one in the car. We backtracked and found the body three miles south of the car with tire tracks headed north. We identified Simpson by fingerprints. You aren't delicate, are you? The blow to the back of his head crushed his skull. It appears he was then rolled over and his face was battered to the point of complete obliteration of any features. Most likely the weapon was a tire iron. Couldn't find one in the SUV."

"Any blood in the car?"

The sheriff narrowed his eyes. "No blood in the car. Now you know everything the media knows. I didn't want you to continue to worry about Simpson returning or be shocked when the hype hits the news."

I need a television.

Colonel and I drove to *Frugal and a Little Fancy*. Gee and Tiffany were in front of a television that was tuned to the local news.

Tiffany waved. "Miss Lady, come listen."

The dramatic teasers with bits of detail were doled out between commercials. After a half hour, an on-scene reporter pointed at the crime tape near the crashed SUV site. Before each commercial break, another teaser hinted at another sordid detail, but after the commercial break, we heard the same thing from ten minutes previously.

"This is boring." I rose from my chair. "I'm going home."

Gee frowned. "Come to my house if you don't feel safe. Or call if you want Tiffany to stay with you."

"Thanks. I will if I need to, but I feel safe with Colonel." His ears perked up, and he headed toward the door.

"Colonel said it's suppertime."

* * *

After I fed Colonel and Mia, I popped a frozen chicken pot pie it into the oven. "While my supper cooks, let's go for a stroll around the block, Colonel."

The evening temperature dipped with the sinking sun, and the air was dry in comparison to the humidity of midday. The cooler air brought out neighbors who toiled in their yards and waved as we passed by. I gawked at weed free flower beds and manicured lawns. A few clouds floated high in the sky, and the birds sang a promise of a clear night.

"This is the second-best time of year in southern Georgia, Colonel. Won't be long before I'll have to put on a sweater for our evening walks. That's the best."

When we returned, the aroma of chicken filled the small house. I brewed a cup of tea to accompany my meal. *I'll bet Woody picked out the chicken pot pie.*

After my bath, I indulged my longing for autumn and dressed in sweatpants and a T-shirt. Mia and I snuggled on the sofa, and Colonel was close by on the floor. Colonel sounded a low growl. I heard footsteps on the front stoop and a quiet tap-tap knock. *Shadows don't knock.*

I peeked out the window and saw Tiffany. I opened the door. "Tiffany, what—"

"We need your help." She reached out to the side and pulled someone to the light. *Carla!*

"Come in."

When they stepped inside, Carla shivered, and I realized she was wet.

"Carla, you need a warm shower. Tiffany, your clothes are still here from yesterday. They'd fit Carla, right?"

"Yes, ma'am."

"I'll brew hot tea. Carla, have you eaten?"

Carla looked at me with wide eyes. *In shock?*

"Tiffany, help Carla to the bathroom and bring me her clothes. I'll throw them into the washer. Have you eaten, Tiffany?"

"Yes, ma'am."

Tiffany's clothes were too big for Carla, but they fit her in length. Carla walked out of the bathroom holding up her pants with one hand. Tiffany and I snickered, and Carla smiled weakly.

"Come to the table for some hot tea and a grilled cheese sandwich. After you eat, we can have ice cream. It's a known fact that eating ice cream warms you up."

After she finished her sandwich and tea, Carla said, "Ice cream sounds nice."

Colonel and I sat on the sofa, Carla sat in the ugly chair with my afghan wrapped around her, and Tiffany carried in a dining chair.

"What happened?" I asked.

"Randall parked the car on the roadside and jerked me out. He screamed at me for screwing up his scam at the house. He was so angry, I thought he was going to have a stroke." She lowered her head. "No, I hoped he'd have a stroke. I pushed him, jumped into the car and drove away. I was crying, and a deer jumped in front of me. I swerved and went into the ditch. When I climbed out of the car, I slipped and fell into the water."

Carla pulled the afghan up to her neck. "I heard a car and was afraid Randall had caught a ride and was coming after me. I hid in the woods until I thought it was safe, but the sun was going down, and I got chilled."

"How did you get into town? Wasn't the car like eight or nine miles out?"

"I ran. I'm a runner. I tried to call my sister, but I couldn't reach her."

I looked at her feet. "You keep running shoes in your car?"

"In my backpack bag. Randall insisted that I wear high heels, but I hate them. I changed shoes in the car."

"And you went to Gee's?"

"I called Tiffany, and she met me. I was afraid Randall was after me, but she said he'd been murdered. Then I was afraid whoever murdered Randall was after me."

"I couldn't think of anywhere else to go," Tiffany said. "So we came here. I was afraid Carla had hypothermia."

"I'll be right back. I'm going to move Carla's clothes to the dryer."

Tiffany jumped up. "I'll do it."

When she returned, I narrowed my eyes. "It's time to call the sheriff."

"He'll arrest me," Carla said. "I was the last person to see Randall except for the murderer."

"You might be right, but you'll be in custody and safe, and I know a good lawyer."

"Tiffany?" Carla pleaded.

"I agree with Miss Lady. At least you'll be safe. If you stay here, you'll put Miss Lady in danger, and if you try to hide, you'll never know when the murderer will find you."

"Will you call the lawyer first?" Carla asked.

I called Amber. "Can you come to my house? I have a client here for you, and I'm going to call the sheriff."

"Amber asked me to wait thirty minutes. Tiffany, would you check the dryer for Carla's clothes in about twenty minutes?"

"While we're waiting for the dryer I need to think. We've got some holes." I tapped the table and pursed my lips.

Tiffany and Carla looked at each other. *Thought so.*

"Who do you think murdered Randall, Carla?"

"He made a lot of enemies. It could be almost anybody."

I waited. Tiffany chewed her thumbnail. *Tiffany knows what Carla's holding back.*

"He liked to fight. To hurt people."

Colonel put his face on my knee, and I scratched his head. The dryer buzzed, and Tiffany and Carla jumped.

"Clothes are dry," I said. Tiffany leaped to her feet and returned with Carla's clothes.

"I'll go change," Carla said.

Tiffany answered the knock at the door, and Amber rushed in.

"Who's my client, Karen?"

"Carla. Tiffany and I will take Colonel for a walk around the block. We'll be a while. I haven't called the sheriff. I thought maybe you might want to."

I grabbed a flashlight even though the moon was bright.

"I'm sorry we came to your house. I was scared and didn't know what to do." Tiffany said while we strolled down the sidewalk.

"I'm glad you did. Carla was close to hypothermic shock when you got here and needed to be warmed up right away."

We came to the neighborhood park. "Okay if we sit?" I asked when we neared a bench. Colonel investigated the area.

"You know what Carla was holding back, don't you?" I asked.

"There are several things, but like she said, he liked to fight and had a lot of enemies. And he was a bully."

"Did he ever hurt you?"

"He tried. But Isaiah—" Tiffany scanned the park.

"What?"

"Isaiah and Thomas stepped in. Randall left me alone after that."

"Did Isaiah and Thomas protect Carla too?"

"No. Her sister and her friends—" Tiffany shook her head. "That's for Carla to tell. Not me."

"I understand. Let's walk."

When we returned, Amber and Carla waited next to Amber's car.

"Carla and I are going to the sheriff's office. She's going to turn herself in."

Tiffany's face fell.

"It's okay, Tiffie." Carla hugged her. "I'll do what Ms. Amber says. This is a mess, but I can trust her."

We watched the car taillights. "Do you want me to stay with you, Ms. Karen?"

"No, I'm fine. Why don't Colonel and I give you a ride to Gee's? I'll bet she's worried."

"I'm sure you're right. I planned to walk, but she'd ground me if I did, wouldn't she?"

"After everything that's happened, she'll ground us both anyway."

When we arrived, Tiffany put her hand on the car door handle and cleared her throat. "Would you go in with me?"

"What? A tough girl like you is afraid of an old woman?"

"When you put it like that, yes." Tiffany grinned.

I chuckled. "I don't blame you. Sure I'll go in with you, but I want you to know I'm just as afraid as you are."

The two of us walked inside Gee's house with smiles, but when we saw Gee's face, we froze. Tiffany stepped behind me. Gee glared at us and burst out laughing.

"Tiffany, you can't hide behind that tiny old white lady. I see you. Come in, you two, and you're both grounded."

"Told you," I said. "Gee, I brought Tiffany home safe. Colonel's in the car. Can we go home now?"

"Yes. But wait for Isaiah to follow you home."

"Dang it, Gee. Do you always have to have the final word?"

She flipped her dishtowel over her shoulder like she was tossing her hair. "Sure do try when it comes to you."

"Okay."

"Okay? No but or except?"

"I'm an old lady and scared of you. And you grounded me. However."

I thought about this all the way over to Gee's.

"However?" Gee's eyes narrowed.

"However, you ride to my house with me and back with Isaiah."

"Dang. You are always thinking." Gee shook her head and grabbed her purse. "Let's go."

When I pulled away, Gee said, "What's up?"

"Alfred Gibson from the bank came into the shop this morning while the mayor was there. There was no love lost between the two of them. What's the story?"

"It was a long time ago. Alfred and the mayor's brother John had been good friends all through school, but they both had terrible tempers. They got into a feud, I think over a girl, and one night it exploded into a full-blown fistfight. No one was around. Alfred said John's foot slipped, and he hit his head. Alfred left him. He said he thought John was fine and just didn't want to get up. The coach found John on the gym floor the next morning. John never woke up and died two days later. Alfred bragged to his buddies that he beat up John, but he changed his story after John died."

"Wow. What about Tiffany? She had the same reaction to Alfred as the mayor."

"You would have seen the same reaction from me. Alfred and my sister were seeing each other, and she got pregnant. He got his buddies to claim she messed around with them too. She was devastated. She lost the baby and spiraled into a depression that lasted for years. Tiffany's father was a wonderful man. George was good for Sissy, and they were happy, but he died in a crash caused by a drunk driver when Tiffany was eight. Sissy struggles."

"I'm so sorry to hear that. I'd be glad to help any way I can."

"You are by being there for Tiffany."

"It seems like Tiffany is caught in the middle all the way around. What about Carla?"

Gee snorted. "I never liked Carla. Tiffany said they were friends, but it didn't seem like it to me. Carla ignored Tiffany except when Carla got into trouble. Then she'd call Tiffany to bail her out or cover for her. I never understood why Tiffany let Carla take advantage of her. So what's going on?"

"Carla called Tiffany, and the two of them came to my house. Carla and Amber went to the sheriff's office together this evening. That's about what I know."

"Amber's her lawyer then. Has Tiffany been charged with anything?"

"Not that I know of." I glanced in my rearview mirror. "Isaiah's getting out of his truck."

"I better let you go in your house before my son embarrasses me with a tongue-lashing." We giggled, and Colonel and I went inside.

A shadow waited for me.

"Hello, old friend. I'm home."

The shadow faded.

* * *

I opened my eyes. I'd forgotten to set my alarm, and it was almost four. *Thursday.* Mia padded in. "Ready for breakfast? Where's Colonel?" I stretched and shuffled to the living room, and Mia dashed to her pantry.

I froze. The back door was open. I heard Colonel whine, and I ran outside. Shadows surrounded and converged on me. Shadows wrapped a chain around Colonel's neck and dragged him away from the house. Colonel whined and choked with each tug.

When I pushed the shadows to get to Colonel, my hands caught on fire, and my cast incinerated in the blaze. Colonel broke away, and we ran to the house. Mia stood in the doorway and grew to the size of a horse. She hissed at the shadows, and they threw flames at her. I blocked the blazing streams, and my hair ignited. Colonel planted himself between me and the shadows and snarled. I couldn't pull him into the house with my burning hands. Mia tossed a wool blanket to me, and I wound it around me to smother the flames. A low growl woke me.

I was cocoon-wrapped in my sheet and damp with sweat. My clock glowed: five minutes after four. Colonel stood in my bedroom doorway and growled at the hallway. His hackles were raised. *A nightmare on top of a nightmare?* Normal-sized Mia was on the rug next to my bed. My cast was on my arm.

I crept to the doorway; Colonel's growls grew louder. When I reached the hall, he snarled and charged the back door. I ran after him and slammed into the door with my shoulder before he raced outside. The door jamb was splintered and gouged at the latch. I looked out and saw a figure in a ballcap run down the alley.

I backed away from the door, grabbed my phone, and called nine-one-one.

"You okay, Ms. Karen?" *I love living in a small town.*

"I'm fine, but someone tried to break into my house. Colonel scared him away."

"Jeff will be there in two shakes. Stay on the line with me."

Tess was right. Jeff screeched to a stop in front of my house in less than a minute.

I opened my front door. "Which way?" He asked.

"In the alley." I pointed. "North."

"Stay inside." He sped off.

I realized Tess was still on the phone. "I'm sorry, Tess. I forgot to tell you Jeff was here."

"I heard, Ms. Karen. You want me to call somebody to stay with you? Aunt Gee would be there in a shot. Bad choice of words. Sorry."

I chuckled. "I think I needed that. No need to call anyone. I've got Colonel." *And Mia.*

After I dressed, my coffee finished perking. I poured a cup and heard another screech of tires. I poured the second cup.

"Karen." The sheriff bellowed.

I opened the door. "Coffee."

He glared but stepped inside and picked up his cup on the kitchen counter. "Thanks. What happened?"

Shadows. Were they trying to warn me or distract me?

"Colonel growled and woke me. Someone jimmied the door and ran away when Colonel barked and charged the door."

The sheriff set his cup next to the stove and examined the door. "This will need to be replaced, and you need deadbolts on your front and back doors. Why would anyone want to break into your house? Your car's out front. They'd know you were here."

I refilled his cup. "I'm not the most intimidating person in town, that's for sure, but everyone knows Colonel stays by my side. He might be old, but he's protective."

"It's got to be related to Carla. Did she leave anything here?"

"Not that I know of."

I glanced at the clock. "It's after four. Time for me to leave for the shop."

The sheriff frowned. "I'll follow you. Give me a minute to secure the door." He returned with a board and hammer. He pulled nails out of his pocket and secured the board across the door. "Not pretty, but it'll do."

"You carry boards and nails in your car?"

"Sure. My trunk is a regular handyman workshop."

Gee and Tiffany were parked across the street when I pulled up to the shop.

Gee walked with Tiffany to the door. "Tess called me. I'm going to stay with you and Tiffany until Isaiah gets out of class later this morning."

I had a fleeting vision of Gee sitting at the front of the shop with a shotgun across her lap. I choked back a laugh, and the sheriff turned his head to gaze at the sky.

"Gee, you're welcome to stay, but it's okay if you open your store on time this morning. I'm sure the sheriff will keep an eye on us." I unlocked the door, and Tiffany hurried inside. Colonel followed her in and flopped down on his favorite spot. I set Mia's carrier down, and she searched the shop.

Sheriff watched her. "When Mia calls 'Clear' I'll leave. But I'll be back for my Thursday donut." Mia went into the storeroom, and the sheriff left.

"I can't sit here and watch y'all work. You're right. The sheriff will keep an eye on you." Gee pushed back from the counter, and the bell jingled when she left.

I stared at Tiffany's back. "What did Carla leave at my house?"

The back of Tiffany's neck turned red, and she froze. "What makes you think she left something?"

"She either left something, or you took it. That's the only reason I can think someone would break into my house, except it doesn't seem very smart to me. Why not wait until I left for work in the morning? It would still be dark, but no one would be home."

She lowered her head. "Miss Lady, I leave at three thirty."

I raised my eyebrows. "So who do you think it was?"

Tiffany refilled my coffee and sat on the stool at the end of the counter. "If Carla left something at your house and didn't call me, it was her sister, Nancy. I think whoever broke into your house thought you left for work the same time I do."

CHAPTER SIX

The sheriff returned as our first customer. His solemn face softened when Tiffany served him his pink-sprinkled donut and coffee. "I'd forgotten it's Thursday. Thanks, Tiffany."

Tiffany set a second full cup on the counter and grinned.

"Well done, Tiffany. You know your regulars. What's the plan for today?" I sat on the stool next to the sheriff.

"Cranberry-orange scones, Miss Lady. I thought I'd drizzle pink icing on them." She refilled the sheriff's cup and hurried to the oven to pull out her next batch of pastries.

Sheriff Grady drained his cup. "I've got a few things to check, but I'll be back before closing time."

"We'll be here."

When the sheriff opened the door, Amber rushed in. She wore a suit and heels. *Court day.*

"How do you keep these hours, Ms. Karen? I'm ready for a nap."

"The meeting room's all set up. Nap sounds good to me, but isn't the old saying *No rest for the wicked?*" I handed Amber her maple donut and carried coffee to the meeting room.

She chuckled. "I've got another one for you. *Takes one to know one.*" She followed me in and closed the meeting room door. "Carla will be released later today. She's given her statement. I don't know when any information is going to be released to the press by the sheriff's department. She's hired a lawyer from the city, and I'm glad about that."

"Anything I need to know?"

"Yes. Pay attention to the press release and give me a dollar for a retainer to be your lawyer. And I need another donut."

I returned to the meeting room with a dollar and a maple donut.

"Here ya go. *Dollars to donuts.* We've about used up our cliché allowance for the day, don't you think?"

"Maybe even for the week." Amber grinned. She finished her second donut and wiped her fingers on a napkin minutes before the first wave of the book club members rushed in.

Tiffany frowned when I shuffled out of the meeting room. "You rest, Miss Lady. I can take care of the book club and customers."

I sat at the counter. "Thanks, Tiffany. I'll sit for a while to catch my breath."

"It takes extra energy to heal." Tiffany carried another carafe of coffee to the meeting room.

And I'm not as young as I used to be.

The bell jingled, and Shirley dashed in. Tiffany hurried to fix her coffee:

"You have a doctor's checkup this afternoon, don't you, Karen? Want Woody and me to take you? We don't mind. I can pick him up at school and swing by and pick you up. I have appointments with two contractors this morning for repair estimates. I have a third one lined up for tomorrow. Woody and I will write assessments of the contractors for you. We love to work together. Woody's a natural project manager. Thank you, Tiffany. I have a house to show this morning. It's people I know so don't—"

"You and Woody don't need to go to the doctor with me. I love the work you're doing with the house. You stay focused on that. I'll focus on getting well. And thanks for telling me you know the people. Otherwise, Tiffany and I'd close the shop and go with you."

Shirley frowned. "Okay. We'll focus on the house. You focus on getting well. Deal. But you better not miss your appointment."

She hurried out with her coffee and sack. Tiffany strolled to the pint jar and picked out the money for Shirley's coffee and pastries.

"It's been a week, Miss Lady. You were right. I still have the nightmares, but it's better. No. It's good. I'm home."

The bell jingled to announce our next customer. Tiffany's eyes widened, and I turned.

"Hello, Nancy. Come on in. Coffee?"

"Yes, Ms. Karen. And a donut?" She looked at the board. "Sprinkles."

Tiffany set the coffee and donut on the counter, went into the meeting room with the utility cart, and closed the door.

Nancy wore her work shirt and jeans and had a ballcap stuck in her back pocket. The cap fell onto the floor when she sat on the stool. She picked up her hat and plopped it on the counter. She sipped her coffee and then stirred in two packets of sugar.

"Ms. Karen, I heard someone tried to break into your house. I think I know who it was, but I can't tell anyone but you."

I narrowed my eyes. "You know if you have evidence, I'll share it."

"Understood. If I had any evidence, I'd take it to the sheriff too. I think the banker and Russell worked together. I got the idea when I heard Russell and Carla argue about a house loan. Carla wanted to know when the first payment was due, and Russell laughed. I think Carla had a payment book. That's what I think the banker tried to recover from your house."

"Where is it?"

Nancy sipped her coffee and took a bite of donut. "Mmm. This is good, Ms. Karen. It's been a while since I've had a donut from the Donut Hole. I'd forgotten how good they were. I'll take a dozen to the crew. We've got another job right after lunch."

"Where would she hide something in my house?"

"She hid her diary in a vent when we were kids. I never told her I knew."

"The intruder wore a ballcap." I raised my eyebrows.

"The banker's a lot taller, and we don't have the same build."

"I'll get you those donuts."

After Nancy left, I opened the meeting room door. Tiffany sat at the table, and she had a scowl on her face.

"Did you hear?"

"Yes, Miss Lady. I heard."

I sat at the table with her. "What do you think?"

"I think we need to clean the shop and check the vent in your bathroom. Now I'm not sure who the intruder was."

I put an elbow on the table and propped my chin on my fist. "We?"

"I'm in. You going to sit there and relax while I do all the work? Or are you claiming disability?" Tiffany's eyes sparkled.

I headed to the door. "You going to stand there jawing all day?"

Tiffany tackled the dishes, equipment, and stove, and I wiped down the counters. When the shop gleamed, the four of us left.

* * *

Tiffany and Mia waited in the car while Colonel and I walked around the house. I examined the alley for footprints. "No help here, Colonel. There's dog, cat, raccoon, bicycle, car, and motorcycle tracks in addition to a variety of human footprints. So much for my crack investigative skills."

Colonel and I circled back around, and the four of us went into the house. Mia strolled to her pantry, and Colonel flopped in front of the sofa.

"I've got a toolbox under the kitchen sink. I'll grab it, and we can remove vent covers in the bathroom."

Tiffany met me at the bathroom door with her hands on her hips. "There's two vents in the ceiling. None on the floor or on the wall." She stood on her tiptoes and stretched up with her fingertips. "I can't touch the ceiling. No way for me to reach the air vent, but I can stand on the toilet and reach the exhaust vent."

"What do you need?" I opened my toolbox.

She stepped up on the toilet seat. "Flathead screwdriver," she said. "I just need to pop off the cover. What do you have in the drawers that Carla could have used?"

I opened the vanity's top drawer. "Draw's empty." I ran my hand to the back and pulled out a metal fingernail file. "Correction. But it's not mine. Must be from a previous tenant. Lucky for Carla?"

"Maybe. Or she had it with her. She would have left it behind before she went to the sheriff's office. Let's put it to work."

Tiffany slipped the slim metal under the cover, gave it a slight twist, and caught the cover as it fell. She handed me the cover.

"I would have expected more dust." She ran her hand along the inside. "Here. I feel something with the tips of my fingers. No, wait. I pushed it away." She stood on her tiptoes. "Aha." She pulled out what looked like a checkbook cover.

"Here you go. Hand me the vent cover, and I'll put it back on."

I leaned against the counter. "This is a coupon payment book, but it looks like coupons have been torn out and the stubs have dates and amounts. The amounts aren't the same, which is what I'd expect for regular payments, and the dates are chronological, but not regular. For example, here's 156.80 with a date of November 10, and the next coupon says 783 with a date of December 3. This first date is a little over a year ago." I flipped through the stubs. "There are fourteen stubs. Most of the pages are damp."

Tiffany returned my toolbox to the kitchen, and I turned on my laptop in the living room.

"No names on the coupons. Not even a bank name, but they have a bank identification number and account number just like checks or deposit slips."

Tiffany scooted a dining chair next to me while I did an internet search for the bank ID number.

I pointed at a name on my computer. "Here we are. It's the local bank."

Tiffany stared at the screen. "Now what?"

"I have no clue. We can't call the sheriff. What would we say? Nancy told us Carla liked to hide things in vents when she was a kid, and we found a wet coupon book with numbers and dates in a vent?"

"So what do we do?"

"How about lunch? I've got yogurt, or we could go to Ida's Diner. In fact, why don't we walk to Ida's? Might help us think." I picked up my purse.

Tiffany frowned. "What about your doctor appointment? Do we have time for all that?"

"Two o'clock. We'll be fine."

Tiffany brushed her hands together. "I need to wash my hands."

The cicadas buzzed while we strolled down the block.

"It's warmer than I thought, and the bugs are forecasting rain. Did the breeze die down?" I wished I'd worn my hat.

"It's warming up for sure, and the humidity's high. Shall we walk around the block and pick up your car? Or should we turn back?"

"I need a walk. Around the block is perfect."

"I never liked Nancy very much," Tiffany said. "I wonder now if it was jealousy. Carla was supposed to come to me for help, not Nancy. Looking back, I think both of us covered for her."

"So what if Carla asked Nancy to tell me the banker story?"

"If she did, Nancy would do it. Nancy would go for the coupon book too if Carla told her she needed it. I just had a thought. What if Nancy told you about the book so she could take it from you? Do you have it with you?"

"No, I don't. What do you think about Nancy's story about the banker?" I stopped under a tree. "This shade is nice. We need a breeze though."

Tiffany waited with me. "I don't like Gibson, so I'd believe anything bad about him. I'm not the one to ask. What do you think?"

"Would it be possible for them all to be in it together?" I resumed my walk. "Carla, Nancy, and the banker?"

Tiffany stopped. "Are you serious? Aunt Gee says you're always thinking."

"The house is around the next corner. Let's go to lunch," I said.

On our way to Ida's, Tiffany stared out her side window. "If Nancy was right then Gibson and Russell were partners. I could see either one of them double-crossing the other."

"Carla could have been in the middle and may have set them up, so each man thought the other was a double-crosser."

"A possibility," Tiffany said. "But how do we explain the domestic violence?"

"Just a show? But I can't explain why. We need to eat." I pulled into Ida Diner's parking lot.

"Agreed. I need a big juicy cheeseburger and fries."

"I'd love salad and dessert."

We sat at a booth near a window. Tiffany ordered her cheeseburger and fries, and I ordered half a Reuben sandwich.

Tiffany sipped her iced tea. "What's our next step?"

I raised my eyebrows. "I'm not sure but looks like Alfred is coming into the diner."

"The diner's full. Maybe he'll come sit with you if I leave. Good idea?" At my nod, Tiffany waved at our waitress. "Mary Rose, can I have my burger and fries to go?"

"Sure enough, Tiff. I'll grab it for you. What about you, Ms. Karen?"

"You can relax, Ms. Karen. I'll help Aunt Gee." Tiffany smiled.

"Thanks, Tiffany. Tell Gee I'll be there after my doctor's appointment."

Alfred stood near the counter and glanced around the full diner. Tiffany rushed past him with her lunch in a sack. He scanned the restaurant again and then strode toward me. "You expecting anyone, Ms. Karen?"

"Please, sit." I waved toward the vacated seat. "Tiffany had to leave. Haven't talked to you in a while."

"Been busy. You know how it goes." He pulled a napkin from the holder and wiped the damp table in front of him. "I heard about your house. Sure glad you're okay overall."

Mary Rose brought Alfred a cup of coffee. "I put in your usual order, Mr. Gibson."

Alfred poured cream into his coffee and stirred in sugar. "Don't mean to talk business, but have you thought about remodeling the donut shop?"

"It hasn't occurred to me. What do you suggest?"

Mr. Gibson grabbed another napkin and pulled his pen out of his pocket. "I'll show you."

He drew a line and frowned. He pulled out another napkin and drew a longer line closer to the edge. He examined his line and sketched a second line perpendicular to his first line.

I held my breath. *Is the second line at a perfect ninety-degree angle?*

I exhaled when he drew a third line parallel to the first.

"Here's your sandwich, Ms. Karen." Mary Rose placed my plate in front of me. "Your lunch will be right up, Mr. Gibson."

Alfred stared at his incomplete square like he was in a trance and then glanced up. "Oh, Ms. Karen. Please don't wait for me. Eat, eat."

I wasn't being polite. I was in awe of his obsessive focus on drawing a perfect square.

"Thank you, Alfred. Oh, look. Here's your food."

Mary Rose dropped off the steak sandwich and fries on two plates and refilled his coffee. "I'll get you more tea, Ms. Karen."

Alfred stared at his drawing and returned his pen to his pocket. He crumpled the napkin and slid the fries plate in front of him. "Guess we'll be eating together after all."

Alfred ate his fries with a fork and knife. When his fries were gone, he moved the plate to the end of the table, and Mary Rose whisked it away as she zipped past the booth.

I was enthralled. *This is not a man who would bludgeon unless he is Dr. Jekyll and Mr. Hyde. Wonder what he's like under pressure.*

Alfred scooted his sandwich plate to the spot previously occupied by the fries. My guess was the plate was equidistant from both ends of the table. I had eaten only half of my sandwich because I stopped to wipe my hands with my napkin after each bite. *I never knew being fastidious was a virus.*

"I have ideas for a remodel, but I'm a banker. Maybe I could talk to your contractor and explain my thoughts."

"Shirley's my project manager for construction. I'll talk it over with her."

His face paled. He picked up his knife and fork and took a bite of his sandwich.

Interesting. History between him and Shirley?

Alfred finished his sandwich and pushed his plate to the table edge. I folded my hands in my lap to avoid touching my empty plate.

Mary Rose appeared with a pitcher of tea. "Anything else? Dessert special is peach pie. Made this morning."

"Sounds good to me," I said.

"I need to get back to the bank." Alfred scooted out and put two quarters on the table with a flourish.

"Want coffee with your pie and a small scoop of ice cream on the side?" Mary Rose asked.

"Yes, please. Thank you for your company, Alfred."

He waved as he headed to the cashier. Mary Rose swept the two quarters into her apron pocket. I raised my eyebrows, and she laughed.

"Mr. Gibson is old school. He's easy to wait on and comes in every day."

I moaned when she set the warm slice of pie with the melting ice cream in front of me. "This looks good. How could anyone pass this up?"

"I know, right? I have a piece of pie and ice cream for breakfast every morning. Helps me keep my figure." Mary Rose giggled and put her hands on her ample hips.

After I ate my dessert and drank my coffee, I left an ample tip.

* * *

After the exam, the doctor leaned back. "You're doing fine, Ms. Karen. Come back in two weeks for another checkup. Call if there's any swelling."

"When will the cast come off?"

"Five or six weeks. Depends on how fast you heal."

"Old people heal slower, right?"

He smiled. "Not going there."

When I left the office, the sheriff's car was parked next to mine. He grinned and stepped out. "I saw your car. What did the doctor say?"

"He said I'm fine and five or six more weeks of the cast."

"Good to hear. How do you feel?"

"I'm feeling cranky because I have a cast on my arm, but I'm really fine. I had lunch today with Alfred Gibson."

The sheriff guffawed. "You had a long lunch then."

I snickered. "I had trouble remembering to eat my own lunch. I was mesmerized. I know he used to be a hothead when he was in high school. I wondered how he is now when he's stressed."

The sheriff's face sobered. "After John died, Alfred spent two years in counseling and anger management. He and a couple other guys started an anger management peer counseling group when they saw the younger generation of boys with the same problems they had. Alfred told me it was his mission to help break the cycle."

"Sometimes people fall back into old ways." I opened my car door.

"They do. But I think Alfred would do himself in before he'd ever harm another human being."

"Unless he had a knife and fork." I grinned.

"Didn't see that one coming." The sheriff chuckled as he got into his car.

I picked up Colonel, and the two of us went to see Gee at her shop. Tiffany saw us first. "Miss Lady. You'll never guess. Aunt Gee and I completed my application for the spring semester at the community college."

"I am so proud of you." I sniffed away an escaping tear. "You let me know if you need any help with any of your classes. I'm an excellent teacher, and I have references."

Gee slapped me on the back and almost knocked me down. "Well done, Donut Lady. You are such a quick wit."

"Doc says I'm healing. What else is going on here?" I sat on a recent addition to Gee's shop that rivaled my sofa for the ugly title.

"Did you have a nice chat with Mr. Gibson?" Tiffany asked. "Learn anything?"

"He's the most meticulous eater I have ever seen, and I've seen some doozies. Did you know about that, Tiffany?"

Tiffany's eyes widened. "No, ma'am. Am I in trouble?"

"No, you're not in trouble." I chuckled. "It was a brilliant idea, and I'm glad I had the chance to spend some time with him. Hope I never have to eat with him again though."

"You definitely took one for the team, Karen. I knew he used a knife and fork to eat all his food," Gee said.

"It's my turn to cook tonight. I need to put the lasagna in the oven. And before either of you say anything, I want to walk."

Tiffany left, and Gee rose. "Be right back. I had a busy morning, and I'm parched."

She returned with two glasses of lemonade and napkins.

I wrapped my glass with the napkin to catch the condensation. "Thanks, Gee. When I talked to Alfred, he asked me if I wanted to remodel the shop. When I mentioned Shirley is my construction project manager, he looked ill. Do you know why?"

Gee sat in the chair that matched the sofa and propped up her feet. "He's still afraid of her, huh? Alfred cuts corners everywhere he can. He's cheap. Not frugal. It was six or seven years ago. The bank had several foreclosures. He was too cheap to pay a commission for a real estate agent to sell the homes and decided he'd sell them himself. Shirley sold one of his homes, and he tried to claim he talked to the client first to cut her out of the deal."

I leaned forward. "Shirley prides herself on being professional. What did she do?"

"She had a signed contract. He didn't, of course. She and her partner, who was president of the local real estate association, met with Alfred. I don't know what was said, but he dropped his claim immediately."

"That's a little bizarre. As far as I know, there's no reason a bank couldn't sell a property it owns."

"This part is gossip. Supposedly Alfred wanted the buyer to pay all the typical sellers fees, like the real estate commission, the title insurance, and the annual property taxes, not prorated. I don't know that for sure, but it fits with his reputation for cheapness. Maybe after their chat, he changed his mind."

"I wonder how long she was in his office."

Gee laughed. "Can you imagine? When the inspection report for the home came back, he agreed to every concession the client requested. He never tried to sell another house on his own after that. He hired a loan officer to take care of residential and commercial loans. I've seen Alfred slip out a back door when Shirley appears."

I frowned. "Doesn't seem like much to me."

"We're a small town. Reputations are important. While what the seller pays and what the buyer pays isn't set in stone and can be negotiated, the appearance of a bank taking advantage of a low-income customer would ruin its reputation."

I finished my lemonade and crunched on the ice. "I can see where Alfred would be very concerned about his bank's reputation."

CHAPTER SEVEN

When Colonel and I got home, Mia met us at the door and announced it was time to eat. I put food in their bowls, but I was too hot to eat. I grabbed a glass of water, and Colonel and I sat on the back porch.

"At least we have a little breeze and shade." I swatted mosquitos. "Oops, spoke too soon. Let's go inside, Colonel."

I opened the fridge freezer and surveyed the dinners Shirley and Woody bought for me. "I can't decide. You pick, Mia." Mia flicked her tail three times. "Three? What does that mean?" I pulled out the dinner third from the top. "Swedish meatballs. That sounds good."

I read the box and popped the dinner into the oven. I found salad fixings in the refrigerator but decided against a one-handed chop for carrots and cucumbers. I prepared a lettuce salad.

Shirley called. "How was your doctor's appointment? Is everything okay? Do you need anything? Wait. What? Oh. Woody said I need to slow down and let you talk. I'll put him on."

"Hi, Miss Lady. We wanted to know what the doctor said."

"It's nice to hear from you two. The doctor said I'm doing fine, and my cast can come off in five or six weeks."

Shirley came back on the phone. "We've got the speaker on so both of us can hear. We think we have a good contractor for you. We'll bring you a report on Saturday at the donut shop. Is that okay? Oh. I'm going to let you talk now. Go ahead. This is hard. It's your turn. I'll be quiet."

I laughed. "Saturday is great. Tiffany can take care of things while we talk."

After I hung up, I sat on the sofa and put my feet up. "I needed that call, Colonel. I think I was a little lonesome."

The timer on the stove woke me. I set my place for one at the dining table and listened to the rumbles of thunder while I ate.

Mia disappeared into her pantry, and Colonel fell asleep on his dog bed. After my bath, I padded off to bed.

* * *

The alarm woke me, and I dressed for the shop. Mia slipped into her carrier, and the three of us left. Tiffany was in the shop when we arrived.

"It's nice to have the key to the shop. Thank you," Tiffany said.

"What's on your agenda today?" I sat at the counter. Mia prowled around the shop.

"How about green slime donuts and eyeball donut holes?"

"I need coffee."

Tiffany had a look of horror on her face. "Did I go too far? Am I fired?"

I laughed. "No. I just need coffee. I think it's brilliant."

Tiffany brought me a cup of coffee. "I think we should do something every Friday. And maple donuts and classic for our regular customers."

"So you're planning three different donuts for today? How are you going to make the eyeballs?"

"I'll use the slime donut holes."

"I'll check the calendar, and then I'll help as much as I can."

When I returned from the storeroom, Tiffany looked like she was working in a cloud of flour.

"No meetings this morning. Sadly, we won't have that extra challenge."

"Miss Lady, I was scared you were going to say we had two meetings. This is the best job I ever had."

"It's more interesting for me with you here. Now, what can a one-armed baker do to help you?"

"You want to slime? And put irises in the middle of the eyeballs?"

"Sure. How are you making irises?" I leaned over the counter to see what Tiffany was doing.

"I got sheets of candy buttons at the store yesterday." She waved the sheets.

"How long you been planning this?"

"Only a day." Tiffany cocked her head. "You sure it's okay?"

"Yes, I'm sure. You've got an entire week to plan next Friday. I think you've come up with an exciting marketing idea. Should we call it *Now What at the Donut Hole?*"

Tiffany placed the first batch of donuts into the fryer. "I think we ask Woody."

"Smart. What about scones? What are you going to do for scones?"

Tiffany wailed. "I didn't think about scones."

"Why don't we do slime and plain scones? We can offer our customers a choice. It will give us an informal survey. We'll see what we have left over. If we run out of slimed, we'll slime the ones left. If we run out of plain, we put sprinkles on the slimed ones. What do you think?"

"Good enough to be a Woody idea. I'll get on it."

Tiffany cut and fried donuts and made scones while I drizzled slime and applied irises.

The bell jingled. The sheriff. Tiffany coughed, and I pressed my lips with my fingers. He froze in the doorway and read our board.

"I'll take one of each of the day's specials. But I need coffee." He sat on his usual stool and stared at the board. "Y'all aren't right in the head. I've got some calls to make."

It wasn't long before the on-duty deputy, Roger, came into the shop. "I think I'm going to love Fridays. Y'all are giving new meaning to TGIF. What have we got today?" He read the board and sat on the stool next to Sheriff Grady.

"What do you recommend, Sheriff?"

"The works."

"Tiffany, may I please have coffee and the works?"

He watched her place the pastries on his plate. "Wait. Your apron says *Got Sprinkles?* I need sprinkles."

Sheriff frowned at Roger. "I need sprinkles too."

Tiffany poured Roger's coffee and added cream and sugar. She pulled out two small sauce cups and poured in sprinkles.

"Here you go, gentlemen." She walked into the meeting room and closed the door.

"Is she mad at me, Ms. Karen?" Roger asked with concern in his voice.

"I think she went into the meeting room to laugh. You two are hilarious."

Roger glanced at the meeting room. "Okay if I take my coffee and plate into the meeting room?"

"Fine with me." After Roger closed the door, I raised my eyebrows, and the sheriff coughed.

"Don't you dare say anything to Roger. Or anybody else. You hear me?" I glared at the sheriff and refilled his cup.

"You just destroyed my entire plan for the day."

I snorted. "My job. So what do you think of our new marketing plan?"

"I think it's goofy and brilliant."

"Tiffany's idea. I've challenged her to come up with something next Friday."

"Thanks for the warning."

The bell jingled, and Tess from the emergency center hurried into the shop.

"Okay, Sheriff. What was so important…oh." She looked at the board and grinned. "What do I take back to work with me?"

"I recommend a dozen slimed donuts and a dozen eyeballs." I flipped a small towel onto my shoulder and assumed my best maître d' voice and demeanor.

"Perfect. I need coffee."

"Coffee first. Certainly, madam. And how does madam take her coffee?"

"Just black. Lord, Ms. Karen. I wish you could go back with me and deliver the donuts yourself."

"I don't think that's necessary, Tess. I'll bet you'll do a perfect impression of Ms. Karen's snootiness." The sheriff chuckled.

After Tess left, the sheriff nodded his head toward the meeting room. "I need my deputy back on duty, Ms. Karen."

"Go tap or holler at the door. I'm not stopping you."

"Well, that's a first." He mumbled.

He walked to the front door and announced in a loud voice. "Got to go, Ms. Karen. I'll just let my deputy know."

Roger dashed out of the meeting room. The sheriff winked, and I shook my finger at him. He laughed and followed his deputy out.

The bell jingled. Amber wore her dark blue suit with a pale yellow blouse. "I've got court today. Nothing exciting, which is different. The scoop at the gas station is all the excitement is at the Donut Hole." She gazed at our specials board. "Oooo. I need an eyeball and a slimed scone with my coffee this morning. Y'all have cornered the market on … what? What are you calling your Friday specials?"

"We don't know yet, Ms. Amber," Tiffany said. "We have to talk to Woody. He's our idea man." She handed Amber her coffee and sack.

Before Amber left, two middle-aged women came into the shop together and stared at the board.

"We need half a dozen slimed donuts and a dozen eyeballs. We heard Friday is specials day at the donut shop when we were at the gas station," the older one said.

"We thought that meant a special on price, but this is even better," the second woman said. "We're hosting the weekly Bible study group at our house this morning. We're reading Judges in the Old Testament."

"Our topic this week is Samson. Slime and eyeballs are perfect." They giggled as they carried out their pastries.

Tiffany's eyes were wide, and I laughed. "Now we know who the town jokesters are."

"Miss Lady, I'm going to whip up two more batches of donuts for slime and eyeballs. If we have any leftovers, we can take them to Aunt Gee's shop as promotions or for Isaiah and his friends."

Shirley rushed in. "Why didn't you tell me you were having a Friday special? Is this new? Will there be a special every Friday? Am I too late? Everybody's talking at the gas station. I need whatever the special is. I have one more contractor meeting this morning and another house to show. Somebody needs to take donuts to the clerk at the gas station. Give me another sack of the specials, and I'll drop it off for him."

I pointed at the counter where her coffee and sack waited. Tiffany added a second sack she had marked *Gas Station Special* in large print. Shirley dropped her money next to the register and hurried out.

"What did you put in her sack, Miss Lady?"

"Slimed, eyeball, and a scone."

"I put in three eyeballs and two slimed donuts in the gas station bag. I wasn't sure if young guys like scones."

Tiffany fried donuts and waited on customers while I drizzled and eyeballed. By eleven, our entire morning's inventory was gone except for the two scones and two eyeballs Tiffany had set back for us.

I flipped the sign on the door to *Closed*. Tiffany and I took our coffee and pastry to the meeting room.

"If Aunt Gee hears about this, we'll be in big trouble."

"She'll hear." I snickered.

While Tiffany gathered our dishes, I cleaned the table. "Roger's a nice guy. Did you go to school with him?"

Tiffany's face turned red, and she gazed at her feet. "No. He's only been in town two or three years. He wasn't around when I had my trouble, but he knows about it. He had a rough childhood too. He went a different direction than I did, though. He thinks I should be a teacher or a school counselor." Tiffany kept her head down.

"I agree you'd make a great teacher or counselor. I'm excited about your college career. You're smart and not afraid to work. You'll be successful at whatever you decide to do."

"What's our next step, Miss Lady?"

"We clean up the shop. I think I've earned an afternoon nap."

After I locked the front door, a car stopped in front of the shop. Carla rolled down the window. "Tiffany, got a little time? I need some help."

Tiffany stepped up to Carla's car. I bit my lip and headed to my car. I put Mia's carrier down to pull out my keys. After I unlocked the door, I loaded the carrier, and Colonel jumped into the back with Mia. When I opened the driver's door, Tiffany appeared next to me.

"Sorry. Didn't mean to slow you down. We can go to lunch now." Tiffany's voice was quite loud and clear.

Carla peeled out with a screech of tires.

Tiffany climbed into the passenger's seat. "You don't mind, do you? It was hard to turn her down after years of jumping to whatever Carla says. Can you drop me off at Aunt Gee's?"

"I'm proud of you. Let's drop Colonel and Mia off at the duplex and go to lunch unless you really need to go to Gee's first. I'll treat. We'll celebrate National Eyeball Day. That is a thing, right?"

Tiffany laughed. "We'll check with Woody, but what if every Friday is a National Something-We-Made-Up Day?"

"I love it. I'll bet our consultant will too. So, what did Carla want?"

"She said I had to help her. She was pretty vague. When I asked her doing what, she got huffy and said I never questioned her before. Those words kind of broke the spell. Does that make sense?"

"It does. Where for lunch?"

"Want to swing by Gus's, grab sandwiches, and take them to your place? I'm kind of over being around people for now."

"I agree. My ears could use a rest."

We sat at my dining table with our sandwiches and drinks.

"Wonder why Carla didn't ask Nancy." I took another bite of my favorite sandwich, turkey and swiss.

Tiffany swiped at her mouth with a napkin. "Mmm. Pulled pork with barbeque sauce. Gus's is the best." She reached down and gave Colonel a morsel of pork. "I asked her about Nancy. She said Nancy wasn't available. She was pretty mad that I asked and even madder about Nancy."

"Sounds like her little support system is falling apart. I have brownies for dessert. Doc said I needed to be sure to eat regular meals. I'm sure he meant dessert too."

"You're always right, Miss Lady." Her eyes twinkled.

I reached into the freezer for our brownies. "Roger's a nice guy, isn't he?"

"He is. Do you think he's nice to me because—well, you know. A lot of people I used to think were friends avoid me. Maybe they don't want to be associated with me, or maybe they don't know what to say."

"It took me a while to realize some people have a hardness that has nothing to do with me. We all move on. As long as I have one or two friends, I figure I'm okay."

Tiffany picked up our dishes and took them to the sink. "In that case, I'm okay."

"And to answer your original question, I'm positive Roger is not being nice to you out of pity or anything else. He likes being around you. You can put him in the friend category."

"Thank you. After I wash these dishes, I'll sweep the floors. What else is hard for you to do with one arm out of commission?"

"You're right about sweeping. I never realized it was a two-handed task until my cast. I've been able to do everything else." I frowned.

"Except change your bedsheets, am I right?" Tiffany grinned.

"You read my mind. I usually change the sheets once a week. The thought of going six weeks just crossed my mind. Ugh."

I kicked off my shoes and propped my feet up on my ugly sofa. Colonel snuffled in his sleep and woke me up. Tiffany was gone, and my little house was spotless.

"Tiffany cheated, Mia. She cleaned the entire house. Is she that quiet or was I that exhausted?"

Mia jumped on my lap, and I stroked her back.

"Let's go for a walk, Colonel." Colonel's head jerked at the sound of his name, and he lumbered to the door. We walked to the park, and I found a bench in the shade. Colonel trotted from tree to tree, chased two squirrels, and flopped on the ground next to me. We strolled to the park's dog water station. I rinsed the bowl and poured fresh water for him.

While he drank, I noticed someone with a ballcap was walking down the path toward us. I recognized Nancy when she got closer, and my eyes widened at her black eye.

"Ms. Karen, I was kind of wanting to talk to you."

"Shall we sit on a bench?" I waved at the benches in the shade.

Nancy looked around. "Might be nice. Not so visible from the street."

"How'd you get the black eye?" I asked as we strolled to the benches. Colonel trotted alongside me.

"Wrong place, wrong time." Nancy's laugh sounded forced to me.

She pulled a thick white envelope out of her jeans back pocket and sat on the bench with me. "I'm afraid Carla's trying to drag me into trouble. This is hard. She's my only sister." Tears slid down her face.

"She told me she needed help. I said I was done helping her. We argued, and she punched me. She's never hit me in the face before." She opened the envelope and handed me a creased photo. "It's a snapshot of Carla and her boyfriend when she was a freshman in high school. It was taken about fifteen or so years ago. She doesn't know I have it."

I looked at the picture. The heavy-set boy had dark hair and was an inch or so taller than Carla. He looked familiar, but I couldn't place him.

"I'm sorry about the mess, Nancy. Is there anything I can do to help you?"

She put the photo back in the envelope and sealed it. "Hang onto this for a while. It's the only picture I have of my sister."

"Who's the boy?"

She shook her head. "I gotta go."

"Wait. How'd you find me?"

"I was down the street from your house on my way to see you when you left." She strode into the woods.

"Ready to go home, Colonel? I could definitely use the walk to clear my head."

When I got home, I scooted Mia's litter box away from the wall in her pantry. I lifted the loose tile, slipped the envelope in with the coupon book, and slid the litter box back over the flooring.

Mia stood near her food bowl and yowled, and I glanced at the clock. "You're right. I'm thirty minutes late with your supper. Have you learned to tell time?"

Colonel barked.

"Don't nag. I'm moving as fast as a one-armed baker can."

After I filled their food bowls, I opened the freezer and pulled out the meal on top. "Sweet and Sour Chicken sounds good."

I put the dinner in the oven, opened the refrigerator, and my jaw dropped. "Look at this, Colonel. Tiffany made me a tossed salad with carrots, cucumber, and tomato."

* * *

My alarm sounded. I opened the back door, and Colonel disappeared into the thick fog. I felt panic rise in my chest until Colonel bounded back into view. We went inside, and I fed him and Mia.

"I'd rather walk than drive in fog this thick. Is that crazy, Colonel?" Mia slipped into her carrier. "Okay, we'll all go in the car."

When I arrived at the shop, it was dark. I unlocked the door, and the three of us went inside. I opened the carrier, and Mia dashed to the storeroom.

I glanced at the front window. *Do shadows hide in the fog?* I took the utility cart to the storeroom and loaded it with the supplies for the day.

My phone rang. "I am so sorry, Miss Lady. I didn't want Aunt Gee to drive in this fog, and it's taking longer to walk than I thought. I'll be there as soon as I can."

"Don't worry. I just put a few things on the cart. Be safe. And thanks for calling."

I left the cart and made coffee. Ten minutes later, Tiffany unlocked the front door and rushed in. I was at the counter with a cup of coffee.

"We've got plenty of time. Don't worry. What's the plan for today?"

Tiffany sat at the counter with me. "How about maple and orange glazed with cranberry-orange scones?"

"Sounds good. I checked the calendar. We've got the ham radio club this morning at nine, and the square dance officers meeting at ten."

"I'm on it. Think the mayor will show up today?"

"I'm hoping he does. He's a huge help. Which reminds me. I expect the ballcaps I ordered to be in this next week. I want to surprise him next week."

"He'll love it, but you know he'll still want to wear his apron while he's working."

When Tiffany dropped the first batch of donuts into the fryer, the bell jingled, and Shirley and Woody stepped inside. "We aren't too late, are we? We're here to help. What do you need for us to do? We can—" Shirley pursed her lips, and I pretended not to notice.

"Tiffany will have donuts ready for Woody to drizzle soon. Shirley, you and I can set up the meeting room for the nine o'clock meeting."

I pointed, and Shirley put plates, napkins, and serving utensils on the buffet.

"Karen, before I forget. I've hired a handyman to fix the back door," Shirley said. "He'll be there this afternoon. If that doesn't work for you, I can reschedule."

"That's good. Thank you. Do you remember who Carla's boyfriend was when she was in high school?"

"I think his name was Brennan or Brendon. He was older than her and not from around here. Her parents were not happy, but Carla was wild from the day she was born. She always got her way. Her mother wanted to send her to a private girls' school, but it was too expensive. Should I look into private school for Woody? I've never seen a child as smart as he is. I'm afraid our school system isn't challenging him. Did you ever teach at a private school? Which is better, public or private? I got off track, right? What do we do next?"

"Not much left to do until it's closer to nine. As far as Woody is concerned, he needs a stable environment more than a fancy school. He has family here, and you are a wonderful foster mother. He's really blossomed under your care. I'm proud of both of you."

"Thank you, Karen." Shirley spoke in a soft voice. "Sometimes I need to be reminded it's all good."

The bell jingled, and the sheriff strode in and read the board. "Does that mean all the eyeballs are gone? I'll take an orange glazed."

Tiffany set a plate with two orange glazed donuts on the counter and my coffee cup next to his.

"You doing okay?" He asked.

"I am. The doctor says I'm healing, and Tiffany's doing above and beyond to help me out."

"You've been good for her," the sheriff said in a quiet voice.

He ate his donuts, finished his coffee, and rose to leave. "You know you've got the entire town buzzing about the donut shop and looking forward to next Friday. You might have to hire Roger for crowd control." The sheriff beamed, and Tiffany's neck turned red.

I glowered, and he chuckled as he left.

At eight thirty, the mayor hurried in and headed to the storeroom for his apron. "Any meetings today? Am I late?"

"Two meetings today. The ham radio club meets at nine, and the square dance officers at ten. The radio club may stay late, but they'll just take over our reading table. They may want to bend your ear about a new repeater antenna. Just a head's up."

"Karen, I have a meeting at ten. Woody wants to stay. Is that okay? I'll be back by eleven, so we can have our construction project meeting. We're very excited. But I can't say any more. Zip. Nothing more. My lips are sealed. This is killing me." Shirley bustled into the storeroom and closed the door.

"Is she okay?" The mayor asked.

"She's fine. It's her way to keep from talking too much."

"Whatever it takes." The mayor shook his head, and I snickered.

Mr. Mayor was in place when the ham radio operators poured into the shop. He served coffee and refilled cups.

"Best job I ever had." He winked as he rushed to fill another platter with donuts. At five minutes until ten the hams' meeting relocated to the reading table. The mayor was a donut, coffee, and smiles machine. He kept the square dance officers and the hams supplied with coffee, donuts, and goodwill.

The bell jingled, and Roger walked in.

He strode to the counter and read the board. "Hey, Tiffany. Is today ordinary Saturday?" He chuckled, and Tiffany giggled.

"Here's your coffee and your ordinary donut." She giggled again.

I won't stare. Or gag. I watched the front door for customers.

Roger finished his donut and coffee. Tiffany watched him go out the door. He stopped outside and waved through the window, and she wiggled her fingers.

Good thing the sheriff isn't here.

The mayor appeared next to me. "Going to be interesting to see where this goes."

"You saw all that?"

"Oh yes." He turned back to his meeting room. After the meetings adjourned, he sat with me at the counter with a cup of coffee. "I love this job. And I've meant to tell you I like your pink cast. It suits you."

"Thank you. You are awesome."

A little after eleven, Shirley returned and took over the meeting room clean up. The mayor left with the notes and drawings the ham operators gave him. When Shirley finished, she joined Woody and me and our donuts at the reading table.

"Brings back memories." I took a bite of my maple donut.

"Sure does. Back in the day. When I was a kid." Woody grinned, and we tapped our donuts in a toast.

Shirley pulled out a folder. "This has all our backup material. The estimates from the contractors and our notes from meetings are here. Woody developed a one-page summary report for you." She handed me the sheet and put her knuckles over her mouth.

I looked at the summary sheet and glanced through their backup material. "Woody, you want to walk me through your findings?"

Woody had such a grown-up, serious look on his face I had to blink to be sure I hadn't fallen through a time warp into the future.

"Miss Lady, we liked the middle bid, but Ms. Shirley said sometimes things come up." He pointed to the bottom of the page. "This is money for a cushion just in case. Reserve, right, Ms. Shirley?"

Shirley beamed and nodded.

I looked through the pages again, more slowly. "You two were certainly thorough and well-organized. I agree completely with your assessment and appreciate all the work you did. Do I need to sign any paperwork?"

"Not yet. Our plan is Ms. Shirley will call the contractor and insurance adjuster to work out the details like the payment schedule."

I blinked again. *How old is this child?*

"Told you he was smart." Shirley beamed.

"Yes, you did. Excellent work, Woody. I'm impressed. Very well presented." I put the folder in my lap.

Tittany pulled up a chair. "Woody, we've got something else we wanted to talk to you about. We'd like to have surprise specials every Friday at the Donut Hole. We aren't sure what to call them, though. As a joke, Miss Lady and I called yesterday National Eyeball Day after everyone left. But maybe something like Surprise Friday might be good too. Should we make up a National Something Day for every Friday?"

Woody frowned and looked at the floor. "You could make it a contest. Have people submit their favorite National Something Day."

"Wow. That is brilliant," Tiffany said. "Definitely makes it easier for us."

"Love it. We'll start on Monday for this month. I think it will be fun."

"Ms. Shirley and I can make up a flyer for the contest and the forms for names. We can design the submissions to be a flyer, so all you have to do is post the form and write the National Day on your board. We can have them ready by Monday. Is that okay, Ms. Shirley?" Woody said.

"Sure is. Woody and I work very well together." Shirley beamed.

"Thank you," I said. "You're taking on the hard work, from my point of view."

"Naw. It's fun for us," Woody said.

"We like projects." Shirley pressed her lips closed.

"You're doing great, Shirley." I rose and slid my chair to its corner.

"I did the Saturday inventory, Miss Lady," Woody said.

"I have the list," Shirley said. "We'll do the shopping now and be back before you leave. Will that work?"

"You don't have to do that. I can do the shopping." When I looked at the two sad faces, I cleared my throat. "On second thought, that would be great. I'm supposed to be taking it easy, but sometimes I forget. Thank you."

"Yay!" Woody whooped, and he and Shirley raced out the door.

Tiffany laughed. "Those two are a funny pair. Who would have guessed they'd be so good for each other?"

"Not me, that's for sure," I chuckled.

Tiffany washed the equipment and filled the dishwasher. "I got a strange text this morning." She dried the beaters and mixing bowl. "Have you seen Nancy lately?"

My heart skipped a beat. "Why?"

CHAPTER EIGHT

"I got a text from Nancy around four yesterday. I know it was her because Carla gave me her number one time. It said *Be careful. Stay away from C.,* and she added *Nancy.* At first, I thought it she was threatening me, but now I'm not so sure. What do you think?"

I walked to a stool and sat. "If it were a threat, wouldn't she have said, *Better stay away from C.* or something like that?"

"That's what I thought too."

"Were you and Nancy ever friends?"

"I'd say no, but that's not true. Nancy and I are the same age. Carla is two years older. Nancy and I were good friends until Carla decided I was her friend."

She sat on the stool next to me. "Funny. I never thought about it like that before. Looking back, Carla didn't like any of my friends and kind of insisted I drop them. She told me Nancy didn't like me because she was jealous. I saw stuff like that in prison all the time. Don't know why I didn't see it in my life until now."

Tiffany pulled her phone out of her pocket. "I'm going to answer her."

She sent the text. "I told her *Talk anytime.*"

Her phone dinged. "She replied *Can't.* That's kind of sad, Miss Lady. I'm glad I made the offer. I hope she knows it stands."

Shirley and Woody pulled up in front of the shop, and Tiffany helped carry in sacks and boxes. Tiffany and Woody put the supplies away.

"Woody and I are going to lunch and then to a movie. Want to go with us? We've been waiting for this movie to come out for ages."

"Did you forget about the handyman? He'll be there this afternoon to fix the door, right?"

"You're right. I forgot." Shirley tapped her forehead with her fingers. "I guess I'm more excited about the movie than what I realized. We'll see you later."

Tiffany and I locked up. "Want a ride?"

"No, a walk is good for thinking. Thanks for listening."

When I put Mia's carrier into my car, I saw shadows out of the corner of my eye. *Shadows on a sunny day? Can't be good.*

When I lifted Mia's carrier out of the back of my car, a white crew-cab pickup parked in front of the duplex. A muscular man with a gray and brown mustache and closely-clipped salt and pepper hair stepped out and lifted a toolbox out of the truck bed. He strode up. His hazel eyes twinkled. "Mrs. O'Brien? I'm Jack. I'm here to fix your door. Backdoor right?" He held his hand down for Colonel who sniffed approval. Jack scratched Colonel's back.

"That's right, come on in." *Any friend of Colonel's is a friend of mine.*

"Heard about your house. You doing all right?" He wiped his feet before he entered.

"I'm fine. Healing. I'm Karen." We shook hands.

"Let's look at what you got here. Good job securing this door."

"The sheriff did that."

"You okay if I make some noise? I can do this another time."

"I'm fine. Really. Go ahead."

I selected a book from my small stack of to-be-read and sat on the sofa. The rhythmic sounds of the electric tools and pounding were soothing.

"Mrs. O'Brien, Karen, I've finished the work. Want to inspect your new door?"

I followed him to the kitchen. "This is nice. I see you installed a deadbolt too. Thank you."

Jack gathered his tools and placed them into his toolbox. "Most welcome."

"How about some iced tea before you leave? It's a hot day."

"Thank you, but I don't want to impose."

"No imposition at all. Sit." I waved at the dining table and poured iced tea for the two of us. I opened the freezer door, reached for brownies, and put two on a plate.

"Homemade brownies, if you're interested. I love them frozen, but it takes only a few minutes for them to thaw."

Jack picked up a brownie and took a bite. "This is delicious. Didn't you buy Mr. Rothenberger's donut shop? I've heard great things lately about the Donut Hole."

"I did. He left me all his recipes. I do enjoy the shop."

"I'll have to stop in." He rose. "Thanks for the cold tea and the brownie. That was the best brownie I've ever had. Your husband is a lucky man."

I shook my head. "I'm not married. It's just me, Colonel, and Mia."

"I'm sorry. I didn't mean to pry." He smiled. "I don't get out much. I guess you can tell."

I chuckled. "I go to work and to the park with Colonel. Stop by the shop sometime. It'd be nice to see a fellow recluse."

"I'll just do that. Nice to meet you, Donut Lady."

"You too, Handyman."

We laughed, and I accompanied him to the front door.

He stopped and frowned. "You need a better deadbolt on this door. Okay if I come by next week and install one? I'll stop by the donut shop and let you know when I'll be here."

"That would be wonderful." We shook hands, and he left.

Wonderful? Since when is a deadbolt wonderful? I must be tired.

I carried my book to the sofa, and Colonel joined me. I woke to whining. It was dark, and Colonel stood next to my face.

"I'll bet you and Mia are hungry. It's probably good I napped, but I've read that one page three or four times. Still not sure what it said."

Colonel and I stepped outside. The moon was hidden by clouds, and the wind blew from the northwest. The cicadas buzzed their warning of rain.

After I filled Colonel and Mia's food bowls, I brewed a cup of hot tea.

* * *

The next morning after breakfast my phone rang. *Shirley.*

"Karen, Woody and I'd like to invite you to lunch with us. Don't tell me you're busy. You're not. We've never been to the Ivy Restaurant. Have you? I've heard it's a nice place. We'll pick you up at eleven. Does that work for you? Taking a breath now. You can talk. Your turn."

I stifled a giggle. *She's trying.* "Lunch sounds fun. See you at eleven."

After we hung up, I heard thunder in the distance, and Mia hissed and dashed into her pantry.

"I'll take my bath before the storm gets any closer." Colonel followed me and laid across the bathroom threshold. The shadows drifted to the ceiling in the hall.

After I dressed for my outing, I relaxed on the sofa and read. The sky darkened, and the wind howled. I opened the blinds to watch the storm. The strength of the wind blew the rain sideways.

"I wouldn't want to be out in that, Colonel." He flopped next to the sofa and closed his eyes. The storm raged, and my eyes drooped.

The sound of a knock at the door startled me awake. The sun shined through the blinds. "We slept through the storm, Colonel." He raced to the door and whined.

I opened the door. "I knew it was you, Woody. Colonel told me."

"Are you ready to go? Ms. Shirley can come inside if you need a little more time."

"I'm ready. I just need to put on my shoes and grab my purse."

"Have you ever been to the Ivy Restaurant?" Shirley asked. "I hear their food is delicious. I sold them the farmhouse four years ago, but I didn't realize the chefs planned to turn it into a restaurant. I feel bad I haven't been there yet. I'd forgotten how far out into the country it is, but this is a nice drive after that rain, isn't it?"

"I haven't been there either. What do you plan to order for lunch, Woody?" I turned and smiled.

"I need a cheeseburger and fries. I heard the Ivy was fancy, but my friends at school say it has specials for kids."

"Sounds like the chefs are smart." I gazed at the landscape. "It is a nice day after all for a drive in the country. I've been in a bit of a rut for a while."

"Did Jack get the back door fixed? He's a retired engineer. He helps me out with repairs on my houses. His wife was a good friend of mine. We went through real estate classes together. Ava died five years ago. He fixed a porch on a house two years ago when I couldn't find anybody else to do the repairs on short notice. I had a tenant ready to move in, but the porch wasn't safe. He said he needed something to do."

"He did an excellent job on the back door. He offered to put a more secure deadbolt on the front door next week. You don't mind, do you?"

"That's great. I should have thought of it earlier. I'd forgotten there were goats out here." Shirley pointed at a farm we passed. "Jack's always the primary topic of conversation when the single women in town get together. They keep asking me why Jack and I don't date, but it would be like going out with my brother. Each one says I should put in a good word for her, and we all laugh. Do you know how much trouble I'd be in if I mentioned one woman's name and not another? Jack's like you. He has a collie or a lab or some other kind of big dog. I can't remember his dog's name. I'm surprised he didn't bring her with him to fix the door. He usually does. But most of the houses he fixes for me aren't occupied. I do repairs after the tenant moves out. Oh, look. We're here already."

I glanced at Woody in the back seat. His head jerked, and his eyes opened when the car turned at the gravel driveway. He stretched and yawned.

Woody ordered his cheeseburger and fries; Shirley ordered a small steak and a salad. I opted for the special, coconut shrimp with fries.

"This is good, Shirley. Thank you for the invitation. How's your steak?"

"Really juicy. How's your burger, Woody?"

Woody wiped his mouth and chin. "Yummy."

The waitress refilled our drinks. "Chef says to save room for dessert. He has something special for you." I moaned, and she looked at my plate. "Shall I box up your shrimp? Chef says the fries don't warm up very well. We'll send you home with a small salad."

"You people are awesome."

"We try." A low male voice from the kitchen called out, and we laughed.

The waitress conferred with Woody. When she served dessert, Shirley and I had key lime pie, and Woody had a warm brownie with ice cream and chocolate syrup.

Woody and Shirley ate their desserts. I ate half my pie and pushed back my plate. The waitress whisked my plate away. "I'll add your pie to your box. You'll have a nice meal tomorrow night."

I asked for the bill, but Shirley overruled me. "I'll get it this time, Karen. Next time you can pick where we go, and it'll be your treat."

"Deal."

* * *

I laid my head on my pillow. *Today was a great day.*

Something shook me awake. I opened my eyes. I was back in my prison cell, and panic rose in my chest. The shadows slipped out through the bars.

"Get up, O'Brien," my cellmate growled. "They're coming for inspection. They know."

I jumped up and pulled my thin blanket taut across the cot. I ran my fingers along the bottom rail to clear the dust. "What do they know?" I held a small scalpel in my hand. Blood dripped from my hand and fingers to the floor.

"What are you doing? They'll see the blood. Hide it." My cellmate hissed and jumped from the top bunk.

"How can I hide the blood? Find something to clean it up." I clutched the scalpel and blood spurted from my arm.

She sunk into the floor and rose as a spitting cobra. I ripped the blanket off my bed and threw it over the snake.

She writhed under the cover and screamed. "Karen, help me. Karen!" I yanked off the blanket. My cellmate's eyes glowed green, and she sank her fangs into my neck.

"I can't be here." I struggled to the door. "Let me out." Voices from the hallway mocked my pleas. "I can't be here. Let me out. I can't be here. Let me out."

I ripped the snake off my neck and flung her across the cell. She turned into a human midair and slammed her head on the iron bed. Blood oozed from her head onto her prison uniform. I saw her face.

"Nancy? Is that you? What are you doing here in prison?"

"Prison?" Her skin sloughed off her forehead, exposing her skull. "We aren't in prison." Her arms detached from her shoulders and dropped to her lap. "We're dead."

I gasped in terror and screamed.

Colonel barked. I was in my bedroom. I checked my hand and arm. No blood.

"I'm not dead." I ran to the bathroom and vomited. I lay on the cold floor and sobbed. Hours later, I pulled myself off the floor and splashed water on my face.

"I'm not dead." I stumbled to the kitchen to start my coffee. "Three thirty. Not sure I'm ready for coffee." I took a quick bath and dressed for work.

By the time Colonel, Mia, and I reached the shop, I stopped shaking. The lights were on inside the shop. I parked and picked up Mia's carrier. "I'm not dead."

Tiffany stood at the mixer. She turned as the bell jingled, and her eyes widened when she saw me. "You had a rough night. I can handle today."

"Thank you." I slumped on a stool, and Tiffany brought me coffee.

I watched Tiffany work. "I'll check the calendar. Did you hear anything from Nancy?"

"No, I haven't. I already checked the calendar. Only one meeting today at nine. The men's group from the Methodist church. Why don't they meet at the church?"

"Their leader told me the group almost disbanded over whose turn it was to clean up after their meetings. They'd rather pay dues than argue with each other."

Tiffany scratched her head. "Doesn't seem like it would be that hard to take turns, but we're happy for their business, right?"

"Exactly. Make an extra batch of donuts. They like to take a dozen to the sheriff's office and two or three dozen to the VA clinic."

I sipped my coffee. "My taste buds don't seem to be interested in coffee this morning." I poured out my cup and filled a glass with water. "I like the look of your black shirt with the pink apron. Is that a new shirt?"

Tiffany covered the rising dough and grinned. "Aunt Gee got a box of promo T-shirts with her last furniture order. There's a logo on the shirt, but you can't see it because of the apron bib." She cat-walked to the door and whirled around and posed with her hand on her hip. "What do you think? The latest fashion?" She sashayed back to the counter, and I chuckled.

"I'm going to set up the meeting room. I'm too restless to do nothing." I stacked plates and napkins on the utility cart. "Do you suppose you could send a text to Nancy? Tell her I'd like to talk to her?"

"Sure. I can do that." Tiffany grabbed her phone and sent the text.

Tiffany drizzled glaze on the first batch of donuts, and the bell jingled. The sheriff strode in.

"Wow, sheriff," Tiffany said. "You must have donut radar. These donuts are almost too hot to eat."

"No such thing," the sheriff laughed. "I'll take two."

I poured his coffee and sat at the counter with my glass of water.

The sheriff raised his eyebrows. "No coffee for you this morning, Karen? You on some kind of diet?"

"Wouldn't that be the worst diet ever? The no-coffee diet?"

"I heard you got your back door fixed. Jack does good work. I'll bet Colonel's happy he doesn't have to walk around the house to go to the backyard. Jack's a nice guy, isn't he?" Colonel's ears perked up at his name, and he ambled to the sheriff for his morning face rub.

Tiffany refilled the sheriff's cup and stayed at the counter.

I raised one eyebrow and glared. "Fishing much, sheriff?"

He snickered. "I bet I won't be the last to mention Jack in this shop today."

"I bet you've already been to the gas station."

"You nailed it, Karen. Our town's version of the water cooler."

"I need a good comeback. How about *Oh is that the handyman's name?*"

"Too subtle for our crowd. Maybe squint your eyes and look mysterious."

"Show me."

The sheriff squinted his eyes and batted his eyelashes. Tiffany and I laughed so hard we snorted.

The sheriff cocked his head. "What? Too subtle?"

"I might just do it. Word will get around I've lost my mind, and everyone will come to the donut shop to see."

The sheriff's radio crackled. "Guess I'd better get back to work. Seriously, you always brighten my day. Thanks."

Tiffany crossed her arms and growled. "So Miss Lady. When were you going to tell me about Mr. Jack?"

"Right after you filled me in on Roger." I squinted and batted my eyelashes.

Tiffany guffawed. "Touché, Miss Lady, and you do look demented."

I lifted my right hand, and we high-fived.

The bell jingled, and Shirley rushed in with a large box. "Did I miss something? Did something good happen? Did you tell Tiffany about Jack? Everybody's talking about you and him at the gas station. You might get some glares today. The hardware store's gearing up for a run on sledgehammers to bust doors. I just thought of something. I know you're working on creative marketing. You could have a doorbuster sale on donuts."

My jaw dropped.

"Oh. I guess that's not a good idea. Sometimes I forget to think before I say something."

Tiffany clapped her hand over her mouth and gave Shirley her coffee and sack.

"I almost forgot. Here are the flyers and entry forms Woody made for the contest." Shirley placed the box on the counter. "Let me know if we can help with anything else. I have a parent's meeting with Woody's principal today. The principal suggested we may want to dual-enroll Woody, but I'm not sure what that means. I'll let you know after I get the information. I have to run, or I'll be late."

After Shirley left, I sat on the stool. "I'm tired."

"And for good reason, Miss Lady. My ears are tired too." Tiffany returned to her donuts. "I did kind of like her idea for a doorbuster sale, though."

The bell jingled as the Methodist men filed into the shop. I headed to the meeting room, and Tiffany waved me off. "I've got this."

I reached into the box for the announcement flyers that Shirley and Woody had printed on heavy paper. I found three stands under the flyers. I put one flyer on our reading table and another on the counter. I stood back to judge the placement and readability. *Eye-catching.*

I lifted out the included box with the submission forms. The top and sides of the box were decorated with watercolor pencil drawings of donuts and scones.

Tiffany carried an empty platter out of the meeting room and stopped. "Wow. I can almost smell the donuts on that box. That child has awesome talents."

"The artwork is stunning, isn't it? Would you place this flyer with its stand in the meeting room? Maybe on the buffet? I'll put the submission box by the cash register."

The bell jingled, and Roger swaggered in.

"On second thought," I said, "I want to see how the meeting's going." I took the flyer, stand, and some submission forms into the pink room.

"Whatcha got here, Ms. Karen?" Silas, the retired dentist, reached for the stand and flyer and placed them on the buffet table.

"We are going to make every Friday a special National Day. Do any of you know about our eyeballs we made last Friday out of donut holes?" I beamed while most nodded, and all the men laughed.

"After we closed, Tiffany said we celebrated National Eyeball Day, and we decided to have a special day every Friday. We're creative with our baking but didn't think we could come up with a special day every week without help."

"Brilliant. What better way to get everyone involved than a contest? We're a unique town and will have our own unique holidays every Friday. Are the donuts going to represent each holiday?" Silas passed out submission forms.

"Absolutely. But most likely only in our imaginations."

The men laughed again.

"Who's going to judge the contest and pick the winners?" Skip, the animal control officer, scanned the submission form.

"Tiffany and I are the judges from the shop. We may have guest judges from our local school or other organizations like the 4H, Girl Scouts, or Boy Scouts. You know, our local dignitaries."

"Your submission form looks like it could be a flyer," Silas said. "You had experts working on this didn't you?" He winked.

Skip and two other men went into a huddle. "We can submit a name as a team, right? And more than one name?" Skip asked.

"Sure can." I smiled at the enthusiasm growing in the room. I picked up the empty platter on the buffet table. "I'll be right back. Y'all have run out of donuts."

As I left the room, the bell jingled, and Roger left the shop.

"Donuts for the pink room?" Tiffany took the platter from me. "Thanks, Ms. Karen. We'll talk later." She grinned.

By the time the churchmen left, I was fading.

"Have you eaten today, Miss Lady?" Tiffany asked. "You're dragging. More than just tired."

"I think I forgot my breakfast yogurt."

"Sit, and I'll bring you coffee and a scone."

I took a bite of the cranberry-orange scone. "This is delicious. Did you know I've never had a scone?"

The bell jingled.

Tiffany shook her head. "You need to get out more, Miss Lady." She glanced at the door and raised an eyebrow.

I turned and smiled at Jack.

"Told you I'd stop by. I'll have that deadbolt tomorrow afternoon. I can install it any time this week."

Tiffany put a cup of coffee on the counter next to where I sat.

"What would you like with your coffee, Jack?" I asked.

He gazed at the board. "A classic and a chocolate-dipped."

"Yes, sir." Tiffany moved with such ease that the plate with two donuts appeared like magic in front of him.

He took a bite of the classic glazed. "This is delicious. I used to buy donuts from Mr. R., but I don't remember his donuts being this good. You've put your own twist to his recipes. Excellent."

"Tiffany and I enjoy experimenting with flavors. She's my baker since the doc put this cast on me."

"Well done, Tiffany."

Tiffany waved from the sink where she scraped and rinsed dishes for the dishwasher. "Thank you. I've got the best teacher in the state."

Jack cocked his head. "You're a teacher?"

"Retired. Now I'm a donut shop owner with a talented baker."

Tiffany refilled our cups. She stood in front of us with the coffee pot in her hand and beamed until I glared at her. She scurried away.

Jack pulled out his wallet to pay, and I waved my hand. "On the house for a first-time guest."

"No. I have to pay for my coffee and donuts. You'll go broke giving them away."

"Nope. Because everybody else in town has been here. You're the last of the possible first-time guests."

Jack chuckled. "Got me on that one. Thursday afternoon okay for the deadbolt? Better yet, why don't we go to lunch on Thursday, and then I'll install the deadbolt."

"Sounds nice."

"Really? Good. I'll meet you at your house at what? Noon?"

"Noon works."

"Good. Well. I better be going. Thank you for the donuts and coffee. See you Thursday." He put a ten-dollar bill on the counter. "Tip for your talented baker."

After he left, I pointed at the tip.

"Going straight into my college fund." She grinned. "I'm having lunch with Roger today. I beat you."

"That's wonderful. You know it's not a competition, but you didn't beat me because Jack had iced tea and a brownie at my house. That counts."

"It's not a competition. Doesn't count."

"We're terrible. You know that, right?" I wiggled my eyebrows.

Tiffany whisked away the dishes I had stacked on the counter. "Did you ever hear from Nancy?"

"No. Very odd. I don't know why she didn't answer. It's not her nature." Tiffany rinsed the few remaining dishes and added them to the dishwasher. After she started the dishwasher, she put the last few pots and pans away and walked to the storeroom to hang up her apron.

Nancy's dead.

"I'm not dead," I whispered.

"Did you say something?" Tiffany came out of the storeroom.

"Just mumbling. See you tomorrow."

It was noon. The shadows moved away from the window when Tiffany approached the door.

When I stopped at the traffic light on the way home, Colonel placed his chin on the back of the seat, and I stroked his cheek. "Colonel, I'm exhausted, but I'm afraid to sleep." The shadows surrounded my car.

"I have to nap this afternoon. You folks okay with that?" The shadows faded into the sunlight.

"I'll eat something then I'll read the same page I've read at least ten times. I'll need you to stay close, Colonel."

Colonel laid his head on my shoulder. *Deal*, my dog told me in his own way.

I grabbed a peach yogurt and dropped a slice of bread into the toaster. When my toast popped up, I smeared peanut butter on it. I dipped my spoon into the yogurt, swirled the peach creaminess in my mouth, and took a bite of crisp toast. *Sweet, salty, and crunchy. Mmm.* Mia came out of her pantry and curled up on my feet.

After I ate, I stretched out on my sofa with my old afghan across my legs. Colonel flopped down on the floor next to me. I glared at my book on the coffee table, but I couldn't reach it without getting up. I rolled onto my side and closed my eyes.

When I opened my eyes, it was still daylight. Colonel had moved to the rug near the front door, and Mia was on my feet. Mia jumped off the sofa and stalked Colonel. I sat up and rolled my shoulders.

"I actually feel rested." The shadows hovered in the hallway. "Thanks for letting me sleep."

Colonel woke. "Want to go for a walk, boy? I could use the exercise."

I carried Colonel's leash, and he ran ahead and cleared squirrels out of our path. We strolled toward downtown. It was a new direction with new sights for me and new smells for Colonel.

When we came to Otto Rothenberger's daughter's house, Darlene stopped pruning her roses and limped with her cane to the shade of a tree where she had two lawn chairs. Stray gray curls escaped from under her wide-brimmed straw garden hat. She wore red rainboots, dark blue denim pants, and an orange smock over her yellow shirt. She eased into one of the chairs, removed her pink garden gloves, and dropped them on the ground.

"We had some excitement in the neighborhood earlier. You may have already heard. Alfred Gibbons is a hero."

CHAPTER NINE

"No, I hadn't heard." I joined her in the shade. Darlene waved at the empty chair, and I sat. "Thanks. The breeze and the shade feel good."

"I know. I can't work in the sun as long as I used to." She fanned herself with her hat.

She peered over her wire-rimmed glasses and spoke in a conspiratorial tone. "Amber, the mayor's daughter, runs by here almost every morning. This morning a young thug attacked her from behind and knocked her down. I didn't see it, but the neighbors think he was trying to rob her. Amber put up a fight, which is no surprise, knowing her. Mr. Gibson was planting azaleas in his side yard and heard the commotion. I don't know why he loves those common azaleas. I told him roses are more refined, but he doesn't seem to care. He ran out, grabbed the boy, threw him on his lawn, and sat on him."

I raised my eyebrows.

"I know. Not very genteel for a banker to sit on a hoodlum, is it? Amber put her foot on the kid's neck and, remember I wasn't there, so this is just hearsay. Dared him to move. She told him she'd crush his neck and he'd never walk again if he so much as twitched. I don't think she really said that. It doesn't sound very ladylike to me."

I put my hand to my mouth. I hoped I looked shocked and not like I was about to burst into laughter.

"The neighbors called the law, and Jeff, the sheriff's deputy, handcuffed the criminal and took him to jail. I wished I'd seen it. I heard the commotion, but I hadn't finished putting on my makeup. By the time I got outside, Jeff had driven away. That boy should have known better than to attack a lawyer. Amber can sue him for everything he's worth. He's not the sharpest tack in the box, is he?"

Everything he's worth? I blinked and shook my head. "That's something. Colonel and I better get going. Thanks for the break and for catching me up. You take care, now."

Colonel turned at the next corner. "You ready to head to the park, Colonel? Sounds good to me."

Colonel trotted ahead and waited at the next corner. When I got close, he trotted a few feet away and stopped. He glanced back at me and grinned.

"No, I'm not going to jog with you. You're old too. It's good for you to take a break and wait for me." I scolded, but I ruined it with a giggle.

Tires screeched behind me. I turned, and Jack jumped out of his truck.

"Are you okay? You weren't home. Should you be outside by yourself? I heard about Amber."

I cocked my head. "I'm not by myself. I've got Colonel. And an entire neighborhood of protective people." I waved down the street where a man or woman, most of them elderly, stood with a shovel, rake, or broom near the sidewalk at almost every house.

Jack's face turned red. "Did I tell you engineers have no social skills? It's true. My seven-year-old collie, Roxie, is with me. Can we walk with you and Colonel so the vigilantes can get back to their yard work?" He lowered his voice. "I might need your protection to get out of this neighborhood alive."

I laughed. "Sure. We're on our way to the park."

We walked in silence behind the dogs whose pace quickened the closer we got to the park. When we arrived, I was ready to take a rest on the bench.

"Thank you for coming to check on me. I have to tell you this is the most interesting walk I've had in a long time."

"You know it's the curse of the handyman to fix things, right? Combine that with the social skills of an engineer, and I've just told you my life story. What about you?"

"As a teacher, I see teachable moments everywhere. Took me a long time to realize that not everyone wants to learn. Twelve years in prison gave me a perspective I would have never gotten any other way, but that's carrying a teachable moment too far, even for me."

He shook his head. "Life does do that, doesn't it? After Ava died, Alfred Gibson pushed me to join his anger management team. I realized how angry I was at the world when he told me depression was anger turned inward."

Colonel and Roxie wandered the park and chased squirrels back to their trees.

Jack and I walked to the dog spigot, and he filled the bowl with water for the dogs.

"Want to walk back to my pickup with us? I'll give you and Colonel a ride home from there."

"That would probably be better than creeping behind us in your truck while we walk." I couldn't hold back the smile.

"Oh, Lord. You've got me pegged." His hearty laugh filled the park. A squirrel overhead chattered its annoyance.

We strolled to the truck, and the dogs ran ahead.

"Feels good to laugh. All my laughs have been polite for too long." He mused.

When he parked at the duplex, Jack opened my door and helped me out. "Thank you, Ms. O'Brien, for an enjoyable afternoon." He walked with us to the door. "I'll see you Thursday at noon."

Jack remained on the porch until I closed and locked the door. I knew he'd wait until he heard the deadbolt slide into place before he left. The shadows waited near the pantry door; Mia scooted out and sniffed Colonel.

"We have time to dust and straighten up a bit before supper." The shadows slipped out the back door. "What? Don't want to help?"

Mia chased the dust mop while I ran it over the floors. She pounced on it, and I dragged her across the floor. "Not sure how much cleaning I'm getting done giving you a ride, Mia." She kept her balance on the mophead while I pulled her through the dining room and Colonel barked.

When I stopped, Mia jumped off and head-bumped my leg. "You're welcome, Mia. We don't play enough around here, do we?"

I put my dinner in the oven and gathered the dirty clothes from my hamper in the bedroom and the towels from the bathroom. I pulled the tablecloth off the dining table, added it to the washer, and started my load of laundry.

I flipped a clean tablecloth onto the dining table, but it slid off the end and landed on Mia. She yowled, ran to her pantry, and dragged the tablecloth with her until it caught on the door hinge.

"Sorry I startled you, Mia." I picked up the tablecloth and added it to the laundry. "Maybe a nice placemat is a better idea until my cast comes off."

I poured a glass of tea and enjoyed my dinner from the Ivy Restaurant with my faithful dog under the table and my pouting cat in the pantry.

* * *

The alarm woke me at four. *I could get used to sleeping all night.*

Mia sauntered into her carrier, and the three of us rode to the shop. The lights were on when we parked.

"What's on deck for today, Tiffany?"

"Good morning, Miss Lady. We've got submissions for our national day this Friday." She opened the submissions box and pulled out three sheets. "This first one's dirt day; this one is Christmas. The third one's. Oh my." Her eyebrows flew up. "National Jailbird Day."

"Oh, Lord." I laughed. "We have to do that. Who submitted it? The sheriff?"

"How did you know?" Her eyes were wide.

"Are you uncomfortable with it?" *I hope Tiffany's not offended.*

"Surprised me, that's all. Kind of grows on you, doesn't it?" She snickered.

"We can see what else we get. Maybe this Friday is Dirty Socks Day, but for sure we'll do National Jailbird Day sometime. We'll let the sheriff have second thoughts over his suggestion and sweat a while."

"I love it. Aunt Gee would be in awe if she knew."

"I know she'd keep it quiet, but I think it'd be fun to surprise her too."

"I need to get busy. I checked the calendar. The only meeting today is the Remote Control Flyers executive committee at nine thirty." Tiffany rushed to check her dough and fryer temperature.

I put the submission box next to the register, slipped our three submissions into a folder, and dropped them into my file cabinet in the storeroom.

The bell jingled, and the sheriff sauntered in. He peered at the specials board.

"I was hoping today was Taco Tuesday."

I poured coffee for the two of us. "Don't you go giving Tiffany any ideas."

Tiffany brought the sheriff's plate with a chocolate glazed donut and a maple donut. "Sounds a little tame after our termites and eyeballs last week."

Sheriff sipped his coffee. "It's not fair. It's getting harder to get anything past you two." He polished off his maple donut in three bites. I refilled our cups. He broke his chocolate glazed donut into quarters. I raised my eyebrows.

He chuckled. "Four is more than three."

"Good one, sheriff," Tiffany called from the meeting room.

"Don't you go giving him any encouragement, Tiffany." I called back.

The sheriff gulped down his coffee. "Thanks for another great start to my day."

As the sheriff left, Shirley breezed inside the shop. Tiffany dropped off Shirley's coffee and sack on the counter before she hurried into the pink room to set it up.

"Don't the flyers look great, Karen? Have you had any submissions yet? Am I eligible to enter?" She slipped entries into the box. "Woody and I brainstormed yesterday. Most of the ideas are his, but I thought of one. When are you going to judge the entries? I talked to the principal yesterday, and he suggested art classes for Woody. The assistant principal is looking into the best school for Woody's style. Thanks for the coffee and donuts, Tiffany. Gotta run."

The bell jingled as Shirley left.

I walked into the meeting room. "What do you think about the bell over the door, Tiffany? For some reason, it gets on my nerves. Maybe that's just today."

"I can see where it made sense to have the bell when the meeting room was an office, and Mr. R. was by himself. I'm not sure he had the volume of customers we have. We can take it down and see if we miss it."

"Let's do that. Be interesting to see if anyone else notices," I said. "The only time I ever paid attention to it was when I was by myself. I liked knowing when my first customer came in, but it was always the sheriff."

"I'll look at it after we close. Another thought is I can move it, so the door doesn't hit it, or maybe I could take the clapper out. Then people will still see the bell that has been there forever, but we won't have to listen to it."

The bell jingled, and Tiffany covered her ears. "It is annoying, and I'm going to hear it all morning now, won't I?"

"Hope not. Especially if you mention it every time you hear it." I rolled my eyes.

Our customer was Josh, the young clerk from the gas station. He wore dark green work pants and a dark green shirt with the gas station logo on the pocket. Josh examined the specials board. "Ms. Donut Lady, could I have four chocolate donuts and two maple?" He pulled folded bills out of his pocket and grinned. "And a dozen donut holes. We collected money for Jorge's birthday. He's a great boss."

Tiffany and I cringed when the bell jingled as he left.

At nine thirty, the meeting room was full. Each one of the seven executive committee members came in separately. The bell jingled the arrival of each one.

"Miss Lady, do you suppose you could take care of the pink room for a minute or two? I want to take a quick look at that bell."

"I'd love to." I put two coffee pots and a platter of mixed donuts on the utility cart and rolled into the pink room. I needed the mayor. He would have been interested in the evolution of remote-control airplanes. When I stepped out of the meeting room, the bell jingled, but the sound came from the display case. My head jerked. Tiffany stood by the cash register with the bell in her hand. She rang it again and grinned.

"Well done, Tiffany. I'll put it in the storeroom." I clutched the bell with both hands, and it clunked.

When each remote-control executive committee member left, I heard the front door creak. My face must have broadcast my dismay because Tiffany laughed. "It's okay. I can fix that with a little penetrating oil."

I straightened the meeting room and wiped down the counter while Tiffany cleaned the equipment, ran the dishwasher, and swept the shop. After Tiffany returned the broom to the storeroom, she scanned the shop. "Ready to leave, Miss Lady?"

"You go ahead. I've got a little paperwork to finish up."

When Tiffany opened the door to leave, it creaked, but it didn't jingle. I locked the door behind her. After I finished the day's paperwork, I locked up the shop. The sheriff drove up, and his face was grim. I bit my lip, and Colonel leaned on me.

Nancy's dead.

"Karen, I have news. There's a press meeting going on right now."

I'm not dead.

"Are you okay? Come sit with me in my car, and I'll take you and Colonel home."

"No, I'm just tired. What's the news?"

He took my elbow. "Nancy's dead, and we haven't been able to find Carla to notify her."

I nodded. *Nancy's dead.* "How did she die?"

"A fisherman found her body in the river early this morning. The autopsy is scheduled for this afternoon. No other information yet."

"No idea of where Carla is?"

"No. We wanted to inform her about her sister's death before the news got out. I don't know if we'll be successful. Will you be okay?"

I met his gaze. "I will. Thank you."

When Colonel and I pulled into the driveway, I saw shadows at the front window. I unlocked the front door, and the shadows moved to the hallway. Mia was curled on the sofa. Colonel sniffed her face. She sprang off the couch, tore around the living room, and zipped into the bedroom. The shadows scattered in her path.

"I'd ask what spooked Mia, but that would be silly. She spooked the shadows."

I kicked off my shoes and flopped onto the sofa. I put my feet up, leaned back, and closed my eyes.

My phone rang. "Hey there, Donut Lady. Tiffany and I would like to invite you to dinner tonight. I'll send Isaiah to pick you up."

"I don't know, Gee. I appreciate the offer, but I'm pretty tired."

"You have to eat. I don't think you're eating right. We all get up early, so we'll send you home early. And Tiffany said she'd tell us about Roger. You okay with six o'clock?"

"No mention of Jack, okay?"

"Can't hear you. Bad connection. Six o'clock." She snickered and hung up.

"Gee's in rare form, Colonel."

Colonel padded to the back door, and we went outside for his break. A mockingbird trilled through its repertoire until the neighbor behind us revved up a lawnmower and drowned out the songs. The air filled with the sweet smell of cut grass. A squirrel scampered across our yard. Colonel charged after it, but the squirrel leaped on top of the fence and disappeared behind the neighbor's house. Colonel ambled back to the porch.

"You almost caught him, boy. Good job." I stroked Colonel's neck.

* * *

Isaiah pulled in at six. "You ready for a grillin'?" Isaiah grinned as he drove us to Gee's. "Mama's probably even got a list of questions ready."

"I'm not surprised. No free lunch, they say. Probably goes for dinner too."

"Well, if she gets on your last nerve, mention *Oliver*. But don't tell anybody I told you."

"I like this. I'll save it for my last nerve. Thanks for the ammunition."

"Yes, ma'am. I love to tease Mama."

Gee met us at the door. "Nobody will have to run to the kitchen for seconds. It's all right here. Let's eat." Gee waved at the table she'd set up buffet-style.

"You sit, Miss Lady. I'll serve up your plate," Tiffany said. It didn't take long for everyone to fill their plates and join me at the table.

I took a bite of the fried chicken. "The chicken is wonderful. It's crispy and juicy. Best I ever put in my mouth."

"Tiffany fried the chicken," Gee said. "She's much better at it than I am. I don't even try when she's here."

No dinner table conversation at Gee's because we were too busy eating. Isaiah helped himself to seconds.

I put my fork on my plate. "I'm slowing down. Tiffany dished up the amount of food I asked for, but I forgot about the rolls. Can't pass them up."

"You might have noticed I haven't mentioned a certain young deputy. Tiffany bribed me to wait until next week. It'll be a better story then anyway," Gee said as she cleared the table. "We've got dessert. Isaiah requested banana pudding."

"I haven't had banana pudding since I was a girl. My grandmother used to make it for special occasions." I scooped up pudding, banana, meringue, and a bit of wafer on my spoon. "Mmm. This is just how I remember it. Creamy homemade vanilla pudding layered with vanilla wafers and banana slices and topped with a perfect cloud of airy meringue."

"I've heard some people prefer it cold." Isaiah waved his spoon. "But I've never had any but warm. Why is that, Mama?"

"Because you people would never wait for it to cool down."

"I'd be afraid Isaiah would eat it all before it cooled," Tiffany said.

"I'd do my best." Isaiah stuck out his chest and laughed.

Isaiah and Tiffany cleared the dishes while Gee and I went into the living room.

"Karen, the autopsy on Nancy is taking longer than anyone expected. They've sent bloodwork off to the lab. She didn't have any water in her lungs. She was dead when her body went into the river."

"Do you know if she had any cuts?"

Gee frowned. "What made you ask that? She did have a large gash on her neck. Don't ask me how I know, but it'll all be out when they release the preliminary autopsy results tomorrow."

"No other wounds?"

"Scratches most likely from the river bottom. Her body was stuck in an underwater stump. Her arms were badly damaged during recovery."

I could feel the blood draining from my face, and the room swirled.

"Are you feeling okay? You don't look so good." Gee handed me a glass of water. "Sorry. Guess I was out of line talking about the details."

"No, the details didn't bother me. I just haven't been sleeping well, and you're right. I haven't been eating like I should. It's all catching up with me. Tonight's dinner was delicious and exactly what I needed. Maybe I can get some rest tonight."

"So tell me. What do you think about Jack?"

"You're incorrigible, Gee. He seems like a nice man."

"Whatever. Do you think he's hot?"

Heat rushed from my neck to my cheeks. "Well, my face is. Where did that come from?"

Gee laughed. "Just asking."

"You ready for your chauffeur, Miss Lady?" Tiffany asked. "Isaiah and I will take you and Colonel home now or whenever you're ready. I packed up leftovers for your supper tomorrow night."

"Thank you, Tiffany. I didn't expect a goody bag. Everything must be catching up with me. I'm tired."

"You ride in the front with Isaiah, Miss Lady. Colonel and I will ride together in the back."

Isaiah opened the passenger door for me and held my to-go bag while I slid into his car.

After Tiffany and Colonel climbed into the back, she leaned forward. "Did Aunt Gee tell you about Nancy? I can't believe she's dead. I don't understand where Carla is. Do you think she's hiding?"

"Gee did tell me about Nancy. It's terrible. Where do you think Carla would hide?"

"When Carla wanted to disappear, she'd always call me or Nancy. Nancy's gone, and I haven't heard from her. I don't know who else she'd call."

"Was there anyone Carla was afraid of? I know she and Russell had that act of her being afraid of him, but could there be somebody else?"

"I can't think of anyone Carla would be afraid of, but maybe that's what she wanted me to think. I never saw her as a manipulator until now."

"Carla was afraid of not being in control," Isaiah said.

"You're right," Tiffany said. "Carla had to be in control. She would be dangerous if she wasn't in control."

"Tiffany, do me a favor and don't be alone. You've got Isaiah, Gee, and me. You're welcome to stay with me anytime."

"Ms. Karen's right, Tiff. I'll take you to work and pick you up. I'm going to talk to Mama, so she knows to be on her toes too."

"Okay. I know outnumbered when I see it." Tiffany leaned back in her seat. "Miss Lady, did Aunt Gee ask you whether you thought Mr. Jack was hot? She said she was going to."

"She did."

"What did you say?"

"I told her she was incorrigible."

"Dang," Isaiah said. "I sure am glad I'm going to college. Maybe I'll learn what that word means next year. Right now I'm not sure if you told Mama she's brilliant or if you told her to shut up."

Tiffany and I laughed along with Isaiah. "Funniest thing I've heard in ages, Isaiah," I said.

When Colonel and I got home, the shadows were under the kitchen table. "What are y'all doing under there?" I flicked on the light switch, and they disappeared. "What's wrong with me, Colonel? I worry when the shadows are here, and then I worry when they aren't here."

After Colonel went outside for his break, we went to bed. Still no shadows.

My sheets were soft and silky, and my pillow was a cloud. I closed my eyes and snuggled in the smell of fresh linens while I floated on the silky cloud.

* * *

My alarm woke me at four. I opened one eye and turned the alarm off. *I slept all night.* I threw off the sheet and swung my legs over the side of my bed. My feet touched something furry, and I gasped. Colonel sat up and almost knocked me back onto my mattress.

I fed Colonel and Mia, let Colonel out, and grabbed a yogurt. I savored the sweet strawberry flavor and pieces of fresh fruit while I stood in the backyard and breathed in the morning air. I scraped the carton and licked my spoon. "Ready to go, Colonel?" Colonel bounded into the house.

"You going today, Mia?" I set her carrier near the door, and she leaped onto the ugly chair and licked her paw. "Your choice. See you later."

Colonel jumped into the car when I opened the door for him. I slid into my seat. "You know we deserve a great day, right Colonel?"

When I drove up to the shop, the lights were on, and Isaiah was parked across the street. He waited until Colonel and I were in the shop before he drove away.

"Good morning, Miss Lady. How'd you sleep?" Tiffany tested the fryer temperature with a donut hole.

"Straight through. What about you?"

"Same. It was nice. I checked the calendar, and we're open. No meetings. First time for me. Do I cut back on the donuts?"

"No. I got a feeling."

Tiffany tilted her head and frowned. "You know Isaiah told me you were a witch. Aunt Gee said he was teasing me. Sometimes, though I wonder because your feelings are always right."

"I'd be really annoyed to find out I was a witch. Would have been handy to know a time or two earlier." I wiggled my nose, and Tiffany giggled.

"We haven't had strawberry glaze for a while. I know we'll need maple tomorrow. How about frosted coffee today?"

"Sounds good to me. Is there a recipe, or will you improvise?"

"I'm thinking just powdered sugar and concentrated cold coffee."

"Maybe add a little butter and a smidgen of cocoa powder. I'll get a pot of strong coffee brewing. If it doesn't taste right to us, we can salvage it with more cocoa powder and call it mocha."

Tiffany weighed the flour for her second batch of donuts. "I'm going to write all this down before I leave. It'll be nice to have ideas to fall back on." While the dough rose, she mixed strawberry glaze for her first batch.

I held up the pot of concentrated coffee. "This looks like coffee sludge to me. Will you set up an ice bath in a sink? I'll pour this into a pan. It'll cool faster."

I brewed a fresh pot of coffee and emptied the box of national day submissions. "Here's National Airplane Day, National Propeller Day, National Flight Path Day."

Tiffany laughed. "Sure can tell who was here yesterday, can't we?"

"National Thank a Pilot Day. These are actually pretty good. National Spirit of St. Louis Day. We should pick one of these for this Friday."

"Let's ask Woody to pick." Tiffany slid her second tray of donuts into the display case.

"I'll ask Shirley if she and Woody can come by after school today." I carried the stack of papers to the storeroom file cabinet and put two empty cups on the counter in preparation for the sheriff.

The sheriff came in the door and looked up. "No bell?"

"Retired." I poured coffee, and Tiffany placed two donuts on a plate.

The sheriff eyed his plate. "What's that?" He asked.

I rolled my eyes. Tiffany grinned. I pointed at myself and raised my eyebrows, and she nodded.

"Donuts," I said.

The sheriff chortled. "I asked for that, didn't I?"

"Yes, and we appreciate it. You made our day. Try it. We'd like to know what you think."

The sheriff narrowed his eyes and took a bite. "Hmm. Coffee? It reminds me of Cuban coffee. Strong, creamy, and sweet."

"Too sweet?" Tiffany asked.

"Nope. Perfect. Can I have another one? In a sack for later, just to be sure."

Sheriff finished his coffee and strawberry donut and whistled while he left with his sack.

"We've got a winner, Tiffany."

My phone rang. It was the hospital's main number. My hand shook as I answered.

"Miss Donut Lady? This is Emma Hayes. I'm volunteering at the hospital this morning. It's kind of a long story, but we need donuts. A tour bus of seniors was on the highway south of town, and the driver didn't feel well. A retired nurse on board ordered him to drive to the hospital. I'm sorry to ramble, but can you hear all that noise in the background? These people are rowdy. The Emergency Department doctor said the nurse saved the driver's life and probably the entire bus because he was in the middle of a major heart attack. But the thing is, we've got forty-two cranky people in our waiting room. Their next planned stop was for breakfast, but it'll be two more hours before the replacement bus driver will be here. I called the library, and they'll bring us books and magazines. We've got coffee, tea, and juice, but we sure could use donuts."

"Emma, we'll be glad to help out. We'll be there in fifteen minutes."

"What?" Tiffany asked after I hung up.

"The hospital waiting room is overrun with forty-two hungry people from a tour bus. They need donuts while they wait for a new bus driver. We'll put up a note on the door and close the shop."

"We don't need to do that. Isaiah doesn't have a class this morning. I'll text him to pick me up. He won't mind. I'll start another pot of coffee. There shouldn't be anything else for you to do except wait on customers while I'm gone."

"Thank you, Tiff. I'd like the shop to stay open if Isaiah's available."

When Isaiah arrived, Tiffany frowned at the display case. "Miss Lady, I'm afraid we're cutting it close."

"We've got plenty, especially with our scones. We'll be fine."

After Tiffany and Isaiah left, Shirley came in. I laughed when she opened and closed the door three times.

"What happened to the bell?"

"It retired."

"That's funny, Karen. I love your jokes. I'm not in a rush for once. Can you believe that?"

Shirley perched on a stool and stared at the board. "I don't ever remember a coffee scone. Are they any good? That was silly. If they weren't any good, you'd have thrown them out. Your donuts and scones are always great. Where's Tiffany? Is she okay?"

I set her coffee on the counter in front of her, poured a cup for myself, and placed her scone on a plate.

"We got a call from the hospital for donuts for a tour bus. Tiffany's delivering them. She'll be back soon."

I sat next to her and peeked at her face when she bit into her scone. "Mmm. Love this." *Our harshest critic. Tiffany will be pleased.*

"Shirley, I don't remember Carla and Nancy. Who were their folks?"

CHAPTER TEN

"Lorraine and Martin Weston. Do you remember them? You might remember her as Lorraine Carruthers. Her folks sold their place out in the country and moved to a condo on the beach after Lorraine and Martin married. Martin was an engineer and retired early. After Nancy was out of high school, Lorraine and Martin traveled. They were killed in a plane crash three or four years ago in the mountains of Peru. Someone said the Andes mountains, but I wouldn't know because my South American geography is weak. Did you travel much? I don't like to travel. It's too hard to stay caught up with work if I'm gone more than half a day. Can I have another scone? Those are really good. Did Tiffany come up with the recipe? I don't remember it."

Roger came in the shop, glanced up at the silent door frame, and strode to the display case. "Is Tiffany in the back?"

"Tiffany's at the hospital." Shirley's back was to Roger.

Roger's face drained of all color, and he wheeled to leave.

"Wait, Roger," I called. "She's delivering donuts to some stuck travelers. She's fine."

Roger's shoulders relaxed. "Thanks, Miss Lady. I'll just go help her."

"Here, take along a donut for the road. It's Tiffany's latest creation," I said.

"And a scone." Shirley added with her hand covering her mouth. She had just bitten into her scone.

I grinned. "Scone too. You want coffee?"

"No, ma'am. I'll grab some at the hospital. Oh, wait. Yes. I'd like a coffee to go."

While I poured his coffee, Shirley chuckled. "Good idea, Roger. The hospital has the reputation of the worst coffee in the county."

After Roger left, I refilled Shirley's cup. "Alfred from the bank said I might want to remodel the shop, and he had some ideas. Do you have time this afternoon to go with me? I love the charm of this old shop, but I'd consider a plumbing or electrical upgrade."

Shirley frowned. "Alfred had ideas? We're not interested. We could talk to Todd Rockford. He's the bank loan officer. But if it's a plumbing or electrical upgrade, we should talk to Jack. He's the expert. I'm free this afternoon at one thirty. Do you already have an appointment or were you going to drop in? I'm fine with dropping in. I'll pick you up at the duplex at one. We can talk about the timeline Woody and I set up for the contractor for your repairs."

"One more thing. I almost forgot. Can I go with you to pick up Woody after school? Tiffany and I need him to pick a winner for our Friday national day this week."

"He'll love that. See you at one." Shirley finished her coffee and second scone, placed money on the counter, and left.

Colonel ambled out of the pink room and stretched.

"Hid, did you? Mia teach you that?"

Colonel trotted to me with a grin, and we stepped out front for his break. I sat on a step while Colonel wandered to the grass.

"We could've stepped out back if we still had the door jingles, Colonel, but I've enjoyed all the reactions to the missing bell."

Isaiah's truck pulled up to the front of the shop with a sheriff's patrol car right behind it. Isaiah rolled down his window. "We're back, Miss Lady. We had law enforcement on our tail the whole way. Did I lose 'em?" Isaiah guffawed.

Tiffany mumbled when she got to the shop door. "You are so not funny, Isaiah."

Roger parked and followed Tiffany into the shop.

"Thanks, Isaiah." I waved as he drove off. "Ready to go inside, Colonel?"

Roger sat at the counter, and Tiffany poured coffee for him.

"The hospital was wild, Miss Lady. The replacement bus driver showed up an hour ago, but it took a while to get everyone loaded onto the bus. Ms. Emma said to thank you because the donuts made a difference. Roger did a great job of crowd control." Tiffany beamed at Roger.

"I mostly listened and said *Is that so?*" Roger laughed.

"Your coffee donuts and scones were a hit, Tiffany," I said. "The sheriff and Shirley complimented you on the new creation."

Tiffany gazed at Roger. "I really need to start cleaning up."

Roger cleared his throat. "I need to get back to work. Thanks for the coffee."

"Thanks for the help at the hospital." Tiffany smiled.

Colonel followed me into the pink room. "It is a good room for hiding out, isn't it?" I whispered to Colonel. I pulled chairs away from the table and pushed them back into place.

"There. Done." I peeked out. Tiffany was at the sink, and Roger was gone. I cleaned the counter while Tiffany swept the floor.

"Colonel and I will drop you off at Gee's."

* * *

When Shirley and I walked into the bank, Alfred slipped into his office and closed the door. Todd Rockford rushed to greet us in the lobby. He had black hair, a thick neck, and his bodybuilder frame strained against his gray suit. He was as tall as the sheriff.

Shirley offered her hand, and he clutched it with both of his.

"It's a pleasure to see you again, Ms. Shirley. You've brightened my day coming into the bank." His smile didn't reach his eyes.

"Ms. Karen, I understand you might be interested in remodeling the old donut shop. Come into my office and let's talk."

"Mr. Gibson mentioned he had some ideas for updates," I said.

"We can talk about that in my office." Rockford placed Shirley's hand in the crook of his arm and waved in the direction of his office.

Shirley nodded, and the hairs on the back of my neck stood up. I stepped behind the two of them.

When we reached his office, Rockford held a chair for Shirley. She raised her eyebrows and sat. He placed his hand on the back of the other visitor's chair, and I glared. He jerked back his hand and rushed to his chair behind the desk. I shifted my chair slightly to keep the door and Rockford in my view.

"I can discuss the remodeling ideas because I suggested them to Alfred," he chuckled. "The town's image would be vastly improved if the Donut Hole had a more modern look and maybe even a new name. Something like *Asbury Center Crullers*. I have some sketches of how the donut shop fits into my overall plan for the town."

He reached into a drawer and pulled out a file folder. He shuffled through the papers and handed a sketch to Shirley. "This is the overall planned look for the Asbury Center." Shirley held the page so I could see too. The sketch was a long glass-front building with a gray surface from the front of the building to the foreground. Three green circles with dots of color were off to the left side of the page. Two people walked in front of the building, and a bicyclist rode near one of the green circles.

"You can see that the Asbury Center will be eco-friendly. All the businesses are inside the building. People can come to one place for restaurants, local produce, whatever they might need. Kind of like a town cooperative."

"How does this fit in with the updates for the donut shop?" Shirley frowned.

"The donut shop is inside with other businesses." I raised my eyebrows. *You lost us with that one, bud.*

"Is this your proposal?" Shirley narrowed her eyes.

I leaned back in my chair. *I'm enjoying this.*

"You love it, right? If you sign on to the idea, everyone in town will jump on board. I've got a contract right here." Rockford fumbled through his folder.

Shirley rose. "Not what I had in mind. Thanks anyway."

Rockford's jaw dropped. She took a step toward the door, and I jumped up to leave with her.

Shirley's face was pinched when we got into the car.

"Shirley, you are a force. Well done." I grinned.

"That was just about the dumbest proposal I've ever seen. *Crullers,*" she snorted. "His plan wasn't even for Asbury. Did you notice the name in the bottom right corner? You might not have seen it. I think my thumb might have covered it. It said Albany Center. I wonder if he found it on the internet and printed it off. Maybe I left too early. I should have looked at the contract. I wonder who else he's approached. I'll ask around."

"I'd like to talk to Alfred. I don't think this is what he had in mind. Is there bad blood or something between you and Alfred?"

"You might say that. He pulled a stunt a few years ago, and I called him on it. Actually, I called him a crooked larcenist and a penny-pinching tightwad with tunnel vision. He overstepped his bounds in an attempt to save money, and I threatened to report him if he didn't back off. Maybe he learned his lesson. I don't know. He's certainly done a lot for the community since then. I'll give him that. Maybe Woody and I should take him some donuts or something sometime. I don't think he'll sit down and talk, though, if I'm around. I've got an idea. Why don't you ask Jack if he'll go with you to meet with Alfred?"

"I'm not so fired up to upgrade or remodel the shop. I'll think about it. Maybe I'll just give Alfred a call. He should at least know what his ambitious loan officer is touting."

"That plan had so many holes in it. Wonder if the mayor knows about it."

"I thought you were a little taken by Mr. Rockford when we got first there. Were you?"

"His attempt at old-world charm tickled me. But when it comes to business, I'd rather deal with a warty toad than a smooth talker. Come to think of it, Alfred's a warty toad. Maybe we will take him some donuts. I wonder if a warty toad would ever be a smooth talker? Wouldn't that be a pitiful combination? One evening Woody and I sat outside and listened to the frogs. I'd never done that before. They are downright noisy. Definitely not smooth talkers."

"Thanks for going with me, Shirley."

Shirley pulled into the school car loop. Her face lit up, and I knew Woody was nearby.

Woody opened the back door. "Hi, Miss Lady. Are we having a party?"

"No, but that's a good idea. Why don't you two come to my house for dinner tonight?"

Woody bounced into his seat and clicked his seatbelt. "I have only a little homework. I can finish it this afternoon."

"Are you sure, Karen? This doesn't give you much notice to cook. If it was me, I only need twenty minutes to heat up a frozen dinner. Or maybe thirty. I'd have to read the package. Do we still have time to go by the shop for Woody to pick the winner? Woody and I like to eat around six. Would that be okay with you?"

"Yes, we have time for Woody to pick our Friday winner, and I'll have time to shop and cook while Woody does his homework. Six is great."

I hovered while Woody looked through the submissions and stacked them into two piles. He pointed at the shortest stack. "I like these the best. " He fanned them out, examined each one again, and handed me a sheet. "This one."

"National Crop Duster Day?" I laughed.

"Of course. Dust powder sugar on the donuts. National Crop Duster Day."

Shirley beamed. "Brilliant idea, Woody."

"I agree. I know Tiffany will love it too. You're amazing, Woody."

"Let's shake a leg," Shirley said. "Lots to do before six o'clock."

* * *

At six o'clock Shirley and Woody were at my door. She held a bottle of white wine, and he carried a clear vase with a dozen pink roses.

"Look, Miss Lady. We found pink roses. They smell pretty too. See?" He thrust the flowers under my nose.

"You're right, Woody. Those must be heritage roses to have such a wonderful fragrance. I love them. Thank you. Excellent choice."

He grinned, and his brown face grew as pink as my flowers.

"Set them on the dining table, Woody. They make a beautiful centerpiece. And wash up, you two. I'm ready to put dinner on the table. We'll eat family-style and pass the food around."

After we sat, Woody bowed his head. "Thank you for Ms. Shirley, Miss Lady, Colonel, Mia, and good food. Amen."

Shirley's eyes misted. "And thank you for Woody. Amen."

"Woody, serve yourself chicken fried steak and mashed potatoes, and I'll pass you the cream gravy."

"Are these fresh field peas?" Shirley asked. "They're delicious. I haven't had field peas in forever. Woody and I signed up for cooking and nutrition lessons next summer at the community college. The class is called *Mom and Me*."

"Ms. Shirley's going to be the mom. I'll be me." Woody tried to hide his smile behind his hand.

I laughed. "That's funny, Woody. Ms. Shirley will make a great mom, and you'll be a perfect you. Or is that me?"

Woody snickered.

After we finished eating, Shirley and Woody took over the cleanup duty.

"Karen, how did you manage mashed potatoes with one hand?"

"I cheated. They're from the deli at the grocery store. "

"I certainly wouldn't have known." Shirley loaded the dishwasher. "Of course, I drowned my potatoes in a ton of gravy. Your gravy is perfect."

"Do either of you have room for dessert? I made a peach cobbler. It's still warm, and I have ice cream to go along with it."

"I'll have just a smidgen." Shirley dried her hands.

"I'll have a huge ginormous bowlful." Woody rushed to the table.

"Shirley, if I serve up the cobbler, would you mind dishing up the ice cream?"

"Not at all."

"I'll fix your coffee and pour more milk for me." Woody jumped up.

After we ate dessert, Woody cleared the table and fed Colonel and Mia, and Shirley started the dishwasher.

"Thank you again, Karen, for a great meal. We'll scoot. Tomorrow's another school day, and you get up early."

Colonel and I stepped outside for fresh air and his break. When we went inside, Mia joined me on the sofa. I stretched out my legs and opened my book. The shadows slid out of Mia's pantry.

I heard scratching at the back door, and the shadows grew larger. Colonel was asleep on the rug near the front door, and Mia jumped off my lap and dashed to her pantry. The scratching grew more insistent.

I opened the back door, and a tidal wave of water from the back porch flooded into the house. Lying face up next to the door was Nancy's bloated body. Her work shirt was tattered. Her dead eyes stared at me. Her mouth moved. A voice gurgled. "You know."

I screamed and rolled off the sofa onto the floor. I stared at the kitchen floor. It was dry. Colonel barked and nudged me with his face.

"I'm okay. I'll get up. Just a second." I shuddered, and the shadows danced. I had fallen on my broken arm. I sat up, and my arm throbbed. I hung my head and sobbed.

Colonel nudged me again, and I eased to my feet. My knees buckled from the pain in my left hip. I grabbed the sofa arm and caught myself.

"Ouch. We'll see how my arm and hip are in the morning, but I need to check the back porch before I go to bed."

I limped to the back door, flicked on the porch light, and opened the door a crack. No water. Colonel whined, and I opened the door for him to go out. I peeked around the corner. No body.

When Colonel came inside, I double-locked the door and leaned against it until my heart rate slowed to normal.

* * *

My alarm sounded, and I slapped at it until I turned it off. I swung my feet over the side of my bed. My arm ached, my fingers were swollen, and my fingertips throbbed but were still warm and pink. *Too early to call the doctor's office.* I raised my arm so my fingers were higher than my heart. The ache in my arm eased, but my shoulder burned. I slogged through my early morning routine, and Colonel and I left for the shop.

When we walked in, Tiffany stared. "You look awful, Miss Lady. What happened?"

"I think I reinjured my arm. I'll call the doc's office at seven. Woody selected a Friday winner." I eased onto a stool at the counter.

Tiffany turned on the fryer and brought me a cup of coffee. "What did he choose?"

"Ready?" I smiled. "National Crop Duster Day. He suggested dusting the donuts with powdered sugar."

"Wow. That's brilliant. I'll check to see if I need to pick up extra powdered sugar for tomorrow. We have only the book club on the calendar this morning. Pink sprinkles and maple." She narrowed her eyes. "Unless you have a feeling we need to do more than our usual Thursday."

"No feeling." I sipped my coffee. "Except my arm hurts. Would you put the flyer in the holder on the display case? We can advertise our Friday special on Thursdays. Get a little interest going."

The door creaked open. "Good morning," the sheriff said. "You replaced the jingle with a creak. Sounds spooky to me. He opened and closed the door."

"Officially annoying." I frowned.

"Me or the door? Don't answer." The sheriff sat next to me at the counter and peered at my face. "What's wrong with you? You look awful."

"Funny, Tiffany said the same thing."

Tiffany poured coffee, handed the sheriff his donuts, and crossed her arms. "Tell."

"You two aren't going to give up, are you? I fell asleep on the sofa, rolled off, and landed on my arm. And you sounded just like Gee for a second there, Tiff."

"Well done, Tiffany Gee." The sheriff held up his hand, and Tiffany smacked a high-five.

"And we're calling the doctor at seven," Tiffany added.

The sheriff stuffed the rest of his pink sprinkled donut into his mouth, wrapped my fingers in his hand, and pinched a fingernail. "Your fingers are still warm, and your circulation's fine. We don't have to jump into the patrol car with lights and sirens and dash to the emergency room."

"That's good, but do you have a hairbrush in your purse, Miss Lady? Your hair's a fright." She refilled our cups.

"You two are hovering. I might have a hairbrush or a comb in the storeroom file cabinet."

The sheriff glanced at the display case. "Tomorrow's National Crop Duster Day? What will the donuts be?"

"A surprise." I chuckled, and he glared.

Tiffany returned with a hairbrush and waved at the reading area. I sat in my reading chair, and she brushed out the tangles with deft strokes. "There you go. Better."

"Thanks, Tiffany."

The sheriff strode to the door. "I'll check on you later."

He opened, closed, and opened the door three times. "I thought the creaks might grow on you, but nope. They just get louder." He laughed and left.

While Tiffany fried, sprinkled, and frosted the day's donuts and made scones, I loaded the utility cart with meeting room supplies.

Tiffany appeared in the meeting room doorway with her arms crossed. "It's seven, Miss Lady."

I sat at the table, turned my back to her, and called the doctor's office.

When I hung up, Tiffany sat in the chair next to me. I glared. "I'm supposed to go to the hospital today for x-rays. The doc's office will make an appointment and call me back. Happy?"

"Thrilled." She growled and pushed her chair in with a clatter.

The display case was full and the platters for the book club were in place when Amber breezed in. She wore her gray suit and red shirt. "Need my maple donut. I won't be able to stay for the whole meeting today. Would you sneak me a second donut for the road when I leave?" She frowned at my face. "You okay? You look awful."

Tiffany laughed. "I'll grab that donut for you, Ms. Amber."

"So I've been told." I meant to sound icy and aloof, but Amber chuckled.

The book club chatter filled the shop. When I took a break and sat at the counter, my phone rang. Tiffany scooted out of the pink room and sat next to me while I answered the phone.

"Ten o'clock," I growled after my call.

"I'll call Aunt Gee. She'll either want to take you or stay here at the shop."

Shirley rushed in. "The door creaks. Is that a new feature? You look awful. I ran into Jack at the gas station. He said he'd replace the deadbolt on the duplex front door today. You knew that right? Do you have a conflict? I can rearrange my schedule if this afternoon isn't convenient for you. Did I say you look awful?"

Tiffany handed Shirley her coffee and sack and rushed to the storeroom and closed the door.

"Is Tiffany okay? She seemed unusually quiet. The book club sounds like they're breaking up. I need to dash."

I strolled to the storeroom and tapped on the door. "All is forgiven, Tiffany, and Shirley's gone."

She opened the door. "I lost count on how many times your appearance drew the comment which I shall not repeat. Aunt Gee will be here in a few minutes. You know the first thing she's going to say."

"I know. I'll wait in the storeroom for Gee until the book club members are gone."

When I peeked out of the storeroom, the last three book club members passed Gee on their way out.

"I've been warned, Donut Lady. No remarks. I'll save them for later. Isaiah will pick up Tiffany and Colonel if we're not back from the hospital when it's time to close up. Anything else you can think of?"

When we arrived at the hospital, the x-ray technician whisked me down the hallway in a wheelchair. "This won't take long, Ms. O'Brien.

You won't have to wait around here either. The doctor will come by after lunch and review your x-rays, and then his office will give you a call."

"That's a relief. I thought I'd be here all afternoon."

When we reached the waiting room, Gee put down her magazine. "That was fast. How does it look?"

"I'm not qualified to read x-rays and provide a diagnosis." He locked the wheels and winked. "You are a lucky lady, Ms. O'Brien."

Gee chuckled. "Well done, young man. Ms. O'Brien will give you a free donut the next time you're in her shop."

He stared at me. "Really?"

"I will. What's your favorite?"

He glanced around the waiting room, bent down, and whispered. "I really liked them eyeballs."

"You work tomorrow? We can make sure to put them on our menu."

Gee and I watched him strut down the hallway. "You made that young man's day. He was practically dancing."

"I don't think Tiffany will mind. And thanks for asking about the x-ray. I wondered, but I'm not functioning on all cylinders today."

When we returned to the shop, Tiffany was putting away the last of the dishes. "Everything's done, Miss Lady. Do you see anything I missed?"

"Looks great, Tiff. Your generous Aunt Gee promised donuts to the x-ray technician at the hospital. Can we make eyeballs tomorrow?"

"That's easy, Miss Lady. I might drizzle some strawberry syrup to see if I can make them bloodshot."

Gee laughed. "Sometimes you two have way too much fun with this donut business. Ready, Tiff?"

Tiffany stopped on her way to the door. "I oiled the hinges, Miss Lady. No more creaks."

Colonel and I locked up. When I pulled into my driveway, Jack sat in his pickup at the curb.

He opened my passenger's side door, and Colonel bounded out. Jack stuck his head inside. "You and Colonel feel like a picnic? I brought Roxie. We picked up lunch for us at Gus's."

Before I was out of the car, Roxie lifted her face to me, and I rubbed under her chin. Colonel and Roxie did their sniffs and wandered around the yard.

"She's a sweet girl. A picnic sounds great. Do you want us to follow you?"

"Nope. There's plenty of room for the four of us in the truck. Let's go."

When Jack pulled away, he said, "You okay with going to the state park? It's not far."

"I haven't been to the state park in ages. I love being outside, and a ride in the country sounds fun."

I gazed at the green fields of corn, cotton, and soybeans and held my breath when we passed the dairy farm.

Jack laughed. "Wind's blowing the other way. You can breathe."

I pointed at the rows of longleaf pines. "I'd forgotten about the tree farms. I love seeing the tops of the pine trees sway with the wind."

We passed a farmhouse with a garden and the skeleton of a truck in the side yard. Ivy spilled out of the truck's engine compartment, and flowers filled the truck bed.

"There's a story for you," Jack said. "Wonder what it is."

"You've got one week to get that eyesore out of my yard, Henry. One week." I waited.

"I'll bite," Jack said. "What happened next?"

"Henry planted flowers. He was as smart as he was lazy."

Jack guffawed.

"Thank you." I bowed my head and swept my hand like royalty. "I like my bungalow being close enough to the shop to walk, but I'd love to have a little land and a garden. A small one. Not big like Henry's."

"The crops are doing well this year." Jack motioned toward the fields. "We've had the right amount of rain for a change."

When Jack pulled into the parking lot, the dogs' heads popped up, and Roxie whined.

"You're right, girl. Almost there."

After he parked, Jack opened the back door, and the dogs bounded after a squirrel.

He reached into the back of the truck bed, handed me a blue recycle sack with a hardware store logo, and lifted out a small cooler.

"How about here in the shade?" Jack waved at a nearby table and set the cooler on the closest bench.

I peeked into my sack and spied a red and white plaid vinyl tablecloth. I gave it my best one-handed shake, and Jack spread it over the picnic table. I pulled out a dog bowl, and Jack poured water into it from a gallon jug. The dogs' attention diverted from their squirrel chase, and the two of them dashed back and took long drinks. Colonel flopped down in the shade, and Roxie joined him.

"Please sit, Donut Lady." He pulled out two wrapped sandwiches. "You aren't vegetarian, are you? I didn't think about that. Ham or turkey?"

"No, not vegetarian. I like surprises. Give me the one in your left hand."

"Chips, potato salad, or both?"

"Potato salad."

He unwrapped my sandwich, handed me a bottle of water, and closed the cooler.

"We have dessert. I'm just bragging."

I bit into my sandwich. "Turkey and Swiss. Yum."

Jack pointed overhead. A hawk floated in a thermal. It dived into the trees and disappeared. I finished half of my sandwich. I pulled the turkey out of my other half, and Jack called the dogs for a turkey snack.

"Ready for dessert?" Jack opened the cooler and handed me a small white sack. I peeked inside the sack at an oversized cupcake.

"Wow. This looks yummy, but it's big enough for four people."

"I thought so too. I'll cut it in half." Jack pulled out his pocketknife.

After we finished dessert, the sun had replaced our shade.

"Let's head back, and I'll fix that door." Jack rose, collected the trash, and packed up.

"Thank you for lunch. A picnic was a wonderful idea."

Jack opened the door for the dogs. "Glad you liked it. I worked in an office most of my career. I'm always looking for an excuse to be outside."

I sat on the back porch while Colonel and Roxie investigated the yard. Colonel found his ball in the grass, dropped it on the porch, and flopped next to me. Roxie trotted up and barked. Colonel closed his eyes.

"I think he's worn out, girl." I picked up the ball and threw it. Colonel raced Roxie for the ball, but she beat him. He sat in the middle of the yard while she ran circles around the perimeter. Roxie dropped the ball and grinned. Colonel took a step toward her, and she grabbed up the ball and resumed her mad dash around the yard.

Colonel returned to my side, and I scratched his ears. "Good job, Colonel."

Jack joined us on the porch. "Lock's installed. Ready to go, Roxie?"

Roxie pranced to Jack and dropped the ball.

"Let me know if you need anything else, Karen."

After Jack and Roxie left, Colonel and I padded to the sofa. I leaned back, and my phone rang.

"Ms. Karen, this is Mary Ellen. Doc wants you to come in tomorrow at three. He wants you to have a hard cast."

I sat up straight. "Did he say why?"

"Yes, ma'am. Doc said he wants you to have a cast as tough as you."

I made a face in the direction of the doctor's office. "Thank you, Mary Ellen. I'll be there at three."

Colonel lay his head on my lap, and I leaned back for a nap.

* * *

I opened my eyes. The shadows in the hallway shimmered in the soft light of dusk. Mia slept on my feet, and Colonel was on his back with his legs in the air.

"Ready for supper?" Mia leaped over Colonel and raced to the kitchen.

After I fed them, I put a frozen dinner in the oven and turned on a burner to heat up water for tea. The shadows slid from the hallway and shimmered in the pantry doorway.

"What are you doing? You've never been interested in the pantry."

The shadows billowed, and their shimmer swirled to black. The black filled the doorway, rose to the ceiling like smoke, dived to the floor, and snaked into the pantry. The pantry door slammed, the kettle whistled, and I jumped.

I poured water into my cup and started the timer. I stared at the descending seconds and minutes. *I'd forgotten about the pantry.*

I eased the pantry door open and flicked on the light. *No shadows.*

I moved Mia's litter box, lifted the loose tile, and slid out the coupon book and Nancy's envelope. The coupons and envelope felt damp. I sniffed. A little musty.

The timer beeped, and I removed my herbal teabag. I slit open the envelope and sat at the table. The picture of Carla fell out, and I pulled out papers. The first was a protective order, and the second was a marriage license, and the third was the summary page of a life insurance policy. The rest of the eight pages were spreadsheets of addresses with dates and two columns of numbers. I glanced through the numbers that ranged from 155 to 1,075. The second column for each row was more than the first column. Each row in the final column listed two letters, like initials or another type of abbreviation. I sipped my tea and read the papers. *I need Amber to look at these. No, I need the sheriff. No, I really need Shirley and her bottle of wine.*

The marriage license was issued to Carla Imogene Weston and Brandon Theodore Canady ten years ago. The permanent protective order was for domestic violence. The order prohibited Carla Imogene Weston Canady from having any contact with Brandon Theodore Canady. The order was issued nine years ago and didn't expire.

Whoa. I finished my cup of lukewarm tea.

The life insurance policy was three hundred thousand dollars' coverage for Carla Imogene Simpson. Beneficiary was Russell Wilshire Simpson.

I stared at the policy. "I thought I had something for a minute. This is backward."

I rose and shuffled to the back door. Colonel jumped up, and the two of us went outside. It was dark. I paced the perimeter of the fenced yard, and Colonel trailed after me.

"My supper's close to ready. Let's go inside."

I brewed a fresh cup of tea and set the pork and gravy dinner on the table. I didn't have any appetite, but I forced myself to eat a few bites.

After I cleared the table, I returned the papers to their home under the tile. I filled the tub with hot water and poured in bubble bath. I sank into the bubbles that relaxed my tense muscles and eased my racing mind with the aroma of lavender.

I climbed into bed, and the shadows gathered at my door like sentries. I turned off my bedside light.

CHAPTER ELEVEN

Dust and eyeballs. I sat up in bed. My alarm was set to go off in ten minutes. I turned it off.

"Good morning, Colonel. I'm excited about today."

I let Colonel out. When he returned, I poured food for him and Mia into their bowls and started a pot of coffee. I rushed to get dressed and brushed past the shadows as they swirled in the hallway.

"Dust and eyeballs today, shadows." They dissipated.

I set Mia's carrier by the door, and she dashed inside. We arrived at the shop fifteen minutes earlier than usual, but Tiffany had plopped her first batch of donuts into the fryer.

"Good morning, Tiffany. It's dust and eyeballs day. I don't know why I'm so fired up about donuts."

Tiffany lifted her head. "I dreamed about dust and eyeballs. Maybe we need a hobby."

"What kind of hobby do you suggest? Does Gee really create crossword puzzles? We should take up gardening or hiking. Or sewing. I wouldn't mind a farm with goats. Or maybe board horses. I'm officially beside myself. I just unleashed my inner Shirley."

Tiffany guffawed. "I think we make Aunt Gee deliver the eyeballs. Her idea, right?"

"Excellent. As soon as you have two dozen, let me know. I'll call and tell her the order is ready."

I jumped at the sound of heavy footsteps behind me.

Roger strode to the counter. "I know you might not be officially open, but Tess sent me to pick up a dozen eyeballs and two dozen crop dusters."

Tiffany beamed.

I headed to the coffee pot with deliberate steps to calm my nerves. "Have a seat, Roger. I'll pour your coffee while Tiffany gets the order ready."

Tiffany drifted to the counter and watched Roger sip his coffee. He set his cup down and gazed at her.

"I have a feeling we're going to need triple our usual, Tiff." *Sorry, not sorry, to bust the mood, but I need eyeballs. And crop dust.*

Tiffany fluttered her eyelashes and smiled at Roger. She turned and glowered at me. "What? You just now got a feeling?"

My back was to Roger. I batted my eyelashes, and Tiffany stomped to the fryer.

"Is she mad at me?" Roger whispered.

"No. Just lots to do, and I'm good at getting under her skin. And vice versa."

Roger drained his cup. "That's my goal. I want to see her glare. Then I'll know. You know."

I refilled his cup. "Admirable goal. If it helps, I have every confidence in you."

"Here's your order, Deputy." Tiffany trilled the words. I rolled my eyes.

Roger reached for his wallet, and I held up my hand. "Roger, please tell Tess it's our treat."

"No can do. She'd have my hide." He dropped the bills on the counter and left.

"Miss Lady, you want your head back now since I bit it off?"

"Best apology ever, Tiff." I laughed. "I'm sorry too. I'll give Gee a call."

Gee rushed into the shop. "What's the emergency, Donut Lady?"

"We have the eyeballs and crop duster donuts ready for you to deliver to the x-ray technician at the hospital. I knew you'd want him to have fresh, hot donuts."

"What? I never said I'd deliver those donuts."

"But you didn't say you wouldn't. Your idea. Your delivery." I grinned.

"One of these days, Donut Girls." Gee growled and shook her finger when she came into the shop. "I know you're in on this, Tiffany. Don't pretend you aren't." She snatched the boxes and stormed out the door.

"Well done, Gee. You win the award for drama." I waved when she glanced at the shop. She jerked her head away and squealed her tires as she left.

The sheriff opened the shop door and sauntered to the counter. "Was that Gee peeling out? I should give her a ticket, but eyeballs first. And a crop duster."

I poured his coffee, and Tiffany served his donuts. He picked up the eyeball and examined it. "This eyeball partied all night, didn't it?"

He popped it into his mouth. "How many eyeballs is an order?"

"Three," I said.

"A double order is seven." Tiffany winked.

"I need a double order." He bit into his crop duster donut. "I've had powdered sugar donuts before, but this is different. What did you do, Tiffany?"

"Trade secret, but I know I can trust the law. I added a bit of lemon zest to cut the sweetness and ground macadamia nut to create a little grittiness."

"I wouldn't have guessed. Totally amazing. I need a second crop duster. Ms. Karen, you need to put a treadmill in here. Y'all are donut geniuses. I'm afraid to ask about the scones. *Raspberry scones,* the board says. What's the catch?"

"No catch. Well, a small catch," I said. "Some of our scones are filled with raspberry jam. We made those for Woody's class. They squirt raspberry blood when you bite into them. Woody's teacher put in a special request. Teachers are more devious than one might suspect."

"Can I deliver the school scones? Does Woody know?" The sheriff chuckled.

"I don't think Woody knows. Today is Ms. Wilcox's birthday, and her class has been razing her all week about getting old. She expects them to prank her, and squirting blood donuts is her revenge. She sent an email to the parents indicating the day might include a messy activity."

"Yep. I need to do a little goodwill visit at the school. Give me two regular scones so Ms. Wilcox and I can enjoy a scone with the class."

Tiffany boxed up the scones. "I wrapped two regulars in waxed paper."

Shirley rushed into the shop. "I need something special for Woody's class today. It's Ms. Wilcox's birthday. They've got a surprise for her. I can't tell you what it is. She doesn't know a cousin of hers will come to their classroom this morning. He's a famous singer, but I never heard of him. He has a lot of pictures of her from their childhood, and he made a movie or video or something of all the pictures and wrote a song. The kids are excited. One of the parents is a photographer and will take pictures. National Crop Duster Day? I never heard of it."

"Here's a box of donut holes for Woody's class, Ms. Shirley." Tiffany bit her lip.

"I see what you did, there, Tiffany. Well done." The sheriff said.

I handed Shirley her coffee and sack with a regular scone and a classic glazed.

"I'll carry your donut holes to your car, Ms. Shirley."

"Thanks, Tiffany. You know there is nowhere in town that can beat the service at the Donut Hole. Everybody says so at the gas station. I need to rush. All I was supposed to do was pick up a treat for the party. I'm not supposed to stop and talk. Don't tell on me." Shirley bustled out with her coffee and sack, and Tiffany followed her.

When Tiffany came back into the shop, the three of us chuckled.

"I've got to get to school. Sounds like we'll have pictures." The sheriff grabbed the box of scones on his way out.

"I forgot to check the board when I came in. Any meetings today?"

"Yes, ma'am." Tiffany dropped in another batch of donut holes into the fryer. "We've got the motorcycle club scheduled at nine and the library executive board at ten."

"I'll get the room set up and get the large coffee pot brewing, but what I really want to do is go to school and peek in the window."

"Come watch this fryer, and I'll be right back." Tiffany chuckled.

"Let's put up a sign that says *Help yourself. Leave money with Colonel*, and both of us go." I snorted. "Lord, we're funny."

"Yep. Just ask us." Tiffany dropped a batch of donuts into the hot oil and drizzled raspberry blood on the donut holes.

"Happy Crop Duster Day, Donut Gurus." Jack sauntered in at ten and sat at the counter. I poured him a cup.

"What's your pleasure, Mr. Jack?" Tiffany stood at the display case with tongs in her hand.

He gazed at the board. "How about one of each—an eyeball, crop duster, and a scone."

"Ms. Karen," the library president opened the pink room door. "We have some questions. Do you have a little time?"

"Of course. I'll be right there."

"I might have some questions too," Jack said.

"Tiffany, answer the man's questions." Tiffany glared at me.

"Sit here, Ms. Karen. We have a proposal for you." My library friend, Monica, patted the chair next to her. Her silver pen was on the table next to her notepad.

I crossed my fingers. *Maybe I'll get to see her silver pen in action again.*

"We have our annual volunteer appreciation dinner next month," Monica said. "We'd like to have cream puffs for dessert. Is that something you could do?"

"How many would you need?"

President Gayle cleared her throat. "We expect fifty people. Is that too many?"

"I'll check with Tiffany, and we'll research Mr. R's recipes. Three per person seems right for a serving but give us until next week to give you a quote. Would that work?"

Gayle beamed. "That's great. I'll drop by next Thursday to check in with you."

I left the room before they adjourned so I could talk to Tiffany. "They're interested in cream puffs for fifty or so people at a dinner next month. I said we'd research."

"Mr. R's book has a small section on cream puffs and eclairs. We'll need to know how many to make per person so we can calculate a cost." Tiffany refilled Jack's cup.

The library executive meeting adjourned, and the pink room cleared. When Monica left, she twirled her pen, and the door jingled.

"Did you hear that?" I asked.

"What?" Tiffany asked as she pushed the utility cart inside the pink room to clean up.

I sat at the counter with Jack. "Did you get your questions answered?"

"I actually have some answers for you. Shirley told me, and the rest of the grocery line, you were thinking about updating the donut shop. True?"

"Alfred mentioned he had some ideas, but when Shirley and I met with Todd, he presented a project much larger than I wanted to get involved with. Why?"

Jack laughed. "Poor Todd can't get anyone interested in modernizing Asbury. If you were thinking about plumbing and electricity because this building is old, Mr. Rothenberger had me update both systems to code the year before he sold it to you. If you were having problems, I'd fix them. Your inspection should have shown the upgrades when you bought the building."

"I'd have to go back and read it. I remember Shirley told me there were no issues, but I don't remember the details. She might have told me."

"It is hard to stay focused on what Shirley says sometimes. The crop duster is now officially my favorite donut."

"Tiffany's invention. Everyone says they are great."

"What?" Jack raised his eyebrows. "You haven't had one? Let me buy you a donut."

Tiffany rolled the utility cart out of the pink room. "Two crop dusters coming up." She put the donuts on plates, cut one in half, and set the plates on the counter. "Just in case you want to share, Miss Lady."

"You're brilliant." I picked up my half, and we tapped crop dusters in a toast. "Oh yum. I do like this. Pink sprinkles may have a serious rival for the most popular donut."

"That sounds like another contest." Tiffany bit into her half. "Buy the donut you like best."

"You are always thinking." I finished my donut.

After Jack left, the sheriff came into the shop. "I miss the jingle, and you need to know when someone opens the door. Why is it gone?"

"Got on my nerves, but I admit I miss it. What do you think, Tiffany?"

"I wouldn't mind having it back. I keep trying to watch the door for customers."

"Put it back whenever you like, Tiff."

Tiffany rushed to the storeroom and danced out shaking the bell and tapping it with a screwdriver. She screwed the bell in where it had always been, stepped back, and said, "That looks right."

"Wait," the sheriff said. "Let me test it." He opened and closed the door. "Perfect. Jingles on an open and jangles on the close. You hear the difference, right?"

"Sure do," Tiffany said.

"You're both goofy." I wandered to the counter and perched on a stool.

"Fine one to talk. You heard it earlier too," Tiffany mumbled.

I stared at Tiffany, and she winked.

The sheriff stuck out his chin. "In that case, I'm not going to tell you what happened at school." He feinted a reach for the door. "On second thought, I'll tell Tiffany."

The two of them joined me at the counter.

"The principal caught me at the door and sent me to the auditorium. It was half-filled with snickering parents. Ms. Wilcox's class was called last to the auditorium, and after they were seated, her cousin and his band walked out on stage. The audience recognized him, and everyone jumped to their feet. The room exploded with applause and whistles. Ms. Wilcox raised her hands, turned to her class, and bowed in defeat. Her class screamed and pounded on each other's backs."

"Who was the cousin?" Tiffany asked.

"His name is Tom, but I didn't know who he was. I got the feeling he's up and coming. I can tell you he and his band were fantastic. They played for forty minutes, and then Ms. Wilcox accompanied them to their bus. Everyone else trooped to the cafeteria where the parents had organized a potluck lunch. The dripping blood scones and eyeballs were a hit."

"Do you have any pictures?" Tiffany peered at his cell phone.

"Sorry. I was kind of on duty. Gatherings of kids and a celebrity make me nervous. I'm sure you'll see lots of pictures."

Tiffany opened the display case. "Miss Lady, we have two scones and one donut left. No eyeballs."

"Take them for Isaiah. Or Gee, if you're interested in a peace offering that won't do any good."

"I'll head out. See you in the morning." The sheriff opened and closed the door three times before he left with a big grin.

"Tiffany, do you know why Carla would go into hiding? None of this makes any sense to me."

"It's what she's always done. Whenever there was trouble, she'd hide." Tiffany opened the dishwasher and stood back while the steam rolled out.

"Where would she hide?"

"Most of the time she'd come to my house and hide in the shed. She said it was like a playhouse. I'd sneak her food."

"Who would take her food now if she's in hiding?"

She hurried to the storeroom and came out with the broom and dustpan. "Miss Lady, can you empty the dishwasher? If anything's too heavy or bulky just leave it. I'll sweep. Pink room first."

I emptied the dishwasher and scrubbed the counter with cleaner. While Tiffany swept the shop, I sprayed and wiped the pink room table and buffet.

I put my cleaning supplies away. "Did you know Carla's boyfriend from high school?"

"Brendon? Not really. I knew about him, but he wasn't from around here. Carla kept her friends in compartments. That make sense? Mine was pretty much closed after Carla graduated from high school, and she moved away. I heard Carla and Brendon got married, and it was a stormy relationship. I don't think it lasted a year."

"Do you know where he is now? Any gossip?"

"I haven't heard anything. Are you thinking Brendon might be helping Carla?"

"Can you think of anyone else?"

"Like I said, compartments."

Isaiah tapped on the shop window. After Isaiah and Tiffany left, Mia ran to her carrier, and the three of us went home for lunch.

At three o'clock I trudged into the doctor's office. Mary Ellen grinned.

"You're all signed in, Ms. Karen. I'll take you to the cast room."

When she led me into the cast room, the technician was perched on a round stool with rollers.

He waved at a soft vinyl chair next to his stool. "If you sit here, I'll take off the soft cast, and then we'll put on a hard one. You have your choice of colors."

"I've gotten compliments on the pink."

"We'll stick with pink then."

An hour later, he finished the last touch on the hard cast. "It takes seventy-two hours for the cast to harden completely. Here's a sheet that explains how to take care of it. Call if something doesn't feel right. Only three more weeks, right?"

* * *

The timer dinged, and I pulled my dinner out of the oven. The shadows crowded the kitchen. I peeled away the foil cover and stirred the mashed potatoes on the aluminum tray with my fork. I poked at the gravy-covered pork chop and stabbed a piece of cooked carrot. I had no appetite; my mood matched the growing darkness of the shadows. I tossed the aluminum tray and contents into the trash and went to bed.

* * *

I woke at four. *Is Tiffany providing supplies to Carla?* The shadows gathered. *What do I know? What am I missing?* The shadows swirled and boiled. My heart raced, and my skin was clammy. My chest tightened, and my throat closed. The shadows filled the room, and I clutched my neck in horror as they destroyed each molecule of air. I sat up in bed. *I can't breathe!*

Colonel barked, and I gasped. Colonel scrambled, growling and barking, to the back door and scratched in a frenzy to go out. I opened the door, and he tore out of the house and raced through the open gate and down the alley. I called him, and he trotted back. His grin said, "Good run."

Did I forget to close the gate?

After my coffee perked, I sipped the hot, bitter liquid. "I know where Carla is hiding, Colonel. Let's go on a field trip after work."

When I walked into the shop, the bell jingled. *Love the jingle.*

Tiffany stood at the fryer. "I dreamed about filled donuts last night. Cream puffs must have put the idea in my head. Nice change from nightmares. I read through Mr. R's recipes this morning and filled donuts take longer to make. We couldn't have them ready for our earliest crowd, but we could by eight o'clock. What do you think? The recipe book's on the counter."

"I like the idea. Maybe they'd be a Saturday special. We can sure give it a try."

"I thought you'd say that. I've got a batch rising, and we've got raspberry filling. I'll whip up the pastry cream for a vanilla cream filling if you can take over the fryer for a few minutes."

"I'll grab my apron if you'll tie it for me. We're in business. Did you check the calendar?"

"The Running Board meets today. What's that?"

"My name for the 5K Planning Board."

The bell jingled. The sheriff narrowed his eyes. "Something's going on here. You in training, Donut Lady?"

I waved my slotted spoon. "Pour yourself some coffee, sheriff, and help yourself. The donuts in the display case are still warm."

"Can I get an apron like the mayor?"

"Only if I can call Emma so she can get a picture."

He poured a cup of coffee and picked up a plate. "You haven't put anything on the board yet. What we got here?"

"Classic glazed and maple," Tiffany said.

"You want to write on the board for us?" I asked.

"I'll be running the whole joint before long." He grabbed the chalk and scribbled on the board. He stepped back and gazed at the board. "I can't read what I wrote. This is harder than I thought."

"Don't worry about it. Enjoy your donuts and coffee." I moved donuts from the hot oil to the draining screen

The bell jingled, and Roger strode in. Tiffany glanced up from the mixer and beamed. I turned my back to the door and batted my eyelashes at her. She snorted and shook her spatula at me.

Roger squinted at the board. "What's a plastic glass apple?"

"Today's special." The sheriff growled and crossed his arms.

Roger mumbled. "I'm so fired." Tiffany and I laughed.

"You're not fired. Right, sheriff?" I refilled the sheriff's cup and poured another while Tiffany put two donuts on a plate.

"You two need to come back in about an hour for our special. I kind of like the plastic glass apple name, and the apples have what inside, Tiffany?"

"One kind oozes blood, and the second oozes … school glue." She grinned.

"Well, as long as there's no worm in the apple," Roger said.

Tiffany's eyes gleamed.

"Now I've done it. I gave Tiffany ideas."

"Update that resume, Roger." I shook my head, and even the sheriff laughed.

After the sheriff and Roger left, Tiffany asked, "You going to change the sign?"

"No." I squinted at the board. "Roger has an amazing imagination. I'm curious to hear what others see."

The bell jingled, and Woody held the door for Shirley. My heart melted at the love the two of them shared in their smiles at each other.

Woody squinted at the board. "Plastic glass apples." He put his hand to his mouth, and Tiffany and I chuckled.

"What? Where do you see that? Is that what the deputy told you when y'all chatted while I pumped gas?" Shirley stared at the board. "I can't make that out. Maybe I need coffee. And some squizzles or whatever that says."

Tiffany fixed Shirley's coffee while I fetched Woody's milk.

"Two donuts for Ms. Shirley, and a filled donut for Woody," Tiffany said.

"Squizzles and a plastic glass apple?" I asked.

"Yes, ma'am. And the plastic glass apple is held together with school glue."

Shirley's eyes widened, but she bit her lip and waited for Woody take a bite of his filled donut. Woody examined his pastry. When he spied the hole used to fill it, he bit into the donut. Only a little cream filling escaped from the side of his mouth.

"Foaming at the mouth, there, Woody." Tiffany snickered.

He wiped his mouth. "This school glue is really good."

"Glad you like it." Tiffany hurried to fill the rest of the pastries and drizzle and frost before the Running Board meeting started. I started two more pots of coffee.

Shirley, Woody, and I sat at the reading table.

"Is it four more weeks until your cast comes off? I think your house may be ready for you in two weeks. The structural engineer said there wasn't near as much damage as they first thought. I've got the detailed report for you to read, but that's the bottom line."

"Can we have a housewarming party for your house, Miss Lady? Me and Ms. Shirley can take care of everything. Can I invite my teacher?"

"Can it be a small party? Or we can have an open-house celebration here at the shop. What do you think?"

Tiffany stopped at the meeting room door. "I like the open-house celebration idea if we're voting."

"What do you think, Woody? We could decorate the shop." Shirley tapped the table and glanced around.

"It might be hard to keep it small. Celebration at the shop is perfect. Me and Ms. Shirley know a good caterer. But we'd have to have donuts too."

"You're right about the donuts. I'm sure Tiffany will come up with something special."

"Sure will. Already have some ideas." Tiffany carried a platter of filled donuts into the meeting room. She left the door open. Woody and I laughed at the squeals and applause.

"Big hit." Tiffany carried the empty platter to the sink.

Woody came out of the storeroom. "I have the list of low supplies. Anything else?"

"I have a list of the extras for next week." Tiffany handed her list to Woody.

"We'll be back soon," Shirley said.

* * *

"Supplies are all put away, Miss Lady. I'm leaving unless there's something else." Tiffany hung up her apron.

"It's been a great week, Tiffany. Thanks for everything."

I checked the back door before I left. Not my usual routine, but I found it unlocked and secured it.

* * *

The next morning, Colonel checked the backyard, and I sipped my coffee. Our neighborhood mockingbird serenaded us until he was drowned out by the roar of the neighbor's lawnmower. *Wonder if those two have a neighborhood feud going on?*

"Ready for a road trip, Colonel?"

As we traveled on the road out of town, the countryside reminded me of the picnic with Jack. "Colonel, wasn't it nice to get away with Roxie and Jack? I relaxed for the first time in ages, just being outside."

After I pulled into the driveway at the farm, I parked near the chimney. The last time I was here was the night I found Woody after he ran away. The burned-out homestead with the lone standing structure— the soot-stained brick chimney—screamed lifelessness and abandonment even more than it did in the dark. I shuddered.

Colonel and I hiked through the tall grass to the larger of the two sheds, the one where Woody had hidden. I flashed on the memory of his thin, unconscious body lying in the cold, dirty shed.

The hasp was fitted over the loop, and the padlock was in place but hung open. I opened the door. The shed was littered with fast food sacks and wrappers, smashed drink cups, and empty beer cans. The sight of maggots that writhed on a half-eaten burger and the thick odor of stale beer, rancid grease, and spoiled food was so overwhelming I gagged. I closed the door and replaced the padlock over the loop. As I turned to leave, I spied the corner of a small cardboard box half-buried and wedged under the shed near the door.

"Let's find something to dig with." Colonel followed me to the homesite where I found a brick shard. When I unearthed and opened the cigar box, I discovered a copy of another life insurance policy. The insured was Russell Wilshire Simpson for five hundred thousand dollars, and the beneficiary was Tiffany Ruth Armstrong.

My jaw dropped, and I sat back on my heels and reread the policy. I didn't know the agent, but the address was in Conway, only twenty miles north of Asbury.

I took a photo of the front page of the life insurance policy and reburied the box. *Don't need it to be missing.*

I tossed the brick shard into the rubble of the house and returned to my car. When we came to the road, I turned south to Asbury.

"That pretty much took away my appetite for any lunch and fast food in particular." I rolled my window down, and Colonel whined. I rolled his down too.

"Maggots take eight to twenty-four hours to appear. Don't ask me how I know. Maggots are disgusting, but doesn't that mean nobody's been at the shed for at least eight hours? We need music." I turned the radio to a country western station and cranked the volume up. I sang, and Colonel howled.

When we got close to civilization, I lowered the volume and rolled up the windows. "Thank you, radio station. Perfect tunes to clear my head."

Colonel and I went into the house. I kicked off my shoes at the door and padded to the kitchen for a glass of tea. Why would Russell name

Tiffany as the beneficiary of his insurance policy, not his wife? And where is Carla? The shed must have been where she hid out when she was a kid, but how could anyone have stayed in that filth?

"Colonel, I need to talk to somebody about all this, but I don't know who. You're a smart dog, but you're a lightweight in the suggestion department."

* * *

I fed Colonel and Mia and sat at the table with my dinner. I poked the potatoes with my fork and moved the peas around my plate. I picked up my phone and called Amber. It rang around to voice mail. I scooped up a forkful of peas and watched them roll off and fall on the potatoes. My phone rang. *Tiffany.*

"Miss Lady, can you meet me at the shop? I need to talk to you."

I have a feeling. The shadows appeared and swirled at the front door. *Blocking the door?*

"We're just now sitting down to dinner. We can be there in about an hour or so. That okay? Want me to call you when we leave?"

"You don't need to call. I'm at the shop. I'll wait."

After I hung up, I leaned back in my chair. "I've got a feeling. Guess it's you and me, Colonel."

Before I reached the door, my phone rang. *Shirley.*

"Miss Lady? It's me, Woody. Ms. Shirley wasn't feeling so good, so me and her came to the hospital. She said I should call you. Can you come sit with me? I don't want to go to foster care."

"I'll be right there, Woody. You're not going to foster care."

I tried to call Tiffany, but no answer. "Colonel, I don't know how long I'll be. Take care of Mia."

I headed to the door, and Colonel followed me. I pointed at his rug. "Stay." He returned to his rug and flopped down.

When I pulled up in front of the shop, the lights were on. I honked the horn. When I honked a second time, the lights went out. Tiffany locked the shop and ran to my car.

"Something wrong, Miss Lady?" She climbed into the car. Her face was pale.

I pulled away from the curb. "Shirley's at the hospital. Woody called. I don't have any details. We can talk on the way."

"Carla called me. She said to meet her at the edge of town, but I told her no." Tiffany lowered her head. "She said I'd be sorry. She said it'd be my fault if you got hurt. I ran to the shop."

"What do you think she meant?"

"I don't know. I sent a text to Roger, but he keeps his phone off when he's at work. He'll call me when his shift's over."

"Shirley first. Then if you don't hear from Roger, we'll call the sheriff and see what he thinks."

Tiffany glanced in the back seat. "Where's Colonel?" Her breathing was rapid and shallow.

"He's at home. Why?"

"I don't know. I have one of your feelings."

"Call Isaiah. If he's available, ask him to take you to my house to pick up Colonel and Mia, if she'll go into her carrier."

When I parked at the hospital, Isaiah and Woody rushed up to the car.

"We'll go get Colonel and Mia and take them to Aunt Gee's," Woody said. "Mia will come to me."

"We'll be back as quick as we can," Isaiah said. I handed him my house keys, and Tiffany and I rushed to the emergency entrance.

Darlene Rothenberger wore a pink volunteer smock and met us at the information desk. "They've rolled Shirley into surgery for an emergency appendectomy. Not an official diagnosis. The doctor will talk to you later, but it didn't seem right for you not to know what was going on. You let me know how I can help. You hear?" She hugged me and bustled away with her magazine cart.

Tiffany's eyes were wide. "I didn't know Ms. Darlene even knew how to hug. Can I get you some water? If you'd rather have coffee, I'll get you some from the gas station."

"Let's sit. I'll call the sheriff."

Tess picked up the call. "Hello Donut Lady. We heard about Ms. Shirley. Is she out of surgery?"

"Not yet. Is the sheriff available this evening?"

"He's on his way to the hospital. I think he's picking up coffee."

Tiffany snorted. I narrowed my eyes, and she put her hand over her mouth.

The sheriff sauntered in with two covered cups of steaming coffee. "The grapevine didn't tell me you were here, Tiffany. Care for some coffee?"

"No, sir. I'd be wired all night if I drank any coffee."

"Me too, Tiff." He handed me a cup. "But I'm on duty most of tonight anyway. So what's going on besides surgery?"

I raised my eyebrows, and he shrugged. "I got one of your feelings is all." He leaned back in his seat. "I'm ready."

Tiffany cleared her throat. "Carla called me and was angry I wouldn't meet her. She said it would be my fault if anything happened to Ms. Karen."

"I picked up Tiffany, and on our way to the hospital, she worried about Colonel and Mia being at the house alone. Isaiah and Woody have my house key and will take Colonel and Mia to Gee's house."

The sheriff strode outside and talked into his handheld radio. When he returned, he gulped his coffee. "Roger will meet up with Isaiah and Woody and escort them here. Roger and I will check your house and shop together. When's Shirley supposed to get out of surgery? Anybody say?"

I handed the sheriff the shop key. "Isaiah has my house key. No news on Shirley's surgery yet."

After the sheriff left, Tiffany's phone rang. She answered. "Hello, Aunt Gee. Yes, I'll tell her."

"She's on her way?" I asked.

"She's in the parking lot."

Gee joined us in the waiting room. "Haven't heard anything yet?"

"Nothing. Not even unofficially." I rose to stretch.

"She may be in the hospital only a day or so. Isaiah wants Woody to come home with us. Is that okay with you?"

"Thank you, Gee. That's a great idea. Woody was worried about where he was going to stay. He was worried about going into foster care. I need to ask him sometime what that means. He's always been terrified by what he calls 'foster care.'"

Tiffany rose. "If you want me to stay with you, I will." She took my empty cup and tossed it into the trash.

"Thanks, Tiff. I'll be fine. I have Colonel and Mia." *And the shadows.*

Gee pulled her phone out of her purse. "I'll text Isaiah and let him know it's okay to invite Woody."

Tiffany wandered to the door.

Gee leaned close to me. "She's not watching for her cousin." We snickered.

A doctor in green scrubs came into the waiting room and strode toward us. Gee and I rose.

CHAPTER TWELVE

"Ms. Shirley's out of surgery. Everything went fine. She's in the recovery room and will be there maybe another hour, but she should be awake enough in thirty minutes for a quick visit. Where's Woody?"

"He'll be right back. Can Woody and I go in to see her together?"

"I don't see why not. I'll let the nurse know."

Isaiah and Woody rushed in, and Woody ran to the doctor. "Is Ms. Shirley okay?"

"She's fine, Woody. You can go see her in thirty minutes or so. The nurse will come to get you and Ms. Karen."

"Can she go home tomorrow?"

"Maybe not tomorrow, but we won't keep her more than a couple days."

Woody narrowed his eyes. "I can see her in twenty-nine minutes?"

The doctor laughed. "Might be a little longer, but not much. I'll let the nurses know you're counting the minutes."

After the doctor left, Isaiah chuckled. "Way to go, Woody. No sense in messin' around." Woody and Isaiah fist-bumped.

"I'm going to spend the night with Isaiah, Miss Lady. Is that all right? He'll drop me off at school in the morning and pick me up. He said I can sleep in his room on the top bunk. Right, Isaiah?"

"That's right, buddy. And Mama's going to make us pancakes for breakfast."

"I sure am. Pancakes and bacon. How's that sound, Woody?"

"Sounds like Christmas. Which gives me an idea. Can we get Ms. Shirley some flowers tomorrow, Isaiah? I've got some money saved."

I glanced at Gee, and she put her hand on her heart.

Isaiah thumped Woody on the back. "We sure can. We'll get some after school, and you can deliver them in person."

I brushed away a stray tear. "Ms. Shirley will love it."

A nurse stood at the information desk. "Woody? Ms. Shirley is asking for you."

Woody grabbed my hand and helped me up out of my seat, and we followed the nurse down the well-lit hallway. The sound of machines and beeps from the rooms we passed accompanied us.

The nurse stopped. "Woody, Ms. Shirley is sleepy, but she's fine. There are a lot of machines around her, but they are just standard after surgery. She has an IV and oxygen. Standard. You can only stay a short minute, though, because she needs her rest. She'll be closer to her perky self tomorrow when you come to visit after school. Ready?"

"Yes, ma'am."

"I'll be at the nurses' station down the hall." She pointed behind us. "You come to see me before you leave, okay?"

"Yes, ma'am."

The nurse pushed the door open. Woody's hold on my hand tightened, and we walked in. Woody's eyes widened.

"Standard," I said.

He gulped. "Standard."

"Woody?" Shirley's voice was weak.

"Right here, Ms. Shirley." He dropped my hand and was at her side in two strides.

"Where are you staying tonight?"

"With Isaiah. He said I could have the top bunk. And Aunt Gee is making pancakes for breakfast."

"Maybe I'll sneak out of here and join you."

"Good one, Ms. Shirley." He patted her hand.

"Karen?"

"Right here, Shirley. You rest up. We'll see you tomorrow."

Shirley closed her eyes, and Woody and I tiptoed out. Woody led the way to the nurses' station.

"We didn't stay too long so Ms. Shirley can get some rest. And thanks for telling me all those machines are standard. They looked like alien robots."

The nurse turned away from her computer screen and smiled. "You're welcome. She'll surprise you tomorrow. She'll be much stronger when you come to visit after school."

The sheriff, Tiffany, and Isaiah waited for Woody and me.

"Ready to go, Woody?" Isaiah asked.

"Sure am. You be okay, Miss Lady?"

"I'll be fine. Have a good night. Don't keep Isaiah awake too late. He has school tomorrow, you know."

"Mama will make sure we go to bed on time." Isaiah grinned, and the two of them left with Isaiah's hand on Woody's shoulder.

Sheriff Grady narrowed his eyes. "Ms. Karen, Colonel and Mia are in my car. Do you have any plans for where you're staying tonight?"

"You're the official sheriff now, aren't you?" I crossed my arms.

Gee and Emma sauntered into the waiting room. Emma put her hands on her hips. "You going to give us problems or go quietly, Donut Lady? You're staying at our house tonight."

"You called in the cavalry? No fair, sheriff." Sheriff Grady and Emma high-fived. "You in on this, Gee?"

"You know it." Gee and Tiffany high-fived.

"Took four of you though." I walked to my car with my head high. The sheriff opened his car door and lifted out Mia's carrier. Colonel jumped out. Emma rode with us, and we followed the sheriff to their house.

"The guest bedroom's all set up for you. We have a black cat named Sparks. He's a scaredy cat, so you probably won't see him. I don't have a dog bed, but there's a soft rug in the guest bedroom Colonel might like. You're welcome to stay as long as you like. If you want to go to work in the morning, I'll drive or go with you if you like."

"Gee and Grady went by your house, and she packed a few things for you." Emma showed me the canvas bag with the logo *Frugal and a Little Fancy*.

* * *

I woke to the wafting aroma of coffee. I checked the clock, but it wasn't there. *Sheriff's house.* Colonel and I padded down the hardwood floors in the hallway to the gray tile in the kitchen. Emma sat on a white saddle counter stool at her gray and black granite breakfast bar. She closed her laptop and set down her coffee cup.

"You're up earlier than I expected. It's not quite three thirty. Grady just left. I'll step out with Colonel if you like. You want coffee? Or would you rather get a little more sleep?"

"I'll get dressed for work. Coffee is great. Thank you so much for everything."

When I returned to the kitchen, Emma poured me a cup, and I joined her at the breakfast bar.

"Do you have food for Colonel at the shop? Or do we need to run by your house?"

"We have food at the shop." Mia's carrier was open, but when I peered in, she meowed at me. My phone rang at three forty-five. *Tiffany?* "Miss Lady, I've called Tess. The shop is a mess. We've been robbed."

My heart pounded. "Are you okay?"

"I'm fine. I'll go sit in the truck. Oh, wait. Deputy car. I'll call you back."

"Emma, Tiffany said someone broke into the shop. I need to go. She said a deputy car pulled up."

"Do you ride with me or am I following you?" Emma grabbed a sweater and picked up Mia's carrier.

"Follow me." I grabbed my purse and the bag Gee had packed and rushed to the door. Colonel jumped up.

The early morning air was damp and low fog hugged the road. I rolled down our windows, and Colonel sniffed the night air. A block from the shop, I slowed the car to make a turn. Colonel whined and leaned out the window. I reached toward Colonel to pull him back and braked. "Was that a moan, Colonel?"

Emma slowed behind me. I pulled to the curb, and Colonel jumped out of the window. "Colonel!"

I grabbed my flashlight from my car's side pocket and chased after Colonel. I had parked at the corner in front of the dry cleaners, and Emma parked behind me. I raced around the corner, and Colonel growled and dashed into the alley.

I froze at the sound of a low moan.

"You hurt? Need help?" I called out and swept the alley with my light. Shadows lingered near a dumpster.

"Here." A weak voice called. Colonel barked twice and growled.

I stepped closer to the building and headed into the alley. My light caught a dark form next to the dumpster.

"Miss Lady."

I raced to the form. *Isaiah.*

Isaiah was sprawled face down in the dirt. I kneeled next to him and lay my hand on his back. "Isaiah?"

He mumbled, but I couldn't understand him. I moved closer to his head and listened.

"Ambushed."

I slipped my hand under his side. It was wet. When I pulled my hand away, I gazed at the warm blood on my palm. Emma appeared at the alley entrance. "Karen?"

"We need an ambulance."

Colonel faced the far end of the alley with his back to us.

I focused on listening to Isaiah's breathing. It was ragged when he inhaled.

"Miss Lady?"

"Right here, Isaiah. Do you know what your injuries are?" I moved closer to his mouth to hear.

He wheezed. "Knife. In ribs. Cold."

"Emma," I called out. "Do you have a blanket?"

Emma ran to us. "Here's my sweatshirt." We laid her pink sweatshirt across Isaiah's broad back. The faint sounds of a siren grew in intensity.

"I'm going to run flag them down," Emma said.

"Miss Lady?"

"Still here. Ambulance will be here soon. Do you know who it was?"

Isaiah didn't answer. His breathing was shallower.

The siren stopped, and Emma shouted, "Down here!"

The paramedic followed Emma down the alley.

"We've got him now, Ms. Karen."

"Just don't remove the knife."

"Yes, ma'am. We're trained to stabilize it." The paramedic grabbed a gauze pack.

"My hip is cramped. I can't get up." Emma grabbed me under the arms and dragged me away from Isaiah.

"Not the most elegant move, right?" Emma whispered. "Want me to help you stand?"

"Give me a second to see if I can stretch the cramp away." I rolled to my side and straightened my hip. "I'm going to need help."

Emma and I struggled to get me up. My cast made it awkward for us. The ambulance crew rolled Isaiah onto a backboard, loaded him onto the cot, and rolled to the ambulance.

"Just give me a minute, Emma."

She sat next to me on the ground until the ambulance left. "Ready?"

"Yep. We don't have to be delicate. No audience." I scooted to the dumpster and got myself to one knee. Emma stooped down, and I wrapped my right arm around her neck and shoulders. She grasped the back of my pants at the waist and hauled me to my feet.

"Lord that was an ordeal." I shook my pants and fixed the wedgie Emma gave me.

Emma laughed. "Not the most elegant, that's for sure. What next? Hospital or shop?"

"I need to go to the shop. I know Tiffany will want to go to the hospital."

"Makes sense. I think I'll go straight to the hospital. I know Gee will be frantic."

Emma gave me her arm, and I limped back to my car with her help. Colonel led the way. The fog lifted, and the sky lightened. Emma helped me into my car.

"Thanks, Emma."

"See you at the hospital."

Tiffany waited on the curb in front of the shop. She opened the passenger's door and jumped in. "I mixed the first batch of dough while I was waiting. I knew you'd come get me. Tess told me about Isaiah. We're going to the hospital, right? Is he going to be okay? Somebody broke down the back door. The cash register was on the floor, but it wasn't damaged. I never understood why you always left it empty and open."

Tiffany rubbed her forehead. "The safe in the storeroom was untouched. Ms. Shirley's jar, though, was shattered. The pieces of glass were near the reading table. I think the frustrated thief threw it against the wall. The money was gone. No surprise."

"Was anyone there when you went into the shop?"

"When I unlocked and opened the door, the bell jingled. I thought I heard someone run to the back, but by the time I got the lights on, they were gone. Isaiah must have seen them when they ran out the back door and chased them down. Is he going to be okay?"

"He'd been stabbed and was weak, but he talked to me. I'll drop you at the hospital then I'll go back to the shop."

"Let's check on Isaiah, and then decide. I told Mr. Jeff we'd be back. He was taking pictures."

When we arrived at the waiting room, Gee, Woody, and Emma sat together, and Isaiah's friends stood near Gee like sentries.

Woody ran to me and wrapped his arms around my waist. Tiffany ran to Gee and kneeled beside her. Tears streamed down Gee's face when Tiffany hugged her.

Woody and I walked arm in arm back to his seat next to Gee.

"They've taken him into surgery," Emma said. "It will be a while. The doc said leaving the knife in place saved his life. How did you know?"

"Thank you, Miss Lady," Woody spoke in a quiet voice.

"Y'all go on back to the shop." Gee brushed away the tears. "Nothing to do here but wait. Text me when you've got donuts. We could use some."

"Are you sure, Aunt Gee?" Tiffany bit her lip.

"Of course, I'm sure we could use donuts." Gee raised her eyebrows. The sentries snickered.

"You'll keep us up to date on any news, right?" I narrowed my eyes at Gee. Woody nodded.

"We will," Emma said. "Oh, and Woody's not going to school today. We voted."

* * *

"Who do you think it was?" I asked on the way back to the shop.

Tiffany shifted her feet. "Carla. She told me you had money. She said she needed money."

"I think it was Carla too." I parked behind Isaiah's truck. "Check the truck for keys. Looks like Jeff is still there."

The bell jingled when Colonel and I went inside. Jeff sat at the reading table. "Just taking some notes, Ms. Karen. How's Isaiah?"

"In surgery."

"He's a lucky kid. Crazy to run after the lunatic, though. I'm pretty much done here. You'll need somebody to fix that door. You going to call Mr. Jack?"

I rolled my eyes. "You're as bad as Gee."

He laughed. "I'll take that as a compliment. I'll check on you later. You're still making donuts today, right? I swept up the glass and picked up the cash register."

"Thank you, and yes, come back later for donuts."

The bell jingled when Jeff left, and when Tiffany came in. "I've got Isaiah's keys."

She washed her hands and tied her apron. I searched the storeroom and found a wide-mouthed pint jar. After I opened the safe for our till money, I checked the calendar.

"This is unusual. No meetings today. I've got a new Shirley jar." I put the money in the register and Shirley's jar under the counter.

"I thought we'd go with strawberry glazed and maple. We need a little pink this morning." Tiffany fried her first batch of donuts.

"If Carla broke in, she cut it close. She knows what time you show up for work."

"Maybe she expected it to be easier to get in than it was." Tiffany pursed her lips.

While I washed my hands, I glanced down. "Dang. I've got blood on my knees."

"Didn't Aunt Gee pack you some clothes for the sheriff's house?"

"She did. Good thinking, and I'm pretty sure I threw the bag into my car. I'll be right back."

I returned with the bag and changed my pants. "Might be a good idea to keep a change of clothes here, just in case. Both of us. Anything I can do to help?"

"After the first batch cools a bit, you can glaze the strawberry. I already mixed the second batch so I can dip the maple."

Sheriff set off the jingle when he opened the door. "What's going on here? You haven't put anything on the board yet."

While Tiffany served his two donuts, I poured coffee. "Just slackers. Before you leave, would you check the back door? The lock is smashed. We'll need it fixed today, but I need to know if you think we can get by with just a new lock."

The sheriff sipped his coffee. "You know my version of fixing a broken lock. A couple of boards and three-inch nails."

I poured my cup and joined him at the counter. "I suspect the fire marshal might take exception."

"You're right. Guess you're going to have to call Jack." The bell jingled, and the sheriff grinned.

I narrowed my eyes at the sheriff. *Must be Jack.*

"Heard you had a little excitement this morning. How's Isaiah?"

"In surgery, Mr. Jack. We haven't heard anything yet." Tiffany answered.

"I thought I'd take a look at that back door."

I rose from my seat. "Good morning, Jack. Have a cup of coffee first. One or two donuts?"

"You're right, business before pleasure. Thank you. Two."

"Don't you have that backward?" I asked while I poured his coffee.

"This is your business, and it's my pleasure to fix a door." Jack grinned, the sheriff guffawed, and Tiffany giggled.

"I walked right into that one." I shook my head and smiled.

The bell jingled, and Amber rushed in; she wore jeans and her faded sweatshirt. "Oh good. You're here, Jack. Did you already fix the door?"

I sauntered over to stand in front of Jack. I rested my elbow on the counter, propped my chin in my palm, and gazed at him. "Welcome to my world."

He spewed his coffee.

"I win!" I threw my hand into the air and danced. Tiffany laughed and threw her hands into the air and danced too. Tiffany poured Amber's coffee and set a plate with a maple donut on the counter in front of her.

Amber laughed and bit into her donut. "How's Isaiah?"

"Still in surgery as far as we know." Tiffany hurried back to her fryer, and I drizzled and dipped.

Jack finished his coffee and donuts and checked the back door. "The door was kicked in. I'll replace the door, the splintered door frame, and install a deadbolt with a deeper throw."

"What?" I squinted and tilted my head.

"Sorry. Went technical. The hardware store is open. I'll take some measurements and get what I need."

Tiffany fried the last batch of donuts and cleaned the equipment.

"Tiffany, would you like to deliver a batch of donuts?" I raised my eyebrows and glanced at Amber, who nodded. "Amber will drive you to the hospital and come back to help me close up."

Tiffany frowned. "Are you sure?"

"You've done all the hard work. We can finish up here," Amber said.

"I need to hang around until the back door is fixed, and we promised Gee donuts."

Tiffany packed up a box of donuts, and the two of the left.

Text from Gee. "Out of surgery. Looks good. Emma & Woody going to park."

I returned her text. "Thanks. Donuts on the way."

Gee: "E & W change of plans."

I snickered. The bell jingled, and Darlene hurried in and rested on the stool closest to the door. She leaned her cane against the counter, pulled a lacy handkerchief out of her purse, and wiped the beads of sweat off her upper lip. "Got coffee? Can't have a donut. I need to walk more. And a glass of water?"

I brought her a glass of ice water. "Nice to see you, Darlene."

She gulped down her water. "The ladies in my group at church and I were planning to prepare a nice dinner for you and Gee and her family. I was going to host it at my house, but it's grown to a town potluck, and we've moved it to the Catholic church."

I poured her a cup of coffee, and she stirred in cream. "They have the biggest hall. We're planning on serving from five until eight. Y'all can come anytime. Don't feel obligated to stay. We'll take care of the food and socializing."

I leaned against the counter. "I'm overwhelmed. It sounds wonderful."

She sipped her coffee. "Have a piece of lettuce for lunch. This town has a bunch of competitive cooks, and there's going to be a lot of food.

Alfred is sending his boys out with flyers to invite our homeless population. Gus and his crew are organizing van pools to transport folks from the retirement homes to the church. And the hospital volunteers are making a list of people who work tonight so we can deliver to them. We need people to eat all that food!"

Darlene put ten dollars on the counter. "I don't know how much coffee is these days, but I understand Tiffany is saving up college money. It's not much, but I'd like to contribute. See you this evening."

Darlene bustled out. The bell jingled when she left and again when Amber came in.

Amber peered out the front window while Darlene climbed into her car. "Ms. Darlene looked like a house afire. She tell you about the potluck tonight? Even the people I know who can't cook are bringing something."

"That's really amazing. Coffee?" I held up the pot.

"Yes, please. The doctor said the force of the knife broke a rib, but the rib kept the knife from going too deep. Sounds like they got everything repaired. Isaiah's in recovery, and then will be going to ICU. Emma's planning on Woody staying with them until Shirley's released which may be tomorrow."

I sat on the stool next to Amber. "How's Gee doing?"

"A lot better with Isaiah out of surgery. I'm going back to pick up Tiffany, and we're going to open the thrift shop. Gee expected a delivery this afternoon and was stressing about leaving the hospital. See you later."

I scrubbed the bathroom sink and swished cleaner in the toilet.

"I just needed something to do." Colonel flopped in the doorway and watched.

"I'm back," Jack called from the back door. He had a white sack in his hand when he strode to the front. "I picked us up some lunch. I didn't know when you'd have time to eat."

I smiled to keep from laughing. "You know about the big dinner tonight, right? Darlene Rothenberger told me to eat a lettuce leaf for lunch."

Jack set the sack on the reading table. "I'm of the theory it's necessary to stretch your stomach before a big meal. Let's eat. I'm starving."

He pulled out two salads. I snorted, and he laughed. "Gus wouldn't let me get sandwiches. He said we have to save room for tonight. I got iced tea if you want it."

"That's great." We sat at the table and opened the clear clamshell containers.

"Grilled chicken with cranberries, pecans, and blue cheese? This looks great." I took a bite. "Gus's house dressing. Yum. So how strong would a person need to be to break down the door?"

"From the placement of the kick, the person was tall. The door was solid wood, but the old frame splintered from the force. The deadbolt was old-style, not as long as they are now. It still would take someone strong to do it."

"Could a woman have done it?"

Jack set down his fork and narrowed his eyes. "You couldn't have. You aren't tall enough. I can show you if you like. A strong, young woman, the size of Tiffany, could. Does that answer your question?"

"It does. How long do you expect to take in replacing the door? Couple of hours? I'd like to go to the hospital to check on Shirley and Gee."

"At least two, maybe three hours. I need to… technical stuff." We laughed.

Jack cleared our places and took the trash out to the dumpster. I put the four donuts from the display case into a sack and emptied the cash register.

"You know that's smart. Emptying your till and leaving the register open. It saved you from having to buy a new cash register. Mr. R. teach you that?"

"He did. He said a cash register wasn't a secure box, and it was too expensive to replace every time some two-bit crook decided to break in."

"I can hear him saying that." Jack chuckled.

"I'll lock the front door on my way out." I picked up my purse, and Colonel followed me.

"Colonel, I thought I might go see Todd Rockford today, but I don't know why. You got any ideas?" I unlocked the car and opened the back door for Colonel.

CHAPTER THIRTEEN

Colonel whined, and I rolled down our windows. "Fresh air feels good, Colonel. Thanks."

I parked at the hospital, and Colonel led the way, except he meandered to every bush and light pole and raced to me when I was ahead of him.

Gee and one of Isaiah's friends sat in the waiting room. "It's been a long day already, Donut Lady. They're moving him from recovery to ICU. The doc says he's still groggy from surgery, and they'll let me know when they have him situated. Doc says I can only stay a minute or so. Woody and Emma have gone up to visit Shirley. She might be going home tomorrow. Or they might toss her out today."

"I'm going to see how she's doing. You know about dinner tonight, right?"

"Darlene came by and chatted. I never really knew her. All this time we've lived in the same town." Gee shook her head.

I got off the elevator on the second floor. The bright hallway, the clean odor of disinfectant, and the hum of voices and machine beeps greeted me. Shirley's room was at the end of the hallway. Shirley wore a blue and white hospital gown and was propped up in her bed. She was focused on Woody. He was telling a very animated story, and she smiled and nodded. Emma sat next to a window. She saw me and winked.

"Miss Lady! Ms. Shirley might go home tomorrow." Woody bounced on his toes. "Ms. Emma and I went to the park and to the animal shelter and visited the dogs and cats. We saw a lizard at the animal shelter, but it was outside on the wall."

"Sorry I missed seeing the lizard, Woody. How you feeling, Shirley?"

"I won't be doing any lifting for a while, but I'm fine. I'm looking forward to being home with Woody. The food here is hospital food. You know, nutritious." Shirley wrinkled her nose, and Emma and I laughed.

"Ms. Emma and I are going to let you rest now, Ms. Shirley. We'll be back tomorrow, right, Ms. Emma?" Woody skipped out of the room, and Emma waved and dashed after him.

"That boy is full of energy, isn't he? I've missed him." Shirley leaned back. "How's Gee holding up? How's Isaiah?"

I sat in the visitor's chair next to Shirley's bed. "Gee's doing fine. Isaiah's moved to the ICU."

"I had a roommate, but she went home early. It was nice to have someone to talk to, but I'm not sure if she was an introvert or hard of hearing. She didn't say much. The nurses here are nice, but they are busy. It's kind of lonesome. I've gotten out of the habit of watching television. I used to watch it all the time, but I can't find any of my shows. I think they've all gone been replaced with new ones which is too bad. I'm ready to go home and get back to work. I miss Woody. Do you—"

I patted her hand and rose. "I need to get back to the shop. I'll see you tomorrow."

Gee was gone when I stepped out of the elevator. Isaiah's friend and Colonel were outside. "We decided we're outside people, not hospital waiting room people, right, Colonel?"

"You're Thomas, right? Thanks for looking after Colonel for me. I didn't think I'd be as long as I was."

Thomas rubbed Colonel's ear and headed back to the hospital.

* * *

When Colonel and I went into the shop, Jack was sweeping the floor around the back door. "I'm all finished. Let me show you your new door. I installed a deadbolt that's up to code. I can't say no one can break in now, but it will be much harder. Here's your keys."

"Thanks, Jack. How much do I owe you?"

"I'll send you an invoice. How's that?" He picked up his tools. "I've got the truck in the back. How about if I pick you up for dinner tonight? About six?"

"I'm not sure yet what time I'm going. I need to check with Tiffany and Gee, but I'm sure I'll see you there."

"Oh. Okay. Lock the door behind me." He kicked the dirt on the way to his truck.

I locked the door. When I turned, Colonel stared at me.

"What? Tiffany will need a ride to dinner if Gee's not going. I don't need anyone to babysit me. Let's lock up. I'll take you home and then go see Todd Rockford. Maybe by the time I get there, I'll figure out why."

* * *

I went into the bank. "Hey, Ms. Karen. How can I help you?" The teller smiled.

"Thought I'd stop by and see if Todd Rockford was available. I have some more questions."

"Mr. Rockford left early for an appointment. He'll be here in the morning. Want me to make an appointment for you or buzz Mr. Gibson?"

"No, that's fine. Nothing urgent. I'll just catch him in the morning. You coming to the potluck?"

"Wouldn't miss it. Grandma made dinner rolls, and I'm taking half of them. Is that cheating?" She grinned.

"Not at all. See you at dinner." *I need to take something. What would a one-armed baker take?*

I parked at the far end of the row at the grocery store. The store was busy. I pushed a cart to the produce aisle and picked up a bag of precut mixed cabbage and carrots for coleslaw. I had all the ingredients at home for my homemade coleslaw dressing. *Genius.*

The shadows hovered while I mixed up my dressing and tossed it with the cabbage and carrots. "Goes into the refrigerator to mingle the flavors."

After some outside time for Colonel, I left for the thrift shop. Tiffany and Amber were in the back room surrounded by boxes.

"We got the boxes back here with the dolly, but now we don't know what to do. Aunt Gee organizes everything, but I don't know her system." Tiffany flopped on the floor and leaned against a box.

"Whatever we do will be wrong," Amber said.

"Why don't you just leave them? They're just as wrong where they are as they would be after you spend two hours moving them around." The two of them stared at me. I held my breath.

"Brilliant," Tiffany said.

"I love it. I need a shower. See y'all later. Now I have time to make a cobbler."

Tiffany dropped her head. "What can I make for the potluck? What are you taking?"

"I made coleslaw. We can go to the store if you like to pick something up."

"I have all the fixings to make homemade brownies at Aunt Gee's. Can you drop me off? What time were you going to the potluck? Can I ride with you?"

"I was planning on it. What do you think about six o'clock?"

"Gives me plenty of time to bake, cool, and cut my brownies."

When I got home, I poured a tall glass of iced tea. Mia attacked my feet while I shuffled around the kitchen. "Okay, I get it." I sat on the ugly sofa with my feet up, and Mia jumped on my lap. I stroked her back, and she fell asleep. Colonel stretched out on the rug next to the sofa and closed his eyes. I leaned back and listened to the duet of soft snores.

Mia jumped off my lap, and I opened my eyes. "Two-hour nap." I yawned. Colonel woke and trotted to the front door.

I slipped on my shoes, and Colonel and I strolled around the block. The neighborhood mockingbird sang its borrowed songs. I shaded my eyes and gazed overhead. A young hawk screeched in delight when it flew from one tree to another. Buzzards circled on the thermals in the blue sky. The crisp fragrance of the freshly-clipped lawns mingled with the soft aroma of cultivated roses and the sharp scent of marigolds. Colonel whined, and we continued our walk.

"No people, Colonel. Think everyone's cooking? It's a little eerie."

Colonel chased a squirrel to a tree, and the squirrel scampered to the top and chattered its displeasure. Colonel trotted back with a grin.

When we returned to the house, I fed Colonel and Mia and ran hot water into the tub for a bubble bath. I eased myself into the bubbles, and the shadows gathered at the bathroom door. Mia prowled into the bathroom. She stalked the soft blue rug and jumped up on the toilet seat. Colonel came into the room and pawed at the rug until its folds and bumps suited him. He flopped down and rested his chin on the floor.

"Could I have a little privacy?"

Mia leaped over Colonel and raced to the door. The shadows scattered, and Colonel followed her.

"Thank you."

I soaked in the tub until the water cooled to tepid. I stepped out of my water sanctuary with reluctance, dried, and dressed.

I put my bowl of coleslaw into a grocery sack so it would be easier for me to carry. Colonel followed me to the door.

"Stay."

The evening air was crisp. I put my sack on the passenger's seat and went back inside for a sweatshirt. Colonel was on the ugly sofa, and Mia was on the chair.

"See you later."

When I pulled up in front of Gee's house, Tiffany bounced out. "Roger has a couple of hours off this evening so he can come to the dinner. Aunt Gee called. Isaiah was awake and talked to her. She's going to be there too. Aunt Gee said Shirley wanted to come and nagged her doctor. He finally relented, but she had to promise she wouldn't overdo. Woody and Shirley are going to spend the night at Emma's. Aunt Gee said the sheriff volunteered for the night shift." Tiffany giggled, and I snorted.

The parking lot at the church was packed. Men in orange vests directed traffic to parking spots on the grass. Silas waved his flashlight at me. I stopped and rolled down my window. He stepped closer to my car. "We've got a reserved spot for you and one for Gee. Put this on your dash and drive to the front of the church." He handed me a large pink heart.

"Awesome," Tiffany said. "I've never been in a celebrity car before."

"Me neither," I growled.

"Oh, settle down," she said. "You're giving a whole town a reason to get together and party. There's going to be people here who haven't spoken in years. It's magical."

"Yes, ma'am, Aunt Tiffany."

"And don't you forget it." Tiffany waggled her head side to side, and her growl turned into a giggle.

"Magical is good, and we might see some fireworks too." I parked in our celebrity spot on the church grounds. Our parking guide saluted and scurried away to the main entrance.

The parking lot on the side of the church was well-lit, but it was dark where we parked. I couldn't see the uneven ground.

"Is the car locked?" Tiffany asked.

I clicked the car fob and listened for the beep. "Is now." I squinted at my feet and walked with tentative steps.

"Hand me the coleslaw, Miss Lady. That might help. It's hard to see in this dark. I'll run these in and come back to walk with you."

"Here, grab hold." Jack appeared next to me with a flashlight and offered me his arm.

"My eyes are having trouble adjusting to the dark, and the glare of those lights in the parking lot isn't helping."

"Annoying, isn't it?"

"Definitely."

Tiffany rushed ahead, and Jack and I ambled to the door.

"Sure is easier to see with the flashlight. You been lurking out here waiting for us?"

"Maybe." He chuckled. "It was either Roger or me. He's been pacing. I think he's been here since four-thirty."

Before we reached the meeting hall, the roar of cheerful voices, laughter, and clinking plates filled the corridor.

"Beautiful sound, isn't it?" Jack asked.

"I don't think I've ever heard anything like it. Magical."

"Ready to go in? It'll be even louder." Jack pushed the door open, and I winced at the blast of noise. Tiffany and Roger met us at the door.

Tiffany leaned over and shouted. "You won't have to worry about small talk. Nobody can hear. I love it." She batted her eyelashes and put on a fake smile.

The four of us joined the buffet line. Individual voices were indistinguishable in the din. I was in a cocoon surrounded by noise turbulence. I smiled, nodded, and studied the interactions of people nearby. *I'm in introvert heaven.*

Tiffany led the way to a table with four vacant seats. My permanent smile was genuine. *I'm having fun.*

Tiffany and Roger finished eating before we did and relinquished their seats to a couple hunting for a place to sit. After we ate, Jack pointed to the exit, and I nodded. We weaved our way to the door. Woody and Shirley waited outside in the hall.

Woody hugged me and high-fived Jack. "Did you have fun, Miss Lady?"

"I did, Woody. What about you?"

"It was noisy." Woody covered his ears.

"We saw you on your way to the door. Have you ever heard such a racket? I might be cured of talking too much. We're going now too. I'm not tired; you're tired. Right, Woody?" Shirley winked.

Woody laughed. "We're staying at Ms. Emma's tonight. Me and Ms. Emma got a new book for me to read to Ms. Shirley."

The two of them strolled down the hall. Woody chattered, and Shirley nodded.

"Now that's magical," Jack said.

"I need to find Tiffany. I'm not sure if she's riding home with me. I don't know when Roger goes back on duty."

"Why don't you relax?" He waved at an open room across the hall that was marked *Library.* "I'll find Tiffany and see if I can retrieve your bowl. The coleslaw went fast. Did you notice? I'm glad I got some. It was good."

I found a soft chair in the library back corner near a window. *Wonder what Woody's reading to Shirley.*

Snippets from whispering voices outside the window drifted into the library. I glanced at the window and spied the tops of two heads in the shadows—one bareheaded; the other wore a knit cap.

First voice. "You're crazy … here. What about ….?"

Second voice. "What … care? I need … unlocked cars … Get … my way."

The heads moved in opposite directions and were gone from my view.

I opened the door to the dining hall. Jack was at the kitchen door with his back to the dining hall. He shuffled backward with small steps out of the kitchen. A woman stood in front of him and waved her hands in animation. Roger and Tiffany were two tables away from the exit. They leaned toward each other and smiled when their shoulders lightly touched. Roger saw me first. I motioned for him to join me. When he and Tiffany were close, I pointed to the door, and they followed me out to the hallway.

"Roger, I was in the library and heard someone outside the window say something about unlocked cars."

Roger scowled. "When? Who?"

"Just now. I don't know who. Two people whispering. I only caught a few words."

"Thanks." He pulled out his radio and strode away.

"Okay if we wait a bit before we go to the car?" Tiffany asked. "Shall I rescue Mr. Jack?"

"He might appreciate it." I returned to my comfortable chair in the library.

"Donut Lady?" Gee called at the library door.

"In here, Gee. I found a comfortable seat."

"You found a quiet seat. Next big ole feast we have needs to be outside." Gee flopped down into the chair across from me. "The doctor says Isaiah's doing great and the hardest part is going to be convincing him to rest so he can heal."

"The advantage of being young."

"That's the truth. I'd ask what's going on with you, but we don't have all night." Gee cackled.

"I can't imagine anything's going on with me that you haven't already heard about." I chuckled. "Gee, is it possible Carla and Todd Rockford know each other?"

"Interesting question. I wouldn't think so. Carla and her husband hadn't been around town at all since Alfred hired Todd Rockford that I know of. This a stretch, but the scams that Simpson had going on with real estate and Rockford's position of loan officer at the bank might be an intersection."

"You're right. It's a stretch. Would you say Russell or Carla was the brains of the scams?"

"Ignoring the domestic violence angle, I'd say Carla. You saw the two of them work together. What do you think?"

"Russell was definitely in a rage at me, and I understand there were sales agents that he did hurt. But in retrospect, I didn't see any true violence aimed at Carla. Angry words are an easy script to follow. He didn't seem like the brainy type, but that whole scene could have been an act. I don't know."

"Did you kill Russell, Donut Lady?" Gee raised one eyebrow, and I burst out laughing.

"Dang, I needed that. I didn't, and you didn't. Woody didn't, and I'm pretty sure the sheriff and Emma didn't. And we know Shirley didn't, because she would have told us." I chuckled.

"Well then. We've got it narrowed down, don't we?" Gee laughed, and I joined her.

Tiffany and Jack came into the library.

"What's so funny?" Jack asked.

"We just needed a little stress relief." I rubbed my forehead to avoid looking at Gee.

"Okay, don't tell me." Jack frowned and sat at the table near our chairs. "And I won't tell you what Ruth Ann told me about Silas and Darlene."

"Don't be silly," I said. "You couldn't hear a thing in there. And you couldn't make up anything as good as Ruth Ann."

"True. So what's going on?"

I glanced at Gee, and she shrugged.

Tiffany perched on the arm of Gee's chair. "Miss Lady overheard someone talking about unlocked cars in the parking lot. Roger's checking it out."

"And we were discussing ways to make sure Isaiah rests so he can heal," Gee said.

"I can only imagine what the two of you came up with." Jack smiled and rose. Tiffany rolled her eyes.

Gee headed to the door. "Tiffany, I'm going home. You ready to go or are you riding with Donut Lady?"

"I'll follow Karen home if you want to ride with Gee, Tiffany. Or, if you want Karen to take you to Gee's, I'll follow everyone to Gee's and then follow Karen home." Jack beamed.

"I'm coming, Aunt Gee. Want to help me find your brownie pan?"

"Already got it. It's on a table by the door."

After they left, Jack sat on the chair Gee had vacated. "You can leave your car here if you like and ride with me."

"I'm fine to drive, but I wouldn't mind if you and your flashlight walk me to my car." I rose from my chair.

"I can do that. And I'll carry your bowl."

* * *

Colonel raised his head when I came inside the house and slid off the sofa. Mia stretched and kneaded the chair cushion.

"Did you two budge at all? Come on, Colonel. Let's go outside."

I turned on the burner under the tea kettle. When I stepped outside, there was a white truck with a crew cab in the back near the street. Colonel and I strolled down the alley.

"You want to park here or in the front? I'm brewing tea."

"I was trying to be subtle. I knew you'd let Colonel out. I'll park in front."

Jack backed out of the alley into the street. I left Colonel outside and opened the front door.

Jack came inside and hung his head. "I guess I have to turn in my secret surveillance card."

"Yes, you do. You want hot or cold tea? Have a seat." I pointed at the dining table.

"Cold. How'd you spot me?" Jack pulled out a chair, turned it around, and straddled it.

"Gee told Tiffany I know my regulars. I looked for you."

Jack chuckled, and Mia scooted into her pantry. I poured hot water into a cup and dropped in my tea bag. "I have cookies that Shirley and Woody bought for me. You interested?"

"No thanks. I'm still full from dinner. It's been a while since I've had good home cooking."

"Everything was good, wasn't it? I'll be glad when I'm not limited by my cast. I never did much cooking until I moved back to Asbury."

"Ava was a great cook. I have her recipes, but it's not fun to cook for myself. When I do, they don't taste the same."

"You still miss her."

"I do. I always will. She was too young to die. Too alive. You would have liked her. She loved to be outside and loved kids. She taught second grade. She said when kids got to third grade, they couldn't see leprechauns and unicorns anymore. She said she was a second grader. I believed her. The year before she died, she cooked two turkeys on Wednesday, the day before Thanksgiving. I asked her why, and she said the leprechauns needed the turkeys for the soup kitchen, and we were vegetarian. Surprise to me. We had sweet potatoes, cranberry sauce, and pumpkin pie. Best Thanksgiving dinner I'd ever had."

"She sounds amazing."

"She was."

Colonel whined at the back door. I rose to let him in, but Jack beat me to the door.

"I've got this." Jack stepped out, and Colonel dashed to the back fence. The neighbor's trash cans rattled. Colonel barked.

"Look at this," Jack said. I join him on the back porch. A large raccoon lumbered down the alley, and Colonel jumped against the fence and howled.

"Colonel's letting loose his inner wolf," Jack said.

"Good boy, Colonel. Come on, let's go inside." I yawned.

"You're exhausted, and I'm thoughtless. I'm so sorry." Jack frowned.

"It's fine. Thank you for checking on us."

Jack left, and I locked the door. After I flipped the deadbolt, Jack stepped off the porch. The shadows huddled at the hallway.

"Is it supposed to turn cold tonight?"

* * *

I shivered. My feet were cold. I felt my nose. *Cold.* I should have paid attention to the shadows. The clock said three. My feet hit the cold hardwood floor. Colonel padded in and flopped down on the rug at the foot of my bed.

I slipped my bare feet into my shoes —cold— and turned on the hallway light to check the thermostat. The thermometer said fifty degrees. The temperature on the thermostat was set at seventy-six degrees, but the controller was on *cool*.

"I thought the air handler would automatically change to heat. Guess I was wrong." I changed the temperature to sixty-eight and flipped the controller to *heat*. Cold air blew out of the vent.

"I hope it's just taking a little warm-up time. Let's get a pot of coffee going, Colonel."

Colonel stayed on the rug. I pulled a blanket out of the closet and wrapped it around me. Mia was rolled up in the afghan I'd thrown across the back of the sofa.

My phone was still on the dining table. *Forgot to plug it in.* I measured water into the coffee pot, scooped ground coffee into the basket, and turned on the burner.

I shuffled to the bedroom to plug in my phone. While I was there, I made the bed and grabbed a load of laundry.

Who would know about a tie between Russell Simpson and Tiffany? I'm convinced Carla's the one who needed money but was that her voice? Why do I think there's something between Carla and Todd Rockford? Just because she's disappeared, and he wasn't at work yesterday afternoon? That's not logical.

When I returned to the kitchen, the coffee pot was boiling over. I hurried to the stove and turned off the burner. *Should I get an electric coffee maker?* I chuckled. *Easiest question I've come up with all day.* I added *Coffee maker* to my shopping list.

Colonel padded to the back door, and the air handler blew warmer air. I opened the door. "Let me know when you want back in because I'm not going out."

I turned off the burner and poured a cup of scorched coffee. I took a sip and blistered the roof of my mouth.

Colonel whined at the back door, and I let him in. "I'm having a rotten day so far. How are you doing?" Colonel grinned and wagged.

I dressed and filled Colonel and Mia's bowls. Colonel ate. Mia snuggled down into her afghan. "Your food's safe because he's afraid of you, right?" Mia purred.

When Colonel and I got to the shop, the lights weren't on, but Gee and Tiffany were parked in front. Tiffany stepped out of the car. "Aunt Gee wouldn't let me go inside and get to work. Talk to her." She slammed the car door, stomped past me, and unlocked the shop.

I climbed into the car. "You're in trouble, Gee. You're going to get grounded if you aren't careful."

Gee shook her head and chuckled. "I know. I won't do it again. You have no idea what I had to listen to."

"I can imagine. You'll chill tomorrow?"

"Only if you agree that you enchanted me."

I rolled my eyes. "Oh fine. You're enchanting." We laughed, and I climbed out.

When I walked into the shop, Tiffany glared. "So?"

"She said to tell you I enchanted her. I'll check the calendar."

Tiffany had covered her first batch to rise and was mixing the second when I returned.

"I don't remember booking this morning's group. Cosplay?"

"Oh cool. I booked them. I thought I told you. There's a comic con next spring, and they're having a planning meeting."

I leaned against the counter. "I feel old. Comic con?"

"Conference. Cosplay is short for costume play. People go to the comic conference dressed as their favorite character. Most make their own costumes or find stuff at Aunt Gee's shop. If we're not too busy, I'd like to sit in on the meeting."

"We'll plan on it. Let me know if I can help. I'm an excellent seamstress. What costume are you working on?"

"I don't know yet. That's why I so excited about a planning meeting to get some ideas." Tiffany rolled out her first batch of dough. "Do you think I'm silly? Too old for all this?"

"If you're worried about being too old, I'll go with you. We'll give 'em old, but I need to be something wicked."

Tiffany rolled her eyes and chuckled. "You're good at putting things in perspective. I'm not old, and you're too nice to be wicked."

"What are you doing for the special today?"

"In honor of cosplay, I thought I'd make poison."

"That sounds different. How are you going to make poison?" I propped my arm on the counter. "This cast is heavy."

"I haven't figured that part out yet."

I hurried to measure coffee. "I'm behind on my duties. Sheriff's going to show up, and all I'll have to offer him is a nice cup of coffee-flavored warm water."

"I've got it!" Tiffany danced and waved her spoon. "Can you get me red hot candies? I am pretty sure the drugstore has them, and they're open. I'll sprinkle red hots on pink glazed donuts."

"Love it." I grabbed my purse. "How about if we call them demon donuts?"

"I'll write it up on the board. And classic glazed with lemon drizzle. Cranberry-lemon scones."

Colonel and I returned from the drug store in less than ten minutes.

"Perfect timing. I'm ready to sprinkle."

"I bought them out. The pharmacist said she'd send somebody over later for donuts for their breakroom." I glanced at the specials board. "Ooo. Demons and Angels. Well done."

Tiffany dropped the first of her third batch into the fryer, and the bell jingled.

The sheriff stopped and stared at the board. "If I have a demon, will I be possessed?"

I chuckled and splashed coffee onto the counter while I poured his cup. "I don't know. It's your idea, what do you think?" I grabbed a towel and mopped up my spills.

"I think one of each is the safest." The sheriff raised an eyebrow and stared at the plate Tiffany put on the counter. "The angel has a drizzled halo. I'll start with the demon and finish with the angel. Kind of stack them with the angel on top."

"Wow. Philosophical and strategic," Tiffany said.

I poured a cup of coffee and settled on the stool next to the sheriff. "I was wondering about last night and unlocked cars at the church."

"We had a few reports of theft, but none of them were after Roger put the group of parking volunteers on watch. The volunteers walked the rows of cars until everyone left last night. Amazing group of dedicated folks."

The sheriff bit into the demon donut and frowned. "Not my favorite. I like the red hots, but they don't seem to be a part of the donut. Like you threw candy on the glaze."

Tiffany stared at the sheriff. "Which is what I did. I can fix it."

I raised my eyebrows at the sheriff.

He shrugged. "I might not be a food critic, but I know donuts." The sheriff winked, and I laughed.

Tiffany stirred up a batch of glaze and tossed in a cup of red hots. She warmed the glaze to melt the candy, drizzled the new red glaze onto a donut, and served it to the sheriff. "Try this."

"This is excellent. The cinnamon of the red hots sneaks up on you. This is a demon donut." The sheriff ate the remainder in three bites. "One more, please?"

I gave him his second demon while Tiffany drizzled the rest of the batch of demon donuts.

"Does it take two angels to counteract two demons?" he asked. "I hope not, because I'm not sure I can eat four donuts."

"Good triumphs over evil. Every time." I poured his coffee refill.

The bell jingled, and Roger stared at the board. "I never know what I'm going to see when I come in here. Today's it's a demon and two angels." He bit his lip and stood frozen at the door.

CHAPTER FOURTEEN

"Nope, not fired today." The sheriff sipped his coffee. "Although it's not my fault if you leave here possessed." The sheriff elbowed me, and the two of us twittered.

I glanced at Tiffany, and she mouthed, "Old."

I choked on my coffee.

"You okay, Miss Lady?" Tiffany grinned.

I fluttered my eyelashes at her.

"Coffee and a special, Deputy?" Tiffany trilled and poured a cup of coffee.

Roger strode to the display case. "A demon and an angel."

The sheriff rose. "Somebody's got to work around here. I guess it's up to the old guy." He sauntered to the door and left.

Tiffany's eyes were wide, and her cheeks were pink. "Am I fired, Miss Lady?"

I headed to the storeroom for the utility cart. "No, but I'm keeping score."

Roger sat at the counter. "Did I miss something?"

"Always, Roger." I closed the storeroom door and giggled. I rolled the utility cart out of the storeroom and loaded it with cups, plates, napkins, and sugar and creamer.

After Roger left, Tiffany took over the utility cart. "Miss Lady, I asked Roger if he'd like to go to the Comic Con with me, and he said yes. It's months away. What was I thinking?"

"You thought it would be fun?"

"You don't understand anything." Tiffany stomped to the pink room and slammed the door.

"I might," I said to the door.

The cosplay folks came in with smiles and rushed to the pink room. Tiffany filled the coffee carafes and platters without a glance in my direction.

The mayor came into the shop and perched on a stool. "Demons and angels are the special today? What do you recommend?"

I poured his coffee. "The sheriff chased his demons with an angel."

"Sounds theologically sound. I'll do the same." The mayor chuckled. "I hear your house might be ready as early as next week. After all you've been through, seems like a little good news is in order."

"That's great news. I miss my house. Shirley's duplex is nice, but Colonel, Mia, and I like our own space." A roar of laughter from the meeting room broke into our companionable silence.

The mayor glanced around the shop. "Where's Tiffany? Who's meeting today?"

"She's in the pink room with the cosplay folks."

"She's doing well, isn't she?"

"She is." I frowned. "Is there any connection between Melissa Armstrong and Russell Simpson that you know of?"

"Not Melissa, but George Armstrong and Russell were cousins. I think maybe second cousins. Their families were estranged, but I don't know the details. Russell's family wasn't from around here, but he came to visit a couple of times when we were kids. They were inseparable, like brothers." He shook his head. "Long time ago."

"Did Gee know Russell?"

"I doubt it. You'd have to ask her, but George was five years older than her."

"I don't remember any of my parents' relatives. When Dad and then Mom died, I didn't have any family left. But since I've moved back, I have family—Woody and Shirley."

Tiffany stepped out of the meeting room. "You doing okay, Miss Lady? Need any help?"

"All's well, Tiffany. Thanks for checking."

She returned to the meeting room.

"And Tiffany and Gee," I said.

The mayor smiled. "I loved the demon and angel. More winners. Do you think it'd be okay if I joined the meeting?"

"You're our official meeting greeter, of course, it would be okay."

The mayor rushed to the storeroom, grabbed his apron, and stepped into the meeting room to shouts and laughter.

I cleared the counter and put our dishes into the dishwasher. The bell jingled, and Shirley came in slower than I'd ever see her move.

"I'm trying to take it easy. What are demons and angels?"

"A demon might be a little spicy for you. How about an angel donut or a scone?"

Shirley sat at the counter. "Scone sounds good. I'm going to work in the office today. I think we might get a final inspection on your house next week. You might be able to move back sooner than we expected."

I set her coffee and scone on the counter. She bit into her scone. "Mmmm. This is good."

"What do you know about Todd Rockford?" I asked. "I thought I'd talk to him about a smaller scale upgrade than what he proposed to see what he thought."

"I don't know much. I got the feeling Alfred knew him before he hired him. But I don't know how because Alfred's always lived here. You'd think I'd know anybody Alfred knows. Now that I think of it, Todd reminds me of somebody who used to live here, but I can't think who. Must have been a while ago. Maybe he was one of Alfred's boys. Some people look just like they did twenty years ago, and others are unrecognizable five years later. Have you noticed how most people put on weight as they get older? You didn't. You look great. I'm glad we had your hair highlighted. You know I've lost ten pounds since Woody came to live with me. All I used to do was work and watch television. I barely sit anymore except at meals. Woody and I always eat at the table. Oh, look at the time. And my coffee's all gone. Can I have a refill? And I ate my scone. I think I need an angel donut to take to the office."

I handed Shirley a fresh coffee and a sack to go. I picked up the money she'd set on the counter and dropped her change into the Shirley jar.

The meeting ended, and the room cleared. The mayor rolled out the utility cart stacked with dishes. Tiffany loaded the dishwasher, and he carried out the trash to the dumpster.

"I have to leave for a meeting. Thanks for introducing me to the group, Tiffany."

"Thanks for your help, Mayor." Tiffany carried the broom and dustpan into the pink room.

The bell jingled, and my heart sank. Pastor David, the new minister at the community church, strode into the shop. "I have a staff meeting in a half hour. I was at the gas station and heard great things about the Donut Hole. The sheriff said to tell you he sent me. Now I see why." He chuckled.

Tiffany peeked out of the pink room. Her eyes widened, and she eased the door closed with a quiet click.

"Did the sheriff have a recommendation?" I smiled.

"Give me a dozen donuts—half demons and half angels. I feel a sermon in the making."

"Would you like a coffee to take with you?" I asked while I packed his donuts. "On the house with a box of donuts. How do you like your coffee?"

"Thank you. Cream and sugar. I understand if I overpay, the balance goes to Tiffany's college fund. Here you go."

The bell jingled when he left, and Tiffany came out of the pink room.

"So much for thinking you'd back me up no matter what." I glared.

"You'd have hidden too if you could have." Tiffany grinned. "Did he say anything?"

"He bought a dozen donuts and said the sheriff sent him. We need to get even with the sheriff."

Tiffany returned the broom and dustpan to the storeroom and sacked up the trash while I wiped down the table and buffet in the pink room. Tiffany returned from taking the garbage to the dumpster in the back. "I have an idea, but I'm not sure how to do it quite yet. Imaginary donuts."

"That's a bizarre idea. I love it. Now you just need to find a recipe."

Tiffany cocked her head. "Don't you mean we?"

"No. My turn to hide."

"I've got an idea," Tiffany said. "When do we want to do it?"

"Tomorrow. He'll expect us to make him stew first. He won't expect anything tomorrow. How are you going to do that again?"

"You'll see. No, wait. No, you won't." Tiffany cackled. "Can you print up a label for a tray?"

"Sure can. I'll give you a ride home or to the hospital. Your choice. Are we about done?"

"Everything's done. I double-locked the back door. I'd like to go to the hospital. Thanks."

Colonel and I dropped Tiffany off at the hospital.

"I have a feeling, Colonel. Mr. Gibson is the key. Let's go see Todd Rockford. I think I know why he looks familiar."

Todd Rockford met us at the door. "Did you change your mind, Ms. Karen?"

"No, but I need to pick your brain for updating the Donut Hole. What do you know about social media and marketing?"

"I'm not an expert, but I'm happy to share what I know." Todd offered me his arm, and we strolled to his office.

After he closed his office door, he grinned "What's this about? Really."

"Am I that transparent?" I laughed.

"Not at all, but I just have a feeling you could teach me about marketing and social media."

"I'm not good at small talk, Todd. I lost that skill after twelve years in prison. But I lived with a manipulator, and I feel the symptoms like razors. Carla puts out razors."

He gazed at me in silence. He dropped his gaze and crossed his arms. "Yeah," he whispered.

"Nancy gave me a picture of Carla and her boyfriend. That was you. A long time ago. In a different life."

"Yes." He leaned back and narrowed his eyes. "I was in therapy for six years. I legally changed my last name to my mother's maiden name. My middle name is Theodore. My mother suggested the nickname, Todd. I'm not trying to hide anything. I just wanted a fresh start. I never expected to see Carla again. She's not a small-town girl. I belong here. She doesn't."

"Carla told Nancy that she, Carla, needed money. Do you know anything about that?"

"Carla told me the same thing. She…" He closed his eyes and tapped his thumb on his desk.

I waited.

He continued. "Carla wanted me to put pressure on Mr. Gibson. She said he and Russell were partners, and Mr. Gibson cheated Russell. I told her no. She flew off the handle and tried to hit me in the face. But I blocked her arm. I never had the nerve in the old days to protect myself or say no."

"Felt good, didn't it?" I asked.

"Sure did."

"Does Mr. Gibson know about your earlier life?"

"He helped me when I was a kid. He gave me the confidence to break away from Carla. I changed my name while I was in therapy and started college classes online. All my transcripts are in the name of Todd Rockford."

"Did Carla give you any details about how Mr. Gibson cheated Russell?"

"No. I'm not even sure he really did. Carla's such a liar. I wouldn't put it past her to make something up. The only thing she told me I do believe is that she needs money to get away. I just don't know from what."

I glared. "Carla's husband and sister have been murdered. Maybe she's trying to get away from the killer."

He met my stare. "Maybe. But it's not me, Ms. Karen."

"You think Carla killed them?"

"She has the temper and the strength. But I'm not sure she killed Russell, and for all her rough edges and faults, she loved her sister."

I rose. "Thanks, Todd."

He stepped closer, glanced at the floor, and spoke in a soft voice. "My therapy was in an institution. I'm sure prison is different, but I understand what you mean about small talk. Thanks for listening to me."

"Anytime. Anybody ever tell you it gets better after a week?"

"Yes, but then I flash back to those times before it got better."

I put my hand on the doorknob and stopped. "Did your nightmares stop?"

He shook his head slowly. "You can call me anytime."

"You too, Todd."

I shuffled out of the bank; I was deep in thought. Colonel followed me.

"What do you think, Colonel? Nancy said the banker tried to retrieve Carla's coupon book. Which banker did she mean? Alfred or Todd? The coupon book looks worthless. What am I missing?"

Colonel whined.

"Hurts my head too, boy. Todd doesn't think Carla would murder her sister. I'm not so sure."

When I pulled into the driveway, Ginny was kneeling in front of our duplex surrounded by pots of flowers. Colonel jumped out of the car and ran to Ginny with his tail wagging in high gear.

Ginny rubbed Colonel's ears. "Hey, Ms. Donut Lady. Like your new cast. I didn't think you'd mind if I plant some flowers."

"I think it's wonderful."

She reached for a pot. "We've got news. We're pregnant. I think the flowers are a nesting symptom. We asked Ms. Shirley about painting our spare bedroom. She said yes, of course."

"That's exciting. How are you feeling?"

"I get queasy in the morning, but other than that, I'm great. Eli's ecstatic." Ginny leaned back on her heels. "We heard about the troubles you've had. You call us or bang on our door any time. We're gone most of the day, but we're here every night."

"Thank you, Ginny."

"Ms. Shirley said your house will be ready soon. Our mothers are planning to rent your duplex when you move. They've already made arrangements with Ms. Shirley and created a visitation calendar. Eli wants to buy a house. Out in the country. I reminded him that he graduates in six months, and I'm sure we'll be moving. He's already considering a few positions out of state." She grinned.

I laughed. "Y'all may appreciate the help for a few weeks. I sure can't blame new grandmas for being so thrilled."

"The funniest part is they are so different. A grandbaby on the way has turned them into allies. Now don't forget we're here if you need us."

After lunch, I left Colonel and Mia to go to the store. I noticed a gray car pull away from the curb when I turned at the first corner. First on my list was an automatic coffee maker.

I rolled a cart to the small appliance aisle.

"Ms. Donut Lady."

I turned. *Carla.*

She stepped close and put her hand on my cart. "I thought it would be better to talk to you in a store with a lot of people around." She glanced to the left. "I need money. I have to get away. Can we go up front to the sub shop and talk?"

I followed her. She selected a seat that faced the entrance and that had its back to a wall.

"You want coffee or a soft drink?" I asked.

"Diet cola."

"I'll buy, but you'll have to carry your own drink."

When the clerk placed the cold drink and my coffee on the counter, Carla scurried to grab her drink and returned to her seat. No surprise she didn't offer to carry my coffee.

I took my seat and gazed at her face. *Wary, and trying to appear vulnerable. We got us a con act in progress.*

"I have to get away. I'm afraid."

No, you aren't.

"I didn't exactly tell the truth." She hung her head. "Russell planned to blackmail a banker who had been his partner for a larger share. He arranged to meet his partner alongside the road. He told me to wait in the trees where I couldn't be seen. After a car drove up, I heard Russell lose his temper. He was shouting. Then he quit shouting, and I heard the other car drive away. When I came out of the woods, I saw Russell and panicked. I drove away and crashed."

She stuck her straw into the cup and took a long drink of soda. "I think the banker killed Nancy because she wouldn't tell him where I was."

"Which banker?" I held my breath.

"I think the young one. I don't have any proof, or I'd go to the sheriff. I just need to get away until he gets caught."

"Didn't Russell have money?"

Her nostrils flared, and she pinched her lips. "His bank account is frozen. I thought he had cash put away, but it's gone. I think Nancy took it, but she denied it and wouldn't tell me where it was."

"The shop runs on a cash basis, so there isn't any extra. I've got my pension, but my check doesn't come in for another week. I can give you some money next week if that helps."

"No." She slammed her fist on the table. The young man behind the counter headed toward our table. His nametag was on his apron, *Jerry*.

"Can I get you anything else, Ms. Donut Lady?"

I raised my eyebrows and peered at Carla.

"I'm leaving," she growled. "But—"

Jerry stepped next to me, faced Carla, and crossed his arms. Carla pushed past him and bumped his shoulder with hers.

"I called nine-one-one," the cashier said.

"I'll take a small soup," I said.

"Yes, ma'am."

Jerry brought me a bowl of hot soup, refilled my coffee, and picked up the money I'd set on the table. The sheriff strode in one entrance. Roger was positioned at the other door. When the cashier saw the sheriff, she pointed at me. I blew on my hot soup. Jerry dropped off my change.

"What now?" The sheriff sat at my table.

"Carla wanted money. When I said I couldn't give her any money until next week, she lost her temper. These fine young people chased her out."

"Let's get a lid for your soup, and I'll give you a ride home. We need to talk."

Jerry brought a lid for my soup.

"Thank you, Jerry."

The sheriff helped me up.

When we were outside, I stopped. "Couldn't you follow me home so I'll have my car?"

The sheriff scanned the parking lot. "Okay. I'll walk you to your car then you wait for me."

When we got to my house, I handed my bowl and keys to the sheriff and climbed out of my car. He locked my car and unlocked the door.

He set my bowl on the table. "Sorry about your lunch. You going to heat up your soup? Feels cold."

"It's pretty salty. I'll have a yogurt." I pulled out a peach yogurt and sat at the table.

The sheriff joined me. "So tell me what you know."

"Carla says she needs money. She said Russell's bank accounts are frozen, and his cash has disappeared. The one thing I do know is that she's a skilled liar with a temper."

"Do you think she knows who killed Russell and Nancy?"

"She might. Except she's come up with a second story about Russell's death. Her new story is that Russell met with a silent partner while she waited in the woods. When I asked her who the partner was, she was vague. I still think if there was any partnership, she was the partner, not Russell."

"What about Nancy?"

"She said Nancy knew where Russell's money was but wouldn't tell Carla. I don't think she realized the implication of what she said."

"Who do you think this silent partner is?"

"I don't know. Carla implicated Todd. Nancy implicated Alfred."

"Call if you see Carla again. Or anything suspicious." The sheriff scooted back his chair and rose to leave.

I walked out with the sheriff. "I do have a question. Was there a second set of tire tracks at the site where Russell's body was found?"

He frowned. "There were several sets of tire tracks—Russell's and the farmer's were two. It's hard to say how many more there were. Why?"

"I'd forgotten about the farmer."

"The state investigation department's going to start selling donuts if you put them out of business. Don't do that. They're terrible cooks."

"Point taken." I waved and went back inside. "Let's go for a walk, Colonel. I think better when I walk."

Colonel bounded to the door. I picked up my keys, phone, and his leash. When we reached the sidewalk, Colonel turned toward the park.

"It's a long walk, but it's a nice day. Let's go."

Colonel ran to the end of the block and trotted back to me. When we reached the next intersection, he raced to the end and waited with a grin.

Who's the key? Alfred? The silent partner?

Colonel chased squirrels. I closed my eyes and soaked up sunrays. *Warm sun feels good on my old bones.*

Colonel yipped. Jack and Roxie parked, and Roxie bounded to Colonel.

Jack sat on the bench. "Sun feels good. I heard you got a new cast. Want to go out to dinner to celebrate?"

"I'd like to, but I didn't sleep well last night, and today's been a full day."

"You should probably eat, right? The community church has a fundraiser scheduled for their overseas missionary. Meatloaf dinner. You sure you can turn down meatloaf? Doesn't have to be a late night. We can eat, socialize, and have you back at your house by seven."

Not interested in socializing or eating, but I'm too tired to argue.

"You're right. I can't turn down meatloaf, but I can't promise I'll be good company."

Jack beamed. "You and Colonel like a ride home? I'll be back at five-thirty to pick you up."

"We'd love a ride home, and five-thirty is fine."

When Jack filled the park dog bowl with water, Colonel and Roxie trotted for a drink. Colonel watched Roxie's back while she drank her fill, and then Roxie stood guard while Colonel drank.

When I rose from the bench, Colonel and Roxie raced to Jack's truck. Jack offered his arm, and we joined the dogs.

Jack waited outside on the porch while I locked the door and flipped the deadbolt.

"I'm not used to being hovered over, Colonel. I'm not sure I like it very much. I like my space. And privacy. I'm jealous of my alone time."

Colonel turned away and padded into the kitchen.

"You're right. I'm feeling peevish. I'll take a bath."

After my bath, I fed Colonel and Mia. The shadows gathered at the pantry.

"I can take a hint." I scooted Mia's litter box and slid the tile away. I pulled out the coupon book, the envelope, and papers. I compared the spreadsheets to the coupon book and found matches on the worksheets for every item in the coupon book.

"That's interesting, but it tells me nothing. Carla said Nancy knew where Russell's cash was but wouldn't tell her. Do I know where Nancy would hide something? Nancy told me in the nightmare I know. Do I?"

The shadows danced in the hallway. One of the shadows grew and filled the hall. The others slid into the kitchen and under the pantry door.

A knock at the door at five startled me. The hallway shadow disappeared.

No shadows here.

I opened the door, and Jack held a pot of flowers.

"I saw the flowers planted in front of the duplex. I hear you'll be able to return home next week. I thought we could go to your house and plant flowers before we went to dinner. You point; I'll plant." He grinned.

"I'll be right there." I gathered up the papers and dashed into the pantry. I expected to find the shadows, but they weren't there. I slid the tile and the kitty litter box over the papers. When I stepped outside and locked the door, Jack was waiting at his truck. The back of the truck was filled with bushes and flowers in pots,

My eyes widened. "It's going to take all night to plant all these flowers and bushes." I fought back my tears. *I'm officially tired.*

"No, no. We're just going to take the plants over to the house and place them where you want them. You point. Then I'll go over tomorrow and plant. Sorry. I was so excited about the flowers I left out a detail or two."

I managed a weak smile and climbed into the truck.

"This was a bad idea." Jack frowned.

"When you take them off the truck, why don't you put them where you think they'd thrive best. Then if I have another suggestion, I can make it."

"I like that. Very efficient." Jack narrowed his eyes. "Are you sure you aren't an engineer?"

I chuckled, and Jack smiled. "I brought a folding chair for you to sit in. I thought you might be tired."

"That is so nice. Thank you." I teared up and gazed out the window. *Toughen up, Buttercup.*

We arrived at my house. Jack opened my door and helped me out of the truck. "I'm going to work fast. You stop me if you want anything changed."

The roof and damage to the side of the house looked repaired. The worksite dumpster was in the side yard and filled with debris. Large tire tracks marred the yard, and the few bushes that had been close to the house were gone.

"The bushes and flowers were a great idea, Jack. Thank you."

His face reddened, and he nodded. While Jack placed pots of flowers in the yard, I relaxed in the camp chair and listened to the cicadas. *Going to rain tonight.*

"Stop a second, Jack. Did you just put a tall plant in front of one that will be short?"

Jack held a pot of flowers in each hand. He scanned the yard. "Where?"

I pointed.

"You're right. Good catch." He set the plants in his hand down and switched the offending pots around.

After he emptied the back of the truck, he brushed his hands on his pants. "Everything look good to you? Any changes?"

"No changes." I rose from my camp chair, and Jack folded it up.

"We can stay as long or as short as you like."

"Thank you."

Emma greeted us at the door and took Jack's money for our dinner. "There's two kinds of meatloaf. One has brown gravy. The other has red gravy. There are those who call the red gravy catsup. And you know the church dinner secret, right? You don't want to get labeled as novices. Grab your dessert first before the best ones are gone and put it where you want to sit to reserve your seat."

Jack and I considered each dessert. "Pumpkin cake with cream cheese frosting," I said. Jack picked up a piece of lemon meringue pie and snitched two cookies off a plate of four and added them to his pie plate.

"What?" he winked.

I giggled and shook my head.

We set our plates down. "Pros," Jack whispered.

We got in line behind Ginny and Eli.

"We've stalked church dinners since we were undergrads," Eli said. "Best food in town and guaranteed homemade desserts."

"Our first date was at a church dinner," Ginny giggled. "I thought Eli was pious but turns out he was cheap."

"Hey." Eli held up his hands in protest. "You say that like it might be a bad thing. I thought you loved me for my cheapness."

"He always picked out two desserts. When one of the ladies raised her eyebrows, he said—you say it, Eli."

"It's for Mama." Eli cocked his head and smiled.

"With that angelic face. Isn't he a hoot? And half the time, the ladies would sneak him an extra dessert."

"You are such a sweet boy." Eli spoke in a falsetto voice. We laughed.

"Didn't know you lived next door to a dessert fiend, did you?" Ginny asked.

"I'm the Donut Lady. Sweet freaks are my bread and butter." We all laughed again.

"Here's the food. Getting serious now," Eli said.

"I'd like the meatloaf with brown gravy," I said.

"Catsup gravy for me," Jack said.

After we ate, our empty plates were whisked away. "That's a signal for us to leave," I said. "The line is weaving outside the door."

We rode back to my house in companionable silence. When we pulled into my driveway, I said, "Come in. Colonel and I will go into the backyard for his break, and you can supervise."

"What a good idea." Jack chuckled.

After Colonel wandered around the backyard and found the spot he'd been looking for, he returned to the back door. I locked the back door. Jack went out the front door, and I closed the door and threw the deadbolt. Five minutes later, I was in bed.

* * *

The alarm went off at four. Colonel was asleep on the rug next to my bed. Mia slept on my feet. The shadows were low in the hall. Then I heard it. *Rain. Soft rain.*

I filled the coffee pot with water, measured coffee into the basket, and turned on the burner. Colonel stumbled into the kitchen, and I shooed him out the back door. I let Colonel back in, and he shook himself dry and bounded to his breakfast. Mia wandered into the kitchen and dashed to her bowl when I dished up her food.

I poured a cup of coffee to cool and hurried to dress. I spied a black shirt I hadn't worn in a while. *Black looked good with the pink apron.* I tugged at the shirt, and two hangers fell behind one of the storage boxes marked *Books* in my closet. I slid the box out of the way and picked up the hangers. I stared in my closet and frowned. *Something important. What?* The sound of rain broke my train of thought. *Is it raining harder? I'd like to leave a little earlier than usual.*

CHAPTER FIFTEEN

Colonel followed me to the door. "Stay, Colonel. It's raining." He wheeled around and leaped to the sofa. I picked up my umbrella. *I can't hold an umbrella and open the car door at the same time.* I set down the umbrella and unlocked the door. *I can't get my cast wet.* I hurried back to the kitchen, grabbed a plastic bag, and put my arm inside the bag.

The rain was light until I stepped outside. I hurried through the heavy rain to unlock my car, jumped in, and locked the door immediately. *Make the sheriff happy.* The shadows skittered alongside through the showers and dodged puddles. I peered into my rearview mirror. Shadows clung to my trunk.

"I know." I snapped my fingers. "You're right, Nancy. I know. But now what?"

When I parked at the shop, I was still deep in thought. *What can I do?* I glanced up. The light was on at the shop, and Gee sat in her car. She waved and drove away after I went inside.

Tiffany glanced up and grinned. "It's Wednesday."

I searched my memory cells. She laughed. "Your face gave you away. It's Imaginary Wednesday. And we pick national Friday day today. And best of all, aren't the pink ballcaps supposed to be delivered today?"

"You're right. I'll check the calendar."

"I did. We have the Liars' Club this morning. I didn't know they had an official club."

"Imaginary Donuts are perfect for them. What else are we doing?"

Tiffany flipped through her records. "We had frosted coffee last Wednesday. It was a hit. What classic do we want?"

"Let's do classic glazed. I have an idea for our imaginary donuts in addition to the invisible ones. Let's make plain cake donuts. Imagine your own toppings."

"Invisible donuts, imaginary donuts, classic glazed, and frosted coffee. Right?" Tiffany asked.

I rubbed my forehead. "I'm thinking drop the invisible for today and just go with imaginary. Or vice versa. It'll be too time-consuming to explain the difference."

"Agreed. You know your regulars. How about the classic glazed, but we call it imaginary sprinkles. No sprinkles, get it? And frosted coffee. Keep the day simple."

"Perfect. What do we do for scones?"

"Imaginary scones. Just kidding! We could do cinnamon scones with coffee drizzle."

"That sounds good."

Tiffany punched down her first batch of dough. "On it."

I made coffee while Tiffany made the day's donuts and scones. I loaded the utility cart and stopped at the pink room doorway. "How do we choose our national Friday day this week?"

"Dignitaries is what we said. I know, let's ask Josh at the gas station. He's the most popular person in town, right?"

"You are brilliant."

The door jingled, and the sheriff walked in. "Good morning, donut gurus. Do imaginary sprinkles have imaginary calories?"

I poured the sheriff his coffee, and Tiffany set two donuts on the counter at his usual seat.

The sheriff squinted at his plate. "I thought the board said imaginary sprinkles. I see pink and green sprinkles." He grinned and sipped his coffee. Tiffany snorted, and I laughed.

"Do you have time this morning for a donut errand?" I asked. "We'd like to ask Josh at the gas station to name the Friday national day this week. Do you mind asking him for us?"

"I could do that, for a price." The sheriff finished his imaginary sprinkles donut. I refilled his coffee and waited.

"I need extra sprinkles on my frosted coffee." He held out his plate. I scattered imaginary sprinkles with my fingers over his donut.

"Old people are weird," Tiffany said.

"You said that out loud, Tiffany." I put my hands on my hips.

Her face reddened, and she turned her back to me. The sheriff held his palm up, and we smacked a loud high-five.

"Like I said," Tiffany mumbled.

The bell jingled, and Roger sauntered in. The sheriff waggled his eyebrows, and I pretended to choke on my coffee.

"Do the imaginary sprinkles cost extra?" Roger asked.

Tiffany giggled and poured coffee. The sheriff left, and I loaded up the utility cart. Tiffany mixed another batch of dough and checked the fryer heat. Roger carried his coffee and donut back to the cooking area.

I chuckled. *If I had an Employees Only sign, I'd have to put Roger on the payroll.*

The bell jingled. Our delivery woman carried in a large box. "Looks big but it's light."

"Thanks. Just set it on the counter. Care for an imaginary sprinkles or a frosted coffee donut?"

"Frosted coffee sounds great. I'm trying to cut back on my imaginary sprinkles."

We all laughed. "Best one of the day," Tiffany called from the back.

I handed her a donut. She took a big bite and ran out with a wave.

Roger shuffled his feet. "Guess I'll go. You free for lunch, Tiffany?"

"Sure am." She smiled.

I blinked three times, and she shook her spoon.

Roger scratched his head and glanced at me. "See you around eleven-thirty." After he went outside, he tapped on the window and waved. Tiffany waved back.

She glared. "Don't say a word. I'm not in the mood."

"Oh really?" I stuck my chin out. She frowned and pursed her lips.

The bell jingled, and the mayor rushed in. "Good morning. It's Wednesday. I took the morning off."

He came out of the storeroom with his apron. "Tie it for me? Did the ballcaps come in? I saw the Liars' Club on the calendar for today. I'm looking forward to this morning." He stared at Tiffany and me.

"Lighten up, you two. You going to open the box? Can I have my ballcap?"

I poured his coffee. "The honor of opening the box is yours, your honor."

He pulled out a cap and adjusted it. He put it on and examined himself in the window reflection. "I love this cap. How do you get the imaginary sprinkles on?"

Tiffany grinned. "Miss Lady does it. Watch. These need sprinkles, Miss Lady." She waved her hand at a tray of glazed donuts and nodded her head.

I lifted my head and cleared my throat. "Stand back a little, Tiffany. My eyesight's not as good as it used to be." I held up my arm and flicked my wrist in the direction of the tray.

"Oooh. Good shot." Tiffany applauded.

The mayor nodded and applauded too. "Awesome. May I test one of the freshly sprinkled?"

Tiffany served him a glazed donut, and I refilled his cup. We hovered while he took a bite. "Slightly crunchy. Warm donut. Perfect. I love working here. It's magical."

He glanced at the clock. "I need to get busy. The Liars' Club members will be here soon. I'll set the box in the storeroom for you. You can tell me later where you want it to go, and I'll move it. You want your ballcap now, Tiffany?"

"Yes, please."

The Liars' Club members drifted in, and the mayor ushered them to the pink room. The sheriff followed two members as they came into the shop.

"Looks like the liars club." He perched on his stool, and I poured a cup for him. "Asking Josh was a stroke of genius, Ms. Karen. He wants Friday to be National Pet Rescue Day. I told him you'd put out a jar for donations for the local animal shelter, and his boss said he'd match the collection as the anonymous donor."

The mayor stopped on his way to the pink room. "Make that two anonymous donors, and I'll match the collection too."

"This is awesome. I'll ask Shirley if she and Woody will make our sign."

"I'll ask Aunt Gee if she has a large jar with animals. I think she might still have that large cookie jar with dogs and cats on it."

"I'll stop by the shelter and let them know what we'll be doing," the sheriff said. "They might want to advertise some of their senior animals for adoption."

"Tell them if they want to bring some animals here for adoption, I don't mind. The weather's supposed to be nice on Friday, and they could set up under the awning out front."

The mayor rushed out of the pink room. "We need more imaginary sprinkles. Do you have any imaginary sprinkles I can put in a bowl? For extra sprinkles."

"There's a punch bowl on a shelf in the storeroom."

Tiffany stared at me, and I shrugged.

The mayor bustled into the storeroom and returned with the punch bowl. I grabbed a wooden spoon, wound up like a one-armed pitcher, and showered imaginary sprinkles into his bowl. The mayor carried the glass bowl into the pink room with the drama of grunts and groans.

"Oof." He set the bowl down hard on the table. The group burst out laughing and applauded, and he closed the door.

The bell jingled, and Shirley sauntered in. "I'm feeling a lot better. What are imaginary sprinkles? I think I need imaginary sprinkles and a scone. I'm showing a house today. My realtor partner is going to meet me there because it's a two-story house. I don't feel like stairs quite yet. I like the ballcap. It looks good on you, Tiffany. Do you need Woody and me to help with National Friday day again? He talked about it all the way to school. I was supposed to ask."

"I need for you and Woody to make a sign. It's going to be National Pet Rescue Day on Friday. We're going to set up a jar for donations, and I hoped Woody would make a sign for the jar."

"He would love that. Maybe he'll do a sketch of a dog and cat. I'll leave that up to him. He's very creative. Sometimes I feel like I'm feeding macaroni and cheese to a future famous artist, and I get goosebumps." Shirley laid her money on the counter and picked up her sack and coffee.

The bell jingled when she left and sounded again when Gee came in.

"I'll take a frosted coffee with my coffee. A double-dose of caffeine sounds good." Gee sat at the counter. "Isaiah is moving out of ICU. He will probably be coming home in a day or so. Put a couple of imaginary sprinkles in a sack for me to take to Isaiah. Isaiah's friend Thomas is watching the shop for me while I go visit Isaiah. Give me a sack for Thomas too."

Gee left, and the meeting broke up. The mayor stood at the door and shook hands. After the room emptied, the mayor brought dishes to Tiffany. She washed dishes, and he cleaned and swept the pink room.

"Miss Lady, all we've got left is invisible donuts with imaginary sprinklers." Tiffany cleaned the display case.

"Put 'em in the freezer for tomorrow."

The mayor hung up his apron and sat at the counter. "I always love working here. There's something magical about the shop. I walk in an old man and feel like a kid by the time I leave. I get to take my hat right?"

"Yes, sir. That's your hat."

"See you on Friday. I'll be by to add a contribution to the jar."

The mayor left, and Roger came in.

"Ready for lunch? I saw Mr. Jack at the gas station, and he suggested a picnic. How does that sound?"

"Sounds great. I love being outside." Tiffany grinned, and Roger beamed.

"Y'all go on. Everything's done. I've got a little paperwork to do before I leave."

"Roger, do you mind picking up our picnic and then coming back?" Tiffany sat at the counter.

"Don't mind at all. Thought I'd go to Gus's. What would you like?" Roger strode to the door.

"I'm not a picky eater. Gus always has two different subs on his daily special. I'll enjoy either one."

After Roger left, I said, "You didn't have to do that, but thank you."

"You're welcome. Gives me a chance to spend a little time with Mr. R's secret recipes while you work."

When Roger returned, the two of them waited while I locked up. After I got in my car, they held hands and strolled to Roger's truck.

When I got home, Colonel danced, and Mia strutted to the back door. I opened the door, and the two of them rushed out. I sat on the porch, and Mia jumped on my lap. Mia purred, and Colonel patrolled the small yard.

Colonel nosed the door, and we all went inside. After my yogurt, I relaxed on the sofa with my book.

When I woke, the sun was low, and the shadows crept down the hall. Colonel padded to the back door, and I let him out. I closed my eyes and pulled out a frozen dinner. *Chicken with sweet potatoes. Sounds good.*

While my pot of water heated, I tossed a small load of laundry into the washer.

I carried my cup of tea to the sofa, and Colonel sat with me. I scratched his ears. "I know where Nancy hid Russell's cash. I don't know why she had it, though. I know who Russell's beneficiary is on his life insurance policy, and I know why. I don't know who killed Russell and Nancy. I don't even know if it was the same person, now that I think of it. Let's look up the addresses on the spreadsheet after we eat."

The oven timer dinged. I set my dinner on the table to cool and fed Colonel and Mia. I stabbed a piece of chicken with my fork and took a tiny bite. I sipped my drink and pushed the chicken off my fork. I ate a cube of sweet potato and finished my tea. I tossed the aluminum tray into the trash and dropped my fork into the dishwasher.

The shadows were so thick around the pantry, the door was hidden. When I reached past them to open the door, my hand was clammy. I pushed aside the litter box, moved the tile, and picked up all the papers.

I made copies of all the papers and returned the originals to their home in the pantry.

I looked up the first address on the spreadsheet. It sold on the date listed on the spreadsheet, and the sales price, $210,000, matched the first column on the spreadsheet, 210.0. I checked the first ten addresses on the spreadsheet, and the information matched just like the first one did. I checked the payment book dates and amounts and found the addresses for all fourteen on the spreadsheet. On a hunch, I scanned through the spreadsheet and located the earliest date. It matched the first payment in the coupon book. The next earliest date matched the second payment. Mia jumped up on my keyboard. *Time to pet the cat.*

"I have no idea of what this means, Mia." I held her in my arms and stroked her back. I put the coupon book under the litter box. The shadows danced around the bookcase.

"Good idea." I folded each piece of paper and placed it in a book. I started on the second shelf. "Maybe not the most original idea, but it'll do."

Colonel padded to the back door. When he came back in, I locked up. "Let's go to bed."

The shadows swirled to the hallway and billowed into my bedroom. I picked up my pajamas and changed in the bathroom. Colonel lay outside the door.

Even though the light was on, the shadows made my bedroom pitch-black. I put my hand on Colonel's back, and he led me to the bed. I pulled up the covers, and Colonel flopped down on the rug. I listened to his soft snore.

I felt a tug on my sleeve. "Hey, Teach."

I opened my eyes. I was in the prison cafeteria. "You gonna eat that?" The heaviest woman I'd ever seen sat across from me. She scowled and pointed at my plate. I shook my head. She growled and stabbed my meat with her knife.

"What about that?" A fist punched my left arm hard enough to leave a bruise. The woman sitting next to me pointed with her fork at my roll. I nodded. "Too bad." She took it. The woman across from me took my plate. "You don't need any of this." She cackled and handed my plate to a woman sitting at the table behind her. The woman sitting next to me reached down, grabbed a chair leg, and flipped my chair.

I landed on my face. I touched my nose and looked at my hand. *Blood.*

The woman who knocked me to the floor laughed. "You got a boo-boo, old woman?"

I pushed myself to my feet and shuffled out of the cafeteria to the library. I sat at my usual place with my book. A woman grabbed my book. I stood up. She towered over me. She had a baseball bat and smacked the palm of her hand with the tip of the bat.

"You got a problem, Teach?" She elbowed me in the face, and I fell against the table. "You're weak. No more books for you."

I had hit my head and saw stars. She lumbered away with my book. I felt the knot on my head. I stayed on the floor. When the shadows surrounded me, I sat up and wrapped my arms around my bent knees.

Darlene limped to my table. "What's wrong with you?" She hissed. "You let them take your food and knock you down. They're young and big. So what? Get up off your behind. You're cunning. You got skills. You're strong."

I pulled myself up with the table. "Say it." Darlene turned into a tiger. "You're fierce. You're cunning. You got skills. You're strong." She roared. "Say it."

I growled. "I'm fierce. I'm cunning. I'm skilled. I'm strong."

"Again." The tiger grew, and her roar thundered.

"I'm fierce. I'm cunning. I'm skilled. I'm strong."

"Again."

"I'm fierce. I'm cunning. I'm skilled. I'm strong." I shouted.

Colonel barked. I woke.

"I'm fierce. I'm cunning. I'm skilled. I'm strong."

* * *

I looked at the clock. I was fierce, cunning, skilled, and dripping wet with sweat. *Four o'clock.*

I let Colonel out, started my coffee, and ran a tub of hot water. When Colonel came inside, I fed him and Mia and poured a cup of coffee. I took my coffee to the bathroom and poured a generous dollop of bubble bath.

"I'm fierce. I'm cunning. I'm skilled. I'm strong. I deserve a bubble bath."

I checked my face before I climbed into the tub. *No bloody nose. No cut or goose egg on my forehead.*

I slid down into the bubbles. *I'm fierce. I'm cunning. I'm skilled. I'm strong.*

I washed quickly and pulled the plug. I dried, finished my coffee, and dressed.

Colonel was waiting for me at the door. We went to the shop. The lights were on. Gee drove away when we got out.

My ears rang with the tune of my internal song. *I'm fierce. I'm cunning. I'm skilled. I'm strong.*

The bell jingled, and Tiffany glanced up and smiled. "Thursday. Pink sprinkled and maple. Cranberry-orange scones with strawberry drizzle. Aunt Gee gave me the large cookie jar. It's in the storeroom."

Tiffany wore her pink apron and her *Got Sprinkles?* pink ballcap.

"You look like you work in a donut shop. I love that cap on you."

"Why don't you wear one, Miss Donut Lady?"

"Because I'm—" I stopped. I was afraid to say "old" because Darlene might come in and roar at me. "I have no idea. Let me try one on and see how it feels."

"I just happen to have yours right here, Miss Lady." Tiffany grinned and pointed with her spatula.

I put on my hat and went into the bathroom to look in the mirror. *Not bad.* I pushed it back, brought it low over my forehead, and squished the brim in a bit. I liked it a little low on my forehead. I could squint and brood. *Fierce.*

I came out of the bathroom and modeled my cap. "What do you think?"

Tiffany glanced up and shifted her attention to her dough. "Fierce."

"Thanks. That's exactly the look I was going for." *How did she know?*

"I like that about you. Nice and fierce. Like a shark inside a marshmallow."

I laughed. "Thank you."

"I love Thursdays. It's almost like a reset. Always the same donuts and the same club. We do craziness all week then it's Thursday. A breather from the wild week."

"That was beautiful. Poetic. I better get the next pot going. Our regulars look for coffee and donuts, not poetry. More's the pity."

The bell jingled. "Happy Thursday. An actual normal day at the wacky donut shop."

"You have a way with words, Sheriff." I poured his coffee, and Tiffany brought him two pink-sprinkled donuts.

"Wacky Wednesday," Tiffany mumbled.

"Now you've done it." I lowered my head and peered at the sheriff. I used the bill of my cap to add to my accusing look.

"I like the ballcaps. *Got Sprinkles?* You going to change the name of the Donut Hole?"

"I wasn't planning on it. What do you think?"

He finished off his first donut and took a gulp of coffee. "I like Got Sprinkles for a logo on the caps and cups, but I couldn't think of this old shop as anything but the Donut Hole."

I refilled his cup. "I agree. The name goes with the shop and the equipment. It all fits."

"Can you imagine Aunt Gee renaming the thrift shop the *Upscale Anti-cue?*" Tiffany chuckled.

"No, it would be the Upscale Auntie-Gee." The sheriff guffawed. "Gotta get back to work. Thanks for Thursday. Oh. Almost forgot. The shelter will be bringing adoptable rescues here tomorrow."

Amber breezed in. She wore jeans and a flannel shirt. "I was cold this morning. I layered. I heard Joshua named Friday National Pet Rescue Day. Do you have your jar? I'd like to pass it around at the book club to feed the kitty, so to speak. Love the caps."

"Tiffany brought us a jar. Come with me. It's in the storeroom. I haven't seen it yet. And we'll get your hat while we're there."

We couldn't have missed the ceramic cookie jar. It was the size of a five-gallon bucket and was eye-catching and garish. The dogs, cats, birds, and fish were raised, and each one was painted a different bright color.

"Wow," Amber said with reverence.

"We are witnesses to either genius or madness," I said.

"Aunt Gee put twenty dollars in the jar under the condition you don't return it." Tiffany stepped up behind us.

"Gee's the genius," Amber said. "I'm going to carry it into the pink room. It deserves to be the centerpiece on the table."

"Because there's no room for it on the buffet," I added.

"Right." Amber hefted the jar to the meeting room and returned to the storeroom for her ballcap.

Amber loaded up the utility cart and set up the pink room, I made coffee, and Tiffany cranked out donuts.

The bell jingled. Shirley and Woody came in. Woody carried two fourteen by nine picture frames.

"I made the signs, Miss Lady. Ms. Shirley found the frames. I love your sprinkles hat."

"Put your signs on the counter for now, Woody. We have your hat too."

Woody put the first poster, a sketch of two puppies of indeterminate breed, on the counter facing the door and window and the second poster, a drawing of two kittens—one orange, and the other gray with a white face—on the counter near the cash register.

"I put the title on both. Did I get it right, Miss Lady? *National Pet Rescue Day*?"

"Absolutely perfect, Woody."

"Wow. I love that tagline—*If you empty your pocket, you'll have more room in your heart*. Who came up with that?" Amber asked.

"Woody designed and drew the posters. Isn't he talented?" Shirley beamed.

"Remarkably," Amber said. "These are beautiful, Woody. Thank you so much for sharing your skills. Wait. You did these last night? Both of them?"

"Yes, ma'am," Woody said. "I did my homework first, though. Ms. Shirley and I skipped reading so I could finish the posters."

"We need to get to school," Shirley said.

Tiffany stood at the door with Shirley's coffee and sack and Woody's cap. "Here you go."

"See you on Saturday, Woody. Thanks again," I said.

"Thanks for my cap. See you." Woody dashed out to catch up with Shirley.

The book club members arrived, and squeals and laughter filled the shop.

Amber rushed out of the pink room. "Do we make checks out to the animal shelter?"

"Yes please."

Amber hurried back to the meeting.

I slumped on a stool. "Tiffany, that jar's going to become an institution. I had plans to smash it after today. I don't think I'll be allowed. I have no idea where we'll store it until next year."

"Wonder if Aunt Gee knew she donated an ugly duckling that would be loved by everyone?"

"I have a feeling that ugly duckling will be providing a lot of medicine, food, and blankets for the animals at the shelter."

After the book club members left, Amber helped Tiffany clean the meeting room.

"Ms. Karen, where do you want the jar for tomorrow?"

"We could put it on the utility cart close to the reading corner, but near the door. What do you think Tiffany?"

"I was worried about it being on the counter. I think the utility cart and a little out of the way is a good idea. It's not like anyone will miss seeing it. We can have one poster on the counter and the second on the reading table."

"Let's get it set up then," Amber said.

The three of us stood at the door with our arms crossed.

"This looks good," Amber said. "I feel like a decorator."

"That jar is so ugly," I said.

"This from a lady who has an ugly sofa and an ugly chair," Tiffany said. "I've got a little more cleaning to do before I'm done for the day. Can I get a ride to the hospital?"

"Colonel and I are going shopping. The hospital's on our way."

"Thanks for a great day." Amber waved and left.

Tiffany finished cleaning the mixer stand. "That was the last thing. I'm ready."

We dropped Tiffany off at the hospital. I pulled into the parking lot near the garden center. "The last time I tried to buy an automatic coffee maker, we ran into Carla. Be nice to finish our shopping."

Colonel walked with me to the entrance and assumed his security guard stance among the outdoor furniture, bags of soil, and plants. I found my automatic coffee maker and checked out. Colonel wagged when he saw me and my sack. We stopped at the crosswalk, and a vehicle gunned its way past the entrance. I stepped back two steps at the first roar of acceleration. The car narrowly missed a young man with tattoos and a ponytail who had exited behind me and whose longer stride placed him a step ahead of us.

"Hey, you jerk." He shouted as he fell back, off-balance. I dropped my package, widened my stance, and caught him with my torso and one arm.

He steadied himself. "Thanks, ma'am. You've got good balance. You a yoga instructor or something? That guy almost took me out."

Silver car with mud on the plates. Driver with gloves, hoodie, and sunglasses.

Colonel and I made it to the car with no more drama. I rolled down the windows for fresh air.

"I'm fierce. I'm cunning. I'm skilled. I'm strong. It tickled me when the young man asked if I was a yoga instructor, Colonel. It felt awesome."

When we got to the house, Colonel fell asleep, and I had lunch. Mia followed me to the bathroom and curled up on the rug. I scrubbed the tub and polished the faucet. I peered at my reflection. *I still had my ballcap on.*

"I never knew I was the ballcap type, Mia. I'll put it with my purse, so I don't forget it when I leave."

I picked up my book on the way to the sofa. "Remind me to stay awake, Mia. I want to finish my book."

I was getting to the best part when I was interrupted by a knock at the door. "Only ten more pages, Mia. I guess I can't pretend I'm not here. My car's outside."

I plodded to the door and opened it. Jack smiled. "Thought I'd surprise you. Want to go see your house?"

Not really. I'd rather finish my book.

"Have you planted all those flowers and bushes already?"

"Every single one. Ready?" He raised his eyebrows and jiggled his keys. Roxie yipped, and Colonel dashed out the door.

"Let me grab my purse." I picked up my purse, and my cap fell to the floor. *I'm not old, I'm fierce.*

I pulled on my ballcap and adjusted the brim.

"I like that cap. Looks good on you."

Of course.

"Thanks."

"Same logo as the plates. I like it." Jack opened the back door, and the dogs bounded in. When we drove up to my house, I gasped. "It looks like fairies visited. It's beautiful."

"I'm glad you're happy. Some of Alfred's boys helped me clean up the yard. They worked hard. I promised them donuts tomorrow. There's a dozen of them. Warn Tiffany."

I laughed. "It's amazing. Looks like it belongs in a magazine."

Colonel bounded around the yard and marked every few feet. Roxie followed him and remarked each spot.

"I've never seen Roxie mark before." Jack stared at the dogs.

"She's just reinforcing Colonel," I said.

"Backup's good, right?" He chuckled.

I sauntered around the house. Jack and the dogs followed me.

"I'm glad I saw the yard before all your work. Y'all transformed it from dark to a burst of fireworks in the sky."

"I can't take the credit. The boys jumped in and took over. They did it for the donut lady. You're a legend to them. You saved Woody."

I gazed at his face. *I'm not old. I'm a legend.*

"I agree with them." Jack met my gaze and smiled. "You and Colonel interested in dinner al fresco? A quartet's performing this evening at the downtown park. Gus is setting up a food truck with the college hospitality class. Food ought to be good."

"A little music and dinner outside at dusk? Sounds nice. We going to eat in the truck?"

Jack laughed. "You got it. Spoken like a true South Georgia gal who knows the bugs and mosquitoes feast at sundown. I'll take Roxie home for her supper and a walk and pick you up in forty-five minutes."

"Sounds good." *Almost said that's a date.*

When Jack opened the back door, Roxie led the way and leaped inside. Colonel scrambled in behind her.

Well done, Colonel. Not old. Just back up.

Jack parked close to the park. When I climbed out of the truck, I smiled at the sound of the all-male voices of a barbershop quartet. I listened to their medley of toe-tapping songs.

"They're good," I said. "This is going to be fun."

We stood in line at the food truck.

"Look." Jack pointed. "There's Eli and Ginny. They've grabbed a prime table next to the fire. Smart. Fewer bugs. Looks like they brought their own sandwiches and coffee and bought dessert." Jack waved, and they waved back.

Jack bought our dinners before I had a chance to at least buy my own. "I buy dinner next time, Jack. Okay?"

"Deal." He grinned.

Dang. I just committed to a next time.

"Hey, neighbor. We saved your seat." Eli stood and waved at us.

Jack and I weaved our way to their table and sat.

"The advantage of being a college student is that I came down here right after class and claimed the table. And the bonus? Three hours of uninterrupted study time." Eli laughed.

Jack pulled our soup and sandwiches out of the sack. I set my drink on the table and sat next to Ginny.

"What is it you're studying, Eli?" Jack took the lids off our soups.

"Double major. Criminal justice and pre-law. I'm leaning toward the Georgia State Patrol. Their reputation is excellent, and there's a good career path for me."

"It's a little tricky with the baby coming because I'll be the main breadwinner for a while," Ginny said. "We might buy a house here after all."

"But we'll wait until the mothers rent your duplex," Eli grinned. "Then Ginny will have help, but it won't be live-in help."

"How's your house going? I hear you're moving next week," Ginny said.

"You've been to the gas station, haven't you?"

"Of course. I was just asking to be polite. You want to know what time you're moving?" Ginny chuckled.

After we finished our food, Jack gathered the trash. Jack and Eli strolled to the trash can near the food truck.

Ginny waved her hand in front of her face. "Time to leave. The evening bugs have found me."

She and I rose. She motioned to a family with three small children and pointed to our table. The two older kids dashed over, and Ginny helped them into their seats.

"Thank you, Mrs. Townsend," the oldest boy said.

"Tanks, Mrs. Towns," the middle boy echoed.

"Hope we aren't chasing you off. We never leave as early as we planned." The children's mother plopped her squirming toddler onto a chair. Her husband set their food on the table, grabbed paper plates out of the diaper bag, and put portions of chicken and carrots on three plates while the mother handed out drink cups from the diaper bag. "But we've got our mealtime routine down to a science."

Ginny and I headed to the street. I glanced at the road and stared at a silver car that parked across the street. The driver stepped out. *Alfred Gibson.*

CHAPTER SIXTEEN

"You okay?" Ginny asked. "Here's our car." She patted the top of a silver car.

I stared at the car. "Where's your green Jeep?" *Does everyone in town have a silver car?*

"Oh, you haven't seen Eli's car, have you? He parks on the other side of the duplex and doesn't get home in the evening until close to five or six. He tries to get the bulk of his studying done before he comes home."

"You ready to go too?" Jack and Eli joined us.

"I'm ready. I've been reading a book and am close to the end."

"It isn't dark yet. You can let Colonel out without a stalker." He laughed.

When we got to my house, Ginny's jeep was in front of their home; I didn't see Eli's car, but their lights were on. Jack accompanied me to the door. He waited for the click of the deadbolt before he left the porch. *I know my regulars.*

"Want to go out back, Colonel?" When I opened the door, he dashed outside. Mia sneaked out of the pantry and stalked the shadows in the kitchen. I put on the kettle. When Colonel trotted inside, I fed him and Mia and brewed my tea.

Finally. I grabbed my book and flopped on the sofa. The last ten pages were as exciting as I expected. I gasped at the twist when I reached the end and reread the last five pages.

Colonel growled, low and soft. *Footsteps on the porch.* Three knocks in rapid succession at the front door.

I flung open the door, expecting to see Jack. Alfred Gibson gasped and took a half step backward.

I raised my eyebrows. "I'm sorry, Alfred. I didn't mean to startle you. I thought Jack forgot something. He just dropped me off."

His brow furrowed. "I apologize for coming by unannounced. I wanted to talk to you in private."

I peered at his face. I read concern, but no anger or malice. His hands were relaxed.

"Come in. Would you like to sit?" I motioned at the ugly chair.

He eased into the chair and scanned the living room and kitchen. Shadows slid under the chair and billowed behind him. Mia darted to the pantry.

"Nice duplex. Shirley owns it, right?" Alfred cleared his throat. "I wanted to talk to you about Todd Rockford."

I nodded and waited.

"I'm worried about Todd. He was one of my boys. Carla was … is … very manipulative. He had a hard time breaking away from her when he was young. I'm not explaining myself very well. The thing is I'm afraid Carla might be trying to blame Todd for the deaths of Russell Simpson and Nancy Weston. Before Russell died, she showed me a coupon book she said she stole from Russell. She said Russell and Todd were partners in a real estate scam, and she had a key to the coupon book that would prove it. She told me she'd get rid of it if I'd give her money." Alfred pursed his lips.

"Did you?"

"Maybe I should have, but I didn't. I'm not much for spending money frivolously. You may not know that. Carla got angry. Very angry. I've worked with a lot of angry boys, but I've never seen a wave of fury so—I'm not sure what to call it. Evil. Her rage was almost demonic. I honestly believe she intended to harm me. You won't believe this part. Shirley walked into the bank and asked for me. Carla heard her and stormed out."

"What did Shirley want?"

"She and Woody brought me donuts. Shirley said they hoped I'd enjoy them. Can you believe that?"

"No. Actually, yes. Those two are amazing together."

"Shirley and I had a disagreement years ago. I was embarrassed by my actions, but I was a stubborn fool. But back to Todd. I was afraid Carla would approach him with her so-called evidence and talked to him about her. I was relieved when he told me she confronted him, and he tossed her out of his office. I was more than relieved. I was proud of him. That was a huge accomplishment."

"Could Carla have proven that Todd killed Russell and Nancy?"

"No, she was counting on the threat of damaging his reputation for money. Carla's always been about the money."

I frowned. "I don't mean to be rude, but why tell me?"

"Todd has his rough edges, but he's a good man. I'd expect Carla to try to tarnish his reputation any way she can. There are people in addition to Shirley that I've hurt in this town. I need someone in Todd's corner besides me. You've got a reputation in this town for integrity and fairness. I knew you'd at least listen, and I thank you for that."

Alfred rose and offered his hand. We shook hands, and he left.

"Well, Colonel. Do we believe ole Alfred, or did we just witness an elaborate smokescreen?"

* * *

"It's National Pet Rescue Day at the shop today. You going with us, Mia?"

Mia ran to her carrier, and the three of us headed to the shop. When the bell jingled our arrival, Tiffany waved and pointed at a sign on the counter. *Free Dog Biscuits and Cat Treats for Our Furry Friends.*

"Aunt Gee. She also supplied the small pet bowls for the treats."

I picked up a dog biscuit and a kitty treat. "Homemade?"

Tiffany nodded.

Colonel trotted to the counter and sat. Mia jumped up on a stool. I gave each one a treat.

I measured coffee into the large pot basket and added water. "What are our donuts and scones today?"

"Rescue donuts—sprinkled with cinnamon and sugar, pink sprinkled donuts, gas station donuts, and orange you adoptin' scones."

I laughed. "I even know what the gas station donuts are. Eyeballs, am I right?"

Tiffany listed the day's special on the board and waved her marker like a wand. "You are correct, Miss Lady."

The bell jingled, and the sheriff strode in. "Happy National Pet Rescue Day. The Donut Hole is certainly decked out for the pet rescue holiday. The animal shelter will be here with their hopeful adoptees in about an hour. I think Emma has her heart set on taking a furry friend home."

I poured his coffee while he stared at the specials. Tiffany brought him a plate with a rescue donut and a pink sprinkled donut.

He pointed at the cinnamon and sugar donut. "Rescue donut?"

"Yep. A little sweet and a little spicy," Tiffany said.

"That makes sense. What's a gas station donut? Wait, don't tell me. Josh's favorite donut is the eyeballs. Do we have eyeballs today?"

"Yes, we do. Would you like to take Josh a dozen of his favorites?"

"Better yet, I'll call his boss and ask him to send Josh over so he can see the national pet rescue day first hand."

I smacked my forehead. "I forgot to check the calendar."

"There's only one meeting today. The mayor called right before you came in. He's having his staff meeting here today. He said he wanted to take care of the meeting himself. All we have to do is keep the coffee pot full and hot."

"What do you need me to do? Eyeballs?" I put on my pink apron and turned around so Tiffany could tie it for me.

"Eyeballs and pink sprinkled. I think I can keep up with everything else. I'm making eight batches today. I think we're going to have a big day. If we don't, the hospital will be happy with our excess donuts."

The bell jingled, and Roger strolled in. "Wow. You were right, Tiff. That is one ugly, eye-catching jar. I'll feed the kitty."

Tiffany joined Roger at the jar. I raised my eyebrows at the sheriff, and he sighed.

"Roger, I'm assigning you to security duty at the Donut Hole this morning. The donut gurus will need some help. That okay with you, Ms. Donut Lady?"

"Let me check with the chef. Tiffany, can you train Roger on eyeballs and sprinkles?"

"I sure can, Miss Lady. I could use help on the fryer. Should he wear an apron?"

I glanced at the sheriff, who gave an imperceptible nod. "Absolutely. It's required."

Roger hurried to the storeroom for an apron and joined Tiffany at the fryer.

I poured a refill for the sheriff. "You have time for a chat?" I tilted my head toward the pink room.

"What's up?" The sheriff leaned against the buffet while I closed the door.

* * *

"Alfred came to see me last night. He said he was worried Carla might try to implicate Todd Rockford in a scheme with Russell Simpson. He said Carla showed him a coupon book that was supposed to be proof of duplicity involving real estate deals. Alfred was concerned about Todd's reputation as a banker. What do you think?"

"I'd take Alfred's word over Carla any day. He's made mistakes in the past, but he's owned up to them and made restitution where he could. Not everything can be made right, though, and I think he carries deep regrets. Do you think the coupon book exists?"

"Yes."

The sheriff met my gaze. "How did you get it?"

"Carla hid it in my house."

The sheriff slammed his hand down on the buffet. "What? And you're just now telling me about this?"

"The coupon book is something anyone could have created. It's just dates and unrelated amounts. Useless by itself." I fought the urge to bite my lip.

"But of course, you have something else which you are about to tell me." The sheriff narrowed his eyes.

I pulled out a chair. After I was seated, I brushed imaginary crumbs off the table. "Nancy gave me some papers to keep for her. I looked at them Wednesday night. There's a spreadsheet that correlates addresses to the dates and amounts in the coupon book and has additional amounts included with each address. I didn't have time to research the addresses, but my guess is they are house sales."

"Where is all this?"

"My house."

"Let's go."

I picked up my purse. "I left something at home. We'll be back soon." Tiffany's eyes widened, but she nodded.

On the way to my house, the sheriff asked, "When were you going to tell me about all this?"

"I didn't know there was anything to tell until Alfred came to see me."

The sheriff entered the house first. I was relieved to see the back door was intact. He followed me to the pantry. When I scooted Mia's litter box aside and lifted the tile, he chuckled.

"Not bad. Most people have an aversion to litter boxes."

I handed him the coupon book, the envelope, and all the papers. "You interested in coffee?"

He shook his head, sat at the dining table, and went through the papers.

When he got to the last page, he scooted his chair back. "I can't make much sense of this either. I knew Todd's history, and I agree with Alfred about Todd's character. However, I can't tell if the documents were created for blackmail or if they're legit. On the surface, they look like personal records and papers. Did Alfred know you had the coupon book?"

"I don't see how. Carla left the coupon book, Nancy told me where Carla hid things when they were kids, and Tiffany helped me find it."

"I'll drop you off at the shop and take these to the office and assign an investigator."

When I walked into the shop, the mayor waved. "I showed up early. I borrowed a banner from the shelter."

Roger was hanging the banner over the door to the meeting room. *Adopt, Don't Shop.*

The bell announced Alana, the animal shelter director. "I have crates, eight dogs, six cats, and a table. Show me where you want us to set up. I brought a tent too."

Volunteers unloaded the crates, dogs, cats, table, and supplies. Alana pointed, and I nodded. Colonel came outside with us.

"I don't really see where we could set up the tent except in the street. The awning looks like it will shade the animals just fine," Alana said.

"This is so exciting." I scratched Colonel's ear.

"I hope you have extra donuts. I think we'll have a good crowd. It's all the talk at the gas station."

The voices and squeals of the shelter volunteers reached a peak that overwhelmed my ears. I went into the shop. *Not much quieter in here.*

"Just enjoy."

"Enjoy what?" the mayor asked.

My face felt warm. "I didn't realize I'd said it aloud. The commotion and level of noise were getting to me. I was giving myself a pep talk."

"Come into the pink room for a minute."

I took his arm, and we strolled into the meeting room. He closed the door. "Catch your breath, and then you can dive back in."

I listened to the muffled sounds. "Okay, coach. Put me in." He opened the door, and we laughed.

Roger was at the fryer, and Tiffany was at the cash register.

"I'll take over the cash register, Tiff. Roger is getting ahead of you."

"Thanks, Miss Lady. Isn't this crazy?"

The mayor's staff rushed through the door and into the meeting room. Tiffany was sprinkling, decorating, and making scones. She'd set up the coffee as self-serve. I served donuts and took cash and credit and debit cards.

Amber rushed in. "Dad called me. Where do you need me?"

"If you can keep the coffee going and wait on customers, I can save my nervous breakdown for another time."

"I'll be right there." She returned from the storeroom with an apron and a hat. "I helped myself." She hurried to the display case.

Amber's line was ten deep, but the atmosphere was one of social chaos. The shop was filled with laughter, hugs, and lively discussions about cats and dogs. The mayor's staff was greeting customers, pointing to the ugly jar, and chatting.

Shirley and Woody came into the shop.

"Woody's school gave us permission to come for the Pet Rescue Day. We've decided we need a cat."

Woody bounced on his toes. "Ms. Alana's going to talk to us about how to care for a cat, and we have a book from the library."

"Woody, what kind of donut do you want? I'll stand in line, but don't go outside without me."

"Oh, man. I need to look at the cats."

"There are too many people. I'd be nervous. Want to stand with me?"

Woody scowled and followed Shirley to the line.

I smiled and turned back to my next customer. *Woody's acting like a typical pre-teen. Shirley's doing a great job.*

Tiffany handed me a box of donuts. "A dozen donuts." She leaned and spoke in a quiet voice. "I'll buy."

Tess laughed. "I heard that, Tiff. And thank you, but I want to get this one."

The customers streamed in, and donuts streamed out.

Woody perched on a stool at the end of the counter. "We've picked out a cat. Come see. I think we have a name."

The mayor appeared at my elbow. "You go, Donut Lady. I've got this."

Woody led the way to a crate with a yellow cat. "Ms. Alana said the cat is about three years old. She likes me and Ms. Shirley." Woody stuck his fingers inside the cage, and the cat rubbed her head against him. "Ms. Alana says she's marked me. I'm hers. Her name is Chase."

"Chase is a good name for her." I reached in and scratched her ears.

Shirley joined us. "Everything's all taken care of, Woody. Put this sign on her crate. I have a list of items for us to go buy then we can come back and take Chase home."

Woody and Shirley left for their shopping.

"I'll take care of the register for a while, Donut Lady," the mayor said. "Why don't you take a break?"

I made my way to the ugly jar and peeked in. It was close to three-quarters' full. Josh and his boss came inside the shop, and Josh's eyes were wide.

"Did you ever think National Pet Rescue Day could be this big, Josh? There's a lot of people here I don't even know. Might be some from as far away as Conway."

"We talked to Ms. Alana, and all the dogs and cats they brought early this morning are adopted." Josh's eyes were bright, and his face was flushed. "The volunteers went back to the shelter for more, and they might have to go back a third time. Isn't that awesome?"

"Get in line for your specials. Your donuts are on the house today."

Josh read the board. "What are gas station donuts?"

"What's your favorite donut?"

"Eyeball donuts. Gas station donuts are eyeball donuts? Yes!" Josh and his boss high-fived.

I glanced out the window, and Alana was being interviewed by a reporter from the nearest TV station, according to the sign on the side of the large white van parked in front of the shop.

A young man rushed into the shop. "Hey, Josh. This here lady outside wants to talk to you." Josh shook his head. His boss whispered to him, and the two of them went out together.

"Box up eyeballs and rescue donuts for Josh, please Tiffany. And run them out to Josh if you don't mind."

"I'll box them up. Mayor, would you take them out?"

"Be glad to. Does my hair look okay? Never mind. I've got on my hat." The mayor chortled.

Josh and his boss had their backs to the shop. The background for the camera was dogs and cats. The interviewer spoke into the microphone and held it between Josh and his boss. Josh's boss spoke. The mayor stepped outside with Josh's eyeballs. When he opened the box, Josh's hands were animated, and the reporter grinned and put the microphone between him and the mayor. Josh pointed at the dogs and cats and at the donuts, and his hands moved the entire time. The camerawoman put down the camera, and the reporter shook hands with half the town. He waved through the window to all of us. The two of them loaded their equipment in the van and drove away.

"That was exciting to watch." Roger rinsed the fryer and dried it.

"Well done, Roger. You must have had a good trainer. You and the fryer just cranking out donuts."

The bell jingled. A familiar male voice said, "Hey, Miss Lady. Got sprinkles?"

Tiffany screamed and ran to the door. I turned and dropped the spoons I had in my hand.

"Isaiah!" Tiffany squealed.

Isaiah leaned on Thomas, and Gee followed them. She caught my gaze and grinned.

"I wouldn't miss National Pet Rescue Day and my favorite donuts." Isaiah sat on a stool. "Two of everything for me, please Tiff."

"I'll take the same," Thomas said.

Gee strode to where I stood at the meeting room door. "Got coffee?"

I grabbed a cup and poured. "Gee, that's the ugliest jar I've ever seen."

Gee cackled. "And it's yours."

"Yes, it is. I don't really have anywhere to store a huge jar from one year to the next so I will loan it to the sturdy shelf high on the wall in the back of the thrift store. It's perfect for that lonely shelf that never gets used because it's so high."

"You're good. You've just given me a town landmark that I can't turn down. But maybe I'll charge you rent. What do you think about that?"

I shrugged. "Don't care."

"Dang it. I should have known. But I'm telling Isaiah and Tiff you bewitched me again."

I laughed. "You're the best, Gee. You always have a high card."

"I've got something for you. I've fixed your supper. All you need is to cook." She held up the insulated bag she'd carried into the store. "You have a twice-baked potato wrapped in foil. Put it in the oven at three-fifty to heat up for thirty minutes. There's an herbed-crusted pork chop. Heat some oil in a cast iron skillet and fry it two to three minutes on each side, and then cover the skillet with foil and pop it into the oven for five minutes. Don't cook the salad." Gee chuckled.

"Thank you, Gee. My energy's been low, and I think it's because I'm not eating right. This sounds great. Home-cooked with the prep already done."

I put my bag into the refrigerator. "Let me show you Woody and Shirley's cat, Chase. She's a beauty."

We talked to Chase and wandered to visit with the dogs.

"Do you think I need a dog for companionship? And a cat to make sure I don't get any mice in the shop? Kind of like Colonel and Mia guard the Donut Hole."

Alana came up behind us. "Gee, I've got the perfect pets for you. I have a chocolate Labrador retriever. She's five years old. That's considered a senior and hard to place. She's a good girl, but she's lonely.

She's perfect to have at the shop because she's a people-dog. Loves people. Her only downsides are she's a lab and sheds like crazy, and she comes with a cat. He's black except for a white face and chest. He's four. They've been together since he was a kitten. We have them together in the same cage. He's not adoptable because he comes with the large old dog. She's not adoptable because she comes with a sassy black cat."

"One old. One sassy. I need to meet these two," Gee said. "Are they here?"

"They are. We brought them because Mandy loves to be around people."

"Mandy? Nice name. What's the cat's name?"

"Sir Andrew. His owner called him Sandy."

"Mandy and Sandy? I'll get them mixed up." Gee laughed.

"They answer to both names, according to our volunteers. We think their owner might have had dementia and couldn't remember who was Mandy and who was Sandy."

"I'll get Isaiah. He's always wanted me to get a dog. I'd ask what you think, Ms. Enchantress, but you bought a donut shop to get a dog and cat."

"True."

Isaiah put his arm around his mother. "I love Mandy and Sandy. Did you know Sandy's a Tuxedo Cat? Ms. Alana gave me a list of food and supplies for both of them. Thomas and I can go shopping for you."

"Tuxedo Cat? Not only sassy but classy. If you and Thomas staff the thrift shop for me, I'll do the shopping. I don't want you to overdo."

"Can we take Mandy and Sandy with us?"

"You can as far as I'm concerned," Alana said. "Just return our crate to the animal shelter."

"Mama?"

"Go right ahead. I'll take care of the paperwork and shopping. See you in a little bit."

When I went inside, Tiffany and Roger sat at the counter. The kitchen equipment was gleaming, and the shop itself was spotless.

"We are officially out of donuts. This has been an unbelievable day." Tiffany still wore her cap but had taken off her apron. Roger's apron was gone too. "All our aprons need to be washed before tomorrow. I'm taking them home."

The mayor headed toward the door with his apron over his arm. "I'll wash my apron. And I'm never taking off my cap. This was an incredible day. Roger and I counted the money in the ugly jar, Donut Lady. The total's on your desk. We took the cash to the bank and deposited it in the animal shelter account. Since we were doing banking, Tiffany made out a deposit slip for your net register cash, and we deposited that too. Your checks are in your safe. Ms. Alana has the animal shelter checks. She'll take care of depositing them. I'm going home for a nap."

There was nothing left to do in the shop, and the animal shelter folks had cleared out. I carried my dinner bag from Gee to the car, and Colonel, Mia, and I headed home.

I put the instructions from Gee on the counter and the bag in the refrigerator. I grabbed my usual yogurt while I had the refrigerator open.

The new book I ordered was in the mailbox when we got home. I brewed a cup of tea and made myself comfortable with my tea, yogurt, and book. When I was about a quarter of the way through the book, I set it down.

"Want to go for a walk, Colonel?"

Colonel and I walked around the block. The cicadas sang their song of impending rain. The neighbors hid from the afternoon heat and humidity. Colonel wandered the yards slower than his usual pace.

"No birds singing, Colonel. Seals the deal on rain, don't you think?"

By the time we got back to the house, the clouds were thick, and the sky was dark. When we went inside, the shadows were darting down the hallway, around the living room and kitchen, and into the pantry. When all the shadows were inside the pantry, they exploded into the kitchen and boiled and rolled into the living room.

"Y'all are more agitated than usual. Rain got you riled up?"

I put my potato in the oven and pulled out my large cast iron skillet. Gee said everything tastes better with cast iron.

I turned on the burner under the kettle and set the table for one.

A long rumble of thunder broke the silence. A low, menacing growl began deep in Colonel's throat and strengthened in intensity. The shadows swirled to the back door. Mia dashed to her pantry. Colonel's growl became louder.

I heard a knock that escalated to pounding at the back door. *Must be Eli checking up on us.* I cracked the door to look. A gloved hand pushed, and the door flung open. *Carla.*

She wore black leather gloves and a black hoodie. Her hands were clenched, and her pupils were constricted, almost pinpoints. I stepped backward between the table and the stove. She moved forward in a stalking motion.

I'm fierce. I'm cunning. I'm skilled. I'm strong.

"I'm tired of your games. Nancy told me you had the real estate transactions and my money before she died. It's all your fault I had to kill her." She pounded her fist into her hand, and Colonel stepped closer to me.

"So why did you kill Russell?" I held my breath.

She sneered. "He was weak. He said he wanted out." Her eyes narrowed. "Nobody walks away from me. It was his fault. He left the tire iron on the seat."

She was within three feet of me. She rushed toward me and raised her arms to the height of my neck. Colonel snarled a vicious growl and bared his teeth. He was ready to spring. Carla faltered and shifted her gaze to him.

I pivoted my body to the left and swung my hips and shoulder into a punch to bash her nose with my cast. I connected with a crunch, and my cast was bloodied. She screamed and clutched her bloody face with both hands. I swiveled and snatched up the cast iron skillet with my right hand. I dropped my arm back to use the weight of the skillet as momentum for the forward motion and arced the skillet into a swing. The heavy skillet slammed into the side of her head near her temple and ear, and she went down. I ran past her and out the back door. Colonel and the shadows were with me. A sudden crack of lightning sounded like a shot, and I ran for my life to the other duplex. The lights were on, and I pounded on the door. Eli came out with a pistol at his side.

"Carla. She tried to attack me." I leaned on the door for support.

Eli ran to my house, and Ginny helped me into her home. Colonel padded along.

"Blood on your cast. You okay?"

"Not mine."

I'm fierce. I'm cunning. I'm skilled. I'm strong.

Ginny guided me to her sofa, and I dropped onto the soft cushions in relief.

She joined me and dialed nine-one-one. "We need a deputy. Carla attacked the Donut Lady at her house."

"Might need an ambulance," I said.

Ginny nodded. "And send an ambulance. No, not for Ms. Karen. Come to the alley."

Ginny hung up. "I'll make coffee. Would you rather have tea?"

"Tea please."

"Have you eaten?" Ginny measured coffee into her coffee maker.

I blinked away tears. "She interrupted … my potato is in the oven, and my pork chop and salad is in the refrigerator."

"Maybe Eli can rescue your potato and bring it here. Would you like some crackers and cheese with your tea?"

I shivered. "I'm okay."

Ginny tossed an afghan from a chair to the sofa and grinned. "You're more than okay. You're a beast. And you're getting crackers and cheese."

The shriek of sirens from all directions pierced through the rumble of thunder.

CHAPTER SEVENTEEN

The sheriff ran up to Ginny's back porch and burst through the door.

"You okay, Karen?" he asked.

"Yes."

He spun around and left. More cars pulled into the alley and out front. Ginny answered the knock at the front door.

Roger strode in and sat in the chair across from me. "The sheriff sent me for your statement. I think you're grounded, Miss Lady."

Ginny chuckled.

"That would be a relief, Roger," I said.

He pulled out a notepad and pen. "So what happened? First, are you hurt?" He pointed to the blood on my cast.

"I'm not hurt. I hit Carla in the nose with my cast."

Roger stared at me. "Can you start at the beginning?"

"Carla knocked on my back door. I answered the door, but before I could close it, she burst inside. She told me she killed Nancy and Russell."

Roger stopped writing. "What did she say exactly?"

"She said Nancy told her that I had Carla's papers and money. Carla said Nancy told her that before she killed her, and it was my fault."

Ginny gasped and sat next to me. "You know it's not, right?"

I nodded.

Roger frowned. "Do you have Carla's papers and money?"

"The sheriff has the papers Nancy gave me, and I think the money might be in my storage unit where Nancy stored my things after the tornado."

"What happened next?"

"I asked her why she killed Russell."

"Oh Lord, Miss Lady. You know Ms. Gee would say that takes the cake." Roger shook his head. "Why did you do that?"

"It seemed like a good idea at the time."

"Sheriff's not going to believe my notes," Roger mumbled. "Gonna be fired for making up stories."

Ginny covered her mouth with her hand.

He poised his pen over his pad. "What did Carla say?"

"She said he wanted out, but nobody walks away from her. She said it was his fault because he left the tire iron on the back seat of their car."

Roger wrote. "Then what?"

"She headed toward me, and I hit her in the nose with my cast. That's where the blood on my cast came from."

"Solid hit, huh?" Roger grinned and ducked his head.

Ginny and I glanced at each other. I frowned to keep from laughing, and Ginny bit her lip.

"Then you ran over here?" Roger sounded hopeful.

"Yes, but first I hit her upside the head with my cast iron skillet. Then Colonel and I ran over here."

"You what?" Roger looked up from his writing.

"Hit. Her. With. The skillet."

"Told you," Ginny said. "Beast," she mouthed.

I snorted at Ginny.

"Miss Lady, if the sheriff doesn't ground you, I will." Roger shook his pen at me and resumed writing.

Ginny chuckled, and Eli hurried inside.

"Everything okay here?" He narrowed his eyes at Ginny and me.

"Everything's fine. Want some coffee? Deputy?" Ginny asked.

Eli strode to the stove.

"None for me." Roger tapped his pen on his pad.

"What did you leave out, Ms. Karen?" Roger glared.

Ginny scooted closer to me. Ivan, her cat, leaped to the vacant spot on the sofa.

"Colonel growled when she came to the door. I should have paid better attention."

"Nothing else?"

"Not that I know of. Why?" I tilted my head and furrowed my brow.

"Just asking." He turned his focus to his notes.

Good technique. He's going to be a stellar interrogator.

"Ms. Karen, I turned your oven off, but they wouldn't let me bring you the potato. It smelled good," Eli said.

"Do you want a ham and cheese sandwich or grilled cheese?" Ginny asked.

"Or a grilled ham and cheese. We're a full-service sandwich shop." Eli opened the refrigerator.

"Grilled ham and cheese sounds great. Thanks." I carried my cup of tea to the table.

Eli pulled the fixings out of the refrigerator.

"Grilled ham and cheese is Eli's specialty. Good choice, Donut Lady. We have two kinds of chips. Regular and ranch. Which do you prefer?" Ginny asked.

"I think regular with grilled ham and cheese."

The sheriff came through the back door into the kitchen.

"Ms. Karen, we'll be out of your house pretty soon. Carla was unconscious when we first arrived but was coming around on the way to the hospital."

The sheriff strode over to Roger and read Roger's notes.

"What?" The sheriff's head jerked up, and he stared at me.

Ginny leaned close. "I think the sheriff just got to the part about the frying pan. What on earth made you think of that?"

"I don't know. I reached out in desperation, and it was there."

Roger flipped his notebook closed, and the sheriff joined me at the table.

"When you finish your sandwich, do you feel up to going to the storage unit?"

"I'd like to. The keys are in my purse. It's in the living room, and I think my phone is on the dining table."

The sheriff rose. "The temperature dropped with the front that rolled in. You have a sweater or something?"

"My sweatshirt's on the back of a dining chair."

When the sheriff returned, I put on my sweatshirt, and Colonel trotted to the door.

"Do you mind if Colonel rides along?"

"Not at all. Come on, Colonel. Let's go."

He took my arm and led me to his patrol car. The rain had turned to a light sprinkle.

When the sheriff parked in front of the brick building, I handed him the storage unit keys. The storage units and the office were surrounded by a ten-foot, sturdy iron fence, and the area was lit with floodlights. I stepped over puddles, and Colonel splashed from one to another.

The sheriff unlocked the gate.

"My unit's in the second row. About midway." I led the way.

The sheriff unlocked the unit and clicked on the inside light. "There's not much here, is there?" He scanned the room.

"That was my thought when I came to check." I walked to the trunk. "There's a box in here."

The sheriff lifted the lid. "Nancy packed it?" He lifted the box and shook it. "Not very heavy."

"All the other boxes like this were delivered to the duplex."

My knees were weak, and I glanced around for something to sit on. My sturdy coffee table faced the trunk. I sat on the coffee table while the sheriff pulled out his pocketknife and slit the brown sealing tape. He opened the box flaps and whistled long and low.

"Packets of twenty-, fifty-, and hundred-dollar bills. This was Russell's money? How did Nancy get it?"

"I'm not clear on the details. Carla told me so many different stories, I'm not sure what's true. I'm guessing Nancy may have stolen it from Carla. Maybe she thought if she hid it, she'd be safe from Carla. Or maybe Carla gave it to her for safekeeping."

"What else you got?"

"What's with you law enforcement types? Roger asked me almost the same question."

The sheriff chuckled. "Guess he's been hanging around me. There's something else, isn't there?"

I took my phone out of my purse. "I don't know what this means either." I found the picture I took of Russell's will. "Here. Look at this."

The sheriff gazed at the picture and zoomed in for a closer look. He sat on the trunk. "Tell."

"I went to the Carruthers when Carla disappeared to see if she was there—"

"Of course, you did." The sheriff shook his head.

"I think she'd been hiding there because there was a mess in the shed where I found Woody. Fast food wrappers and half-eaten food. I caught a glimpse of something buried outside the shed. When I dug it up, I found a cigar box with a copy of Russell's will. I took a picture and put it back and reburied the box."

"What's the connection with Simpson and Tiffany?" The sheriff glared. "I know you. You'd have checked."

"Tiffany's father and Russell were cousins. There wasn't any other family left."

The sheriff sighed. "You want to come out of retirement and teach investigative techniques to my new detectives? No, I take that back. I need fresh donuts." He closed the box. "What else you got?"

"I think that's it."

"What's your theory about the cash?"

"I think it's from Russell and Carla's scams. I think Carla was the brains, but Russell squirreled away the money. It's just a feeling I have."

"Good enough for me. And you're fired. No more investigating on your own." He rose and offered me a hand up. "I almost hate to ask, but do you have any questions for me?"

"Do you know how to get blood off a cast?"

The shadows danced around the box.

ACKNOWLEDGEMENTS

Huge thanks to my husband for his patience while I wander off into the world of my imaginary friends.

Thanks to my family and friends for their support, and to my beta readers and fierce editor.

Thank you for reading. If you enjoyed the Donut Lady's story, tell a friend, post a review, subscribe to the Judith A. Barrett newsletter, and read SWEET DEAL REVEALED, DONUT LADY COZY MYSTERY, BOOK 3.

After the Donut Lady witnesses a friend's estranged husband in a sketchy incident, he's found dead. Is Karen too close to revealing the truth? Her nightmares saved her once, but the murderer takes it to a personal level. She's on her own.

Subscribe to Judith's newsletter! Look for the Subscribe button on www.judithabarrett.com

ABOUT THE AUTHOR

Judith A. Barrett, award-winning author, lives in rural Georgia on a farm with her husband and two dogs. She writes thrillers, post-apocalyptic science fiction, and cozy mystery novels. Stories with a twist!

When she isn't writing, Judith is working in her garden, hiking with her husband and dogs, or rocking on her front porch while she watches the sunset.

Website http://judithabarrett.com

Subscribe to the eNewsletter via her website

Let's keep in touch!